The Maid of Kent Murders

Also by Amy Myers

Marsh and Daughter Mystery series:
The Wickenham Murders
Murder in Friday Street
Murder in Hell's Corner
Murder and the Golden Goblet
Murder in the Mist
Murder Takes the Stage
Murder on the Old Road
Murder in Abbot's Folly

Tom Wasp Victorian Mystery trilogy:
Tom Wasp and the Murdered Stunner
Tom Wasp and the Newgate Knocker
Tom Wasp and the Seven Deadly Sins

A MARSH & DAUGHTER MYSTERY, BOOK 9

THE MAID OF KENT MURDERS

Amy Myers

LUME BOOKS

LUME BOOKS

Published in 2022 by Lume Books

Copyright © Amy Myers 2022

The right of Amy Myers to be identified as the author of this work has been asserted by them in accordance with the Copyright, Design and Patents Act, 1988.

All rights reserved. No part of this publication may be reproduced, stored in a retrieval system, or transmitted in photocopying, recording or otherwise, without the prior permission of the copyright owner.

ISBN 978-1-83901-473-4

Typeset using Atomik ePublisher from Easypress Technologies

www.lumebooks.co.uk

Authors' Note

The story of Richard of Eastwell, together with the glory days of the Old Vic theatre with Richard Burton and John Neville, have long lodged themselves in my memory, and I am glad to have had this opportunity to revisit Richard of Eastwell and to provide Marsh & Daughter with a conundrum that stems from the London theatre scene of the past. Sir John Wilbourne bears no resemblance either to Richard Burton or John Neville but he treads in their footsteps. In writing a series, its main characters increasingly become familiar friends and so *The Maid of Kent Murders* has also allowed me not only to join Peter and Georgia Marsh for this update on their work but to find out what has been happening to them and their family.

For all this, my gratitude goes to Lume Books for their encouragement of Marsh & Daughter and I am also indebted to my agent Sara Keane of Keane Kataria and to the Lume Books' editors for their sterling and incomparable help. My thanks also to Martin and Sally French, Alice Rees, the invaluable tree surgeon Jeremy Ault and my husband Jim for his tolerance of repeated trips over the years to visit the ruins of Eastwell Church, Richard of Eastwell's burial place.

List of Characters

Active participants

Peter Marsh: one half of Marsh & Daughter
Georgia Marsh: the other half of Marsh & Daughter
Percival FitzRichard: eccentric owner of The Maid of Kent
Bernie Beane (née FitzRichard): Percival's daughter
Tony Beane: Bernie's husband
Gerald Randall: owner of Cobshaw Hall and head of the Tudor faction
Brenda Randall: widow of Thomas Randall, Gerald's brother
Sophy Randall: Gerald's granddaughter
Dave Cook: chair of the parish council and head of the Planters faction
Mick Buckley: works for the Randalls and prominent Tudor
Geoff Sanders: a Planter. Former gardener at The Maid of Kent
Louis Sanders: a Planter; Grandson of Geoff
Edward Colduggan: prominent actor
Rowena Watts: prominent actor
Howard Green: property developer
Elena: former wife of Peter Marsh
Jill Frost: daughter in law to Luke Frost

Luke Frost: Georgia's husband

Detective Superintendent Will Whittan: Marsh & Daughter's chief police contact

Detective Inspector Jack Cotton: Marsh & Daughter's liaison officer

Past participants

Serena FitzRichard (Percival's stepsister), Montague FitzRichard (Percival's father), Brian Cook (Dave's great-uncle), Sam Buckley (Mick Buckley's grandfather), Jacob Randall (Gerald's father), Sir John Wilbourne (actor)

Chapter One

'It says *Blood Royals only*,' Georgia said doubtfully.

In fact, she was increasingly doubtful about this whole venture. Joke or not, the placard over the door in front of them was clear enough. Only royalty could enter. Not that any member of the royal family would ever be stepping inside this uninviting back entrance to a run-down pub in rural Kent. Nevertheless, this door was the only provision that the Maid of Kent inn made for mobility scooters and so her father Peter had to use it, weird or not. This visit required the presence of both Marsh and Daughter.

'Blood royal, eh? In we go then! I always said there was more to the Marsh family history than we knew,' Peter commented cheerfully, as she pushed the door open for him to drive the scooter majestically through.

Sitting in large grounds for a pub (which were surprisingly well kept in comparison with the building itself), the Maid of Kent had changed greatly since Georgia had last visited it donkeys years ago when she had come here with her brother Rick. Then it was a well-kept, smart, timber-beamed medieval hostelry, its walls gleaming white in the summer sunshine and its beams a tasteful dark brown. Now it looked dilapidated and uncared for: it badly needed repainting, the bedraggled flowers in the hanging baskets were beseechingly flopping over in search of water and dead-heading and even the inn sign—presumably displaying the maid of Kent herself—looked battered and world-weary. No Michelin stars for this place then. No stars at all, which was a set-back in view of their current mission.

Georgia shivered. What she had been looking forward to as a sunny May Day outing no longer seemed so inviting.

'Tally-ho!' Peter murmured as he steered his scooter past the toilets and through another door that Georgia was holding open for him. What lay beyond was still a mystery—and possibly not an attractive one.

She blinked. Mystery indeed! Greeting them on the wall facing them only a few feet away and encased in an ornately carved frame was a life-size replica of the famous fourteenth-century image of King Richard II, grandly seated on his throne with sceptre and orb. His young face under the heavy-looking golden crown stared out at them reproachfully for entering his realm uninvited.

'This place,' she remarked uneasily, 'is distinctly odd.'

Peter agreed. 'This chap on the wall must be here because he was the son of Joan, the Fair Maid of Kent. It's a strange welcome though.'

Coming from Peter, the eternal optimist, this confirmed Georgia's increasing sense that they'd made a mistake in coming here. Too late to duck out now. A choice of direction awaited them, as there were no helpful signs to reception or the main bar. They could turn left, turn right, or nip along a side passage a few feet further on. None of the choices looked promising.

'Excelsior!' Peter decided. 'Let's turn left on the grounds that it's the least likely to lead us to our destination. This is the kind of weird place for that to work.'

'This kind of place' grew weirder with every step. The walls and ceilings of all the corridors they were passing through were all but completely covered with paintings, photos, drawings and newspaper cuttings; a few were in gilt frames, many of them just stuck on with sticky tape. Some were instantly recognisable: Errol Flynn as Robin Hood was standing proudly beside King Richard I, Laurence Olivier was triumphantly riding into battle as Henry V, the Princes in the Tower were cowering from their assailant, King John was signing the Magna Carta and Henry II was penitently paying homage for the murdered Becket.

Peter stopped, obviously as bewildered as Georgia. 'Anything strike you as odd about all these paintings and adornments, dear daughter?'

'They seem,' she replied, 'mostly to be kings and queens of England. Early kings and queens. I haven't seen any Normans or Anglo-Saxons. Nor Henry VIII. And good old Queen Vic is missing.'

'So far they're all of Plantagenet royalty,' Peter agreed, negotiating a turn round a corner of the corridor. 'Presumably because the pub honours Joan, Fair Maid of Kent. Not that Joan seems to have spent much time in Kent for all her father was the Earl. Still, she's obviously remembered here with great enthusiasm.'

'*No, she isn't!*'

This came out with a howl of horror as an old man startled them by shooting out of a door that had been masquerading as part of the wall because it too was covered with royal art. He was thin, wiry, and must be in his mid-eighties, Georgia guessed, as he stood glaring at them over his spectacles and blocking their passage. He looked like an eccentric Roald Dahl character out of the books that enchanted her stepson Mark's daughter Rosie. Georgia had taken full advantage of her position to read to Rosie and her young brother Robbie all the books she herself enjoyed as a child. Mark was the son of her husband Luke Frost and his first wife.

Unfortunately, this gentleman before them was looking extremely grim.

'Can't you read?' he shouted. 'For Plantagenets only. *Royal* Plantagenets. You don't look in the least bit royal.'

'I do my best,' Peter replied meekly. 'Is there another entrance for this contraption I'm riding?'

The new arrival looked perplexed. 'Perhaps there isn't.' He sniffed. 'You'd better come in. I suppose you're the Marshes.' He stared over his glasses at them suspiciously.

'Georgia Frost,' Peter waved a hand grandiosely in her direction. 'Professionally Georgia Marsh of Marsh & Daughter. I'm Peter Marsh.'

The grim face was now beaming. 'I've been expecting you. Percival Henry FitzRichard at your service.' They were treated to a deep bow. 'And,' he added as he resumed an upright position, 'the Fitz does *not* imply illegitimacy. I am of the true blood, descended from King Edward III himself. Now,' he swept on before Georgia could ask how this came about, 'I'm told you wish to organise a concert to be held in our gardens.'

'Yes, and—'

'Plus a banquet for twenty-five to take place thereafter at £50 a head, with heralds and trumpets extra,' he continued grandly.

'That,' Peter said firmly, 'is not yet decided.'

Percival looked astonished. 'But trumpets to herald the feast are—'

'At the moment,' Georgia intervened, highly amused, 'the hire of the grounds and provision of drinks and nibbles are all we definitely require. The rest is yet to be settled.'

'Perhaps that's best,' Percival said regretfully. 'However, we are renowned for our sausage and chips. As for the financial arrangements, if you care to visit our bar, I will ask Bernie to join you.'

'Bernie?'

'My daughter, Berengaria. Wife of King Richard I. I speak of the original Berengaria, that is,' he corrected himself. 'Ah, all those Crusader castles, eh? Have you seen Richard's Room?'

Georgia cast a despairing look at Peter who promptly took over. 'Not yet. What—?'

'You must, you must. Some time or other,' he added thoughtfully, disappearing with a regal wave of dismissal into his 'office'—or so Georgia presumed from the brief look she had at his hideaway.

He was only gone for a moment before he reappeared, shouting after them, 'And kindly bear in mind that we are not, quite definitely *not*, Joan, the Fair Maid of Kent. We have our own maid. And our own murders. Is that clear?'

Murders? Was that really what he said? Georgia battled to make sense of it. What on earth did he mean by 'our own maid'? Before Georgia could ask him though, Percival Henry FitzRichard had promptly vanished again.

'Murders?' Peter pondered. 'Wonder what they are?'

'Don't go there!' Georgia recommended. Usually, she'd have been right with him over that, but not today. They were here to arrange a concert.

Talk of past murders was guaranteed to set Peter going, naturally enough as the partnership of Marsh & Daughter investigated unsolved cases of such tragedies. They researched and then recorded them in book form with her husband Luke as stern publisher. Her father's previous career had been in the Kent Police until a bullet put paid to that and resulted in his being confined to moving around on a mobility scooter; the Marsh & Daughter projects allowed him to follow his personal passion for the cold cases, sometimes buried deep in history, sometimes more recent. The snag was that with both, they had to bear in mind that cold cases could turn into hot ones if they had repercussions in the present day.

'Do we really want to hold the concert in this place?' Peter sighed as they travelled along yet another corridor. 'I know it would be held in the gardens, not inside, but even so it's risky. Josephine Mantreau and Lucien Marques are a world-famous soprano and cellist respectively and they're giving up a lot to come here. Much as I love sausage and chips, I can't see our audience fancying them at a memorial banquet for Rick.'

'This was Rick's favourite pub,' Georgia pointed out. 'So it's only fitting to have the memorial in his honour here. Besides, from what we know of Josephine and Lucien they'll get a kick out of this place.'

'The audience won't. They'll politely lick their ice-creams, down their pints of beer, chew their sausages and think we're mad.'

He was right, and Georgia knew it. Saturday, August 17th would be the anniversary of the day her brother Rick had died. He had set off for that trip to Brittany with the world his oyster after graduating and simply disappeared. It was only after many years of fruitless searching that they had at last managed to piece together what had happened to him. He and Josephine, now famous but then a budding singer, had fallen in love, but Rick had died while saving Lucien, then a child, from death, after a disaster in the River Danube. Despite its now obvious limitations though, Georgia was still convinced that this memorial concert should go ahead *here* with all the music he had loved so much.

'I submit,' she said. 'The food can be sorted out later, and we'll fix the bare essentials for it here. We could always taxi everyone to Canterbury for supper if need be. Now let's go in search of Berengaria, our Plantagenet princess.'

As they turned into yet another corridor, they saw a door ahead and although they could hear no cheerful hum of customers it was clear that they had arrived at their destination. As they entered the door by the side of the huge bar, the dark old tables and pews looked serviceable enough, and indeed welcoming. So did its attractive low-beamed ceiling and walls and yet the room lacked conviviality and clients. Georgia began to lose hope. For a start, there was no one behind the bar, always discouraging.

At one table at the far end on their left was an elderly lady on her own, sitting very upright with a cup and saucer before her and fixing the newcomers with a piercing gaze as though she were the owner. At her feet was a very yappy dog who was guarding his mistress like one of the lions in Trafalgar Square. The lady must be about eighty, too old to be Berengaria, Georgia decided

At the opposite end of the room was a shrunken man with a bristling beard who looked well into his eighties and was fixing an unfriendly gaze on them, although his young companion lounging back in his chair beside him looked more approachable. Only one table was occupied in the centre of the bar room, again by two men, one in a bright pink shirt who looked in his late fifties, burly with an air of power about him, the other much younger, perhaps forty or so, and even more well-built. Both looked reasonably affably towards them, but nevertheless the message all round was clear. Strangers had invaded their territory and ground rules had to be applied towards such illegal immigrants.

Peter took no notice of the silence, bidding them all a cheery good morning as he drove the scooter up to the unattended bar and turned to survey his audience. Selecting the lone lady, he enquired of her: 'Miss FitzRichard perhaps?'

The silence deepened sharply, broken only by the frantic barks of the dog and a guffaw of laughter from the central table.

'Perhaps you mean Mrs Beane,' the lone woman answered, not quite as icily as Georgia had expected. 'There's a bell to ring on the counter.'

It wasn't needed because as Georgia moved towards it, a door behind the bar opened and a woman in her late fifties or early sixties hurried in, introducing herself as Bernie Beane. Sturdy and pleasant looking, she bore no relation to the Plantagenet queen, nor did she look in the least dotty, thankfully, as she ushered them round the bar and into her inner sanctum. Glory be, Georgia noticed, there were no paintings or drawings of kings and queens of England here, only a very efficient looking computer, files and a painting of the Maid of Kent pub in better days.

'Much community spirit round here, is there?' Peter dared to ask, manoeuvring the scooter skilfully through the door.

Bernie chuckled. 'Depends who's in. We're the only pub for a mile or two, so we get them all, the Randalls crew from Cobshaw Hall and Dad's Maid of Kent mob.'

'That sounds very feudal,' Peter commented.

'It is. The village has always pretty much been split between the two, back to the days when the whole village worked for one or the other estates and there were dark doings afoot. Hasn't changed much only now the stakes are different, not so much fighting for your boss as fighting for what you want for the future of the village.'

'And that is?' Georgia asked cautiously. This wasn't sounding ideal for their concert.

Kentish villages, she knew all too well, were no different to villages the world over where local politics were concerned, but it was unusual for strangers to be put in the picture so speedily. Especially potential customers.

Bernie hesitated. 'The pub's up for sale, so that's what's setting off the ructions at present. Tony—that's my husband—isn't a local lad and so he's tolerated by both sides. I'm only tolerated because I'm the one who does the cooking and pulls their pints if our barman isn't around.' She grinned uneasily at them, perhaps regretting such frankness. 'It won't affect you though. Your concert's safe. Nothing will happen for ages, if at all.'

'Why's that?' Peter enquired with interest.

'Like I said. Village is split—Dave Cook—he's chair of the parish council. Sitting in the middle of the bar. Pink shirt. He's all for the community buying the pub and making a go of it by using it as a community centre as well as a pub. That's what anyone with sense round here wants. But her ladyship—Mrs Brenda Randall—having her coffee out there, she's the council vice-chair and village historian. We used to think of this place as an inn with accommodation but there's been none of that for years. Brenda's all for selling to some posh hotel chap she knows, Mr Howard Green,' she said dismissively. 'He'll preserve the heritage, she says. What she really wants is to preserve her blessed ancestry.

'She claims the Randalls once owned the whole of Cobshaw,' Bernie continued, 'including this place, but their days of glory aren't what they were. Anyway, that's why she and Dave aren't bosom pals for all he was once married to her daughter. As I said, the Randalls have to come in here, as well as the other side. This time of day it's frigid politeness, of an evening we have to watch it or it's likely to end in a punch up for the younger lot and a yelling match for the oldies.'

'What caused this split in the village?' Peter asked. Georgia was reeling under this diatribe, beginning to share Peter's doubts about Rick's concert.

'Like I said, it's been this way for ever,' Bernie said gloomily. 'We reckon it began in about the sixteenth century and been on and off ever since. Back in the day as far as I remember it's always been the Planters—that's Dad's Plantagenet lot—and the Tudors who are Brenda's lot, the Randalls. Chief of which is Gerald Randall, her brother-in-law up at Cobshaw Hall, but he doesn't come here too much. Nowadays the Planters and Tudors don't always fight in the open. That's why you saw Dave sitting with Mick Buckley though Dave is a Planter and Mick a Tudor who's normally full of himself and ready to spar like crazy. He runs what they call the estate for the Randalls.'

'But your father can sell the pub to whom he likes so there's not much point their fighting over that,' Georgia commented.

'Ah. Well, yes, Dad can. Trouble is neither lot has come up with a true Plantagenet.'

'A *what*?' Georgia asked.

Bernie giggled. 'Dad owns this place, and he won't sell to anyone unless they're a true Plantagenet by descent like himself. That's what *his* dad insisted on. I gather it's all in the deeds.'

'That must narrow the field,' Georgia said, trying to keep a straight face. 'Is it still valid?'

'Doesn't matter whether it's valid or not. That's what Dad says and nothing will budge him.'

'Then why try to sell the inn when he could just leave it to you?' Peter asked politely.

'Run this place for the rest of our lives? Tony's sick of trying to balance the books—he's my husband. Much as he'd miss the old place—especially as he keeps his precious classic Porsche 356SC in the old stables—he can't wait to get shot of the problems. As for me, I love the building, but hate the politics and—'

'What can't I wait for?' A man of medium height in late middle age appeared suddenly from yet another hidden door. Slenderly built, with a mop of short greying blonde hair, he introduced himself as Tony Beane. Welcoming grin he might have, but Georgia noticed a shrewd gleam in his eye.

Change the subject quickly, she decided. 'Smugglers must have had a whale of a time drinking in this pub years ago. Hidden doors and passages all over the place, I expect.'

'Right, but I wish they'd left some of their whisky behind,' he joked. 'Bernie's been talking about dumping the old Maid, I suppose. Pity really. It has a lot to offer, but it needs more cash than we've got. Not Plantagenets by any chance, are you?'

'Can't claim that,' Peter replied, then added smoothly, 'What were the murders that your father spoke of, Mrs Beane? Not recent, I hope? Connected with *a* maid of Kent but not the wife of the Black Prince, we gathered.'

Bernie grinned. 'He meant Cecilia. She was murdered somewhere around here in the sixteenth century. She's supposed to be buried here too, but whether in the gardens or the house has never been clear. If she existed at all, that is. Tony's a carpenter by trade and he's been all over this place without any luck in finding her.'

'Maybe we'd do better,' Peter joked. 'We investigate cold cases.'

'Good luck to you then. Cecilia is Dad's historical sweetheart, his fair maid. She was a Plantagenet and he will have it that we're all descended from the Plantagenets too.'

'A lot of families claim the same,' Peter pointed out.

'It's the route they take that matters,' Bernie replied gloomily.

'Which is your father's?'

'Like the fair Cecilia, through Richard.'

'Ah. His Majesty. We saw his portrait by the outside door,' Peter said.

'No. This Richard is local. Richard Plantagenet or Richard of Eastwell,' Tony explained. 'Take your pick over his name.'

Of course. That rang plenty of bells for Georgia. His story was well known locally. Eastwell was a small village and large estate buried in the North Downs quite close both to where she and Luke lived and to Haden Shaw where Peter lived. It was also not far away from where they were now standing in Cobshaw.

It had been on the Eastwell estate that Sir Thomas Moyle, the mid sixteenth century owner of an old medieval house, now called Lake House, decided to build a grand new home in the grounds. There was no doubt that Richard of Eastwell was no myth, but his origins had long been the subject of speculation. According to the most familiar story, Sir Thomas had been startled to find his stonemason reading a book—a surprising recreation for workmen at that time, and even more surprising was that the book was in Latin, the language then only of the well-educated.

'The builder was Richard of Eastwell, who explained to Sir Thomas that he was the illegitimate son of Richard III, didn't he?' Georgia said. 'His story was that he'd been forced to take up humble employment after his father's death at the Battle of Bosworth.'

'Wrong, according to Dad,' Bernie said. 'There are lots of views on who he was—one of the Princes in the Tower, for instance—but Dad reckons he alone has the true story and it starts, in his opinion, with our good old Richard being the only living *legitimate* son of Richard III, on the grounds that Richard III married Anne Neville a year or two earlier than their political marriage in 1474. Possible but far from proven. Richard's only acknowledged son born after that died before his father so although there were several illegitimate kids, Dad insists Richard of Eastwell, or Richard Plantagenet as he prefers to call him, had the best claim on the throne.'

'And now he's a ghost haunting Eastwell Park, so the legend goes,' Peter contributed. 'That suggests an unquiet soul, doesn't it? Does one of those multiple murders that your father mentioned have anything to do with Richard?'

Tony chuckled. 'Could be. Where Percival is concerned, who knows? He has his own idea of history.'

'I needed this fresh air,' Georgia said gratefully, sometime later. It was only the first day of May but it looked as if it would be a hot summer ahead and today was a forerunner. Within the pub walls the atmosphere had been stifling both physically and mentally, although Bernie had been meticulous in dealing with the question of the concert in the grounds and what they could and could not provide. Indeed, it struck her that having said her piece, Bernie was only too happy to abandon the subject of the murders at the Maid of Kent, despite her tolerance of her father's devotion to the pub's historical past. At least the concert was now a fixture for August 17th, and local suppliers of chairs and tables plus other things needed as well as contingency plans for coping with rain had been arranged. Even the food had been settled with Bernie unexpectedly agreeable for an outside caterer to be hired.

There had been no sign of Mr Percival FitzRichard after discussions ended, so now, Georgia thought somewhat thankfully, they were free to wander round the grounds to try to visualise their concert taking place in the open-air theatre that the Maid of Kent boasted. It was rarely used now but still maintained. They had just peered into what seemed to be the remains of an old walled vegetable garden and were now passing what might have started life as an Elizabethan knot garden. The smell of lavender wafted over to her and the chirping of the birds indicated their approval of the herbs she could spot. This at least seemed in use although sage, oregano and fennel didn't seem to tally with a menu of sausage and chips.

'A knot garden is a sign that the Maid of Kent might not always have been a pub,' Peter observed.

'Very few pubs have open air theatres in their grounds either,' Georgia pointed out as they rejoined the path through the main gardens. Their initial reaction was how well cared for they were compared with the pub itself. The grass was immaculate, the rhododendron walk—in full bloom—would have graced any National Trust property and the borders, full of greenery and flowers, were delightful.

The pub and the gardens they had just crossed were at the top of an incline of the North Downs, and when they reached the point where they could look down on what lay before them, Peter gave a whistle of admiration. There lay the theatre. The rounded shape of the terraced hillsides formed a semi-circle in front of the stage, providing in effect a circle and stalls. The stage area had bushes acting as wings and a backdrop of bushes and small trees, but Georgia's eye immediately went to two huge beech trees slightly higher up the incline and guarding the theatre at either end.

Guardians, though, always stand apart, watching, waiting, shielding, judging—and unpredictable. Georgia's initial unease when they had entered the Maid of Kent came back to her. Nonsense, she told herself as they made their way down the main entry point for the audience. There's *nothing* odd about this place. That's just my imagination.

Finally, Peter broke the silence. 'To be or not to be,' he said slowly as they took in the magnificent setting.

'To be,' Georgia responded. There was no doubt about that. The concert must go ahead, despite all this rubbish she was dreaming up. True, those two trees looked forbidding, almost gloomy, but apart from that this was undoubtedly a superb place for the concert.

'It's all splendid,' Peter added.

Was she wrong about the lack of enthusiasm in his voice? Surely she must be.

'I can see why Rick must have loved it, if it looked as good as this when he knew it,' Peter continued after a pause, but she still sensed he had reservations. 'Who knows, some birds might join in the chorus when our concert takes place. A few nightingales perhaps.'

'Rick would have loved that.' Georgia paused, then asked awkwardly, 'Have you told Elena of our plans?'

'No, darling daughter, I have not. Not yet. I aim to face all the histrionics at once after it's a done deal.'

She was somewhat ashamed to be relieved. Elena was her mother and Peter's ex-wife who had returned some years ago from France after the death of her second husband. Now she lived next door to Peter in the village of Haden Shaw where ostensibly she was Peter's 'carer'. The situation was delicate however, as his faithful long time carer Margaret had had other ideas. As a result, Elena now did her best to help and 'advise' (to her way of thinking) and was usually gently dissuaded. There were wobbles, but on the whole this truce worked.

'Like it, do you?' The young man who had been in the bar earlier appeared as if from nowhere, as he trundled over towards them on his mower. He was tall, good-looking, and had the seasoned look of a lad who knew what he was doing and loved it, she thought.

'Splendid. Is the theatre often in use?' Peter asked.

'Not so's you'd notice.'

'Why ever not? Weather too bad for outside performances?'

'Folks prefer the karaoke nowadays,' he said shortly.

There was no answer to that. 'I take it you're one of the gardeners here?' Georgia asked him cautiously, bearing in mind her newly acquired knowledge of the village feuds.

He laughed. '*The* gardener. Took over from my grandad. That was him with me in the pub, known as Geoff. Louis Sanders is the name.'

'Why don't they employ more?' Georgia asked, taken aback. This was a lot of garden for one young man and for the concert she'd have to be sure that a garden not a jungle awaited the audience.

'They don't employ anyone. I just do it. I come along when I can and rope in a volunteer or so if I can find anyone.'

'But this is a fantastic amount of work.' She was horrified. 'Why, if it's not used much?'

She thought he wasn't going to answer, but he did.

'I come when I can and—'

'Louis!'

As if on cue, a girl came running along a path down from the higher ground beyond the stage. She was blond, as was he, but it was immediately clear that they weren't brother and sister. She too looked twenty or so, Georgia guessed.

Louis blushed. 'Company, Sophy.'

The girl stopped short, then walked a trifle nonchalantly towards them. Georgia took the hint with a nod at Peter. No hostility emanated from the young couple, but it was clear that she and Peter weren't wanted here.

Georgia couldn't sleep. Luke was slumbering peacefully at her side which made it all the more annoying as she tossed and turned. By the small hours the wind had increased and the threatened storm had clearly arrived from the noise beating at the window. Medlars, their home near Godmersham on the road from Ashford to Canterbury, was plentifully surrounded by trees but never, it seemed to her, in the direction from which any winds decided to howl.

Luke must have sensed her restlessness because he stirred and reached out a comforting hand. 'Spring storms always sound worse than they are.'

'Not always,' she muttered. The heavy wind seemed ominous, boding ill for what should be a happy summer planning for the concert. 'Imagination,' she told herself in vain. She had more on her mind than the storm and that's what was keeping her from peaceful sleep, not the wind. She and Peter had made their way down to the theatre stage and wings area after leaving Louis and Sophy, and she had left the place still with the feeling that a dark shadow had passed over her hopefulness for the concert.

'You're dreaming all this up,' she told herself firmly as she tossed and turned. 'You're thinking of past cases.' That's why she had said nothing to Peter when they were at the Maid of Kent theatre. Soon she might have to do so, because they would be returning to the pub not only for the concert but no doubt for preparatory meetings. Eventually she must have fallen fully asleep again because she was awoken by Luke in broad daylight. He was leaning over her, already dressed, cordless phone in hand.

'Peter,' he said succinctly, as she seized it from him.

She hadn't heard it ring and was instantly alarmed as Peter wasn't usually given to making phone calls before nine at least. She'd overslept and it was well past eight o'clock. 'I've had Will Whittan on the line,' Peter's voice greeted her without preamble.

That meant trouble, she knew. Will had replaced Detective Chief Superintendent Mike Gilroy, Peter's former protégé in the Kent Police. Mike had now retired but Will, thankfully, was inclined to be friendly.

'What did he want?'

'I'd rung him,' Peter confessed, 'when I reached home yesterday to ask about those murders old Percival was talking about. About which Will knew nothing. He pointed out he'd only been in the force for thirty years or so.'

That meant her father had been pushing his luck again. 'What did he ring you for then?' Georgia enquired with dread.

'To tell me the storm brought down a lot of trees at the Maid of Kent during the night. It blew down one of those huge beech trees we saw yesterday, roots and all.'

'But what's wrong?' Georgia counted to ten as he paused. Peter always liked drama.

'Remains,' he finished. 'Probably human.'

Chapter Two

What, Georgia wondered, was she doing here on a dismal morning like this? Did she really think that these remains could be those of Cecilia, maid of Kent, whether fair or not? And as for her reactions to those trees yesterday, surely that was just her own private anxiety causing it? Peter had obviously felt nothing odd yesterday, or he would have mentioned it. She must merely have been caught up in the emotion of their mission for Rick.

Anyway, she had had no choice about coming to Cobshaw today. Peter had insisted that she left immediately, pick him up at Haden Shaw and set off to find out what was happening. Now that they had arrived though, even his enthusiasm seemed tempered with reservations.

'Mere curiosity,' Peter said gloomily, echoing her own thoughts. 'Elena pointed out that curiosity killed the cat. I then pointed out that cats had nine lives so I might as well risk one of them. Whatever risk there might be in seeing an uprooted tree,' he added.

'Half of Cobshaw seems to be curious too,' Georgia said, 'judging by this car park.' True, the Maid of Kent's car park wasn't large, but there must be over twenty vehicles there, including, she noticed, several police cars. Cobshaw was, she calculated, only about fifteen minutes' walk away and many villagers could have taken a short cut from there through the pub grounds to peer at the remains.

Which of them was going to speak first? she wondered, as she and Peter left the car and reached the path to the theatre. She still had lingering doubts and as Peter seemed oddly reluctant to speak she summoned up her courage.

Peter forestalled her. 'About yesterday, Georgia.' he said with an appealing glance at her. 'That theatre—did you—'

'Fingerprints,' she said flatly, forestalling him and relieved that at least it was now out in the open. 'You felt them too? I was afraid it was just me.'

'Fingerprints on time' was their shorthand for their shared sense of atmosphere where there had been violence in the past, particularly violent death, but there had been no resolution for the victims. Their tragedies had passed unrecognised. Instead there was a sense of deep grief or pain that had left its imprint on the place. Unsolved murders seemed to be crying out for justice. Neither Peter nor she needed any ghostly apparitions to present themselves as evidence, for the very locations spoke for them.

Then the practical business of an investigation would have to take over, as Marsh & Daughter had to determine whether a case might still be solved in the cold light of twenty-first century demands and resources—taking into account what the results might lead to. In cases where this proved impossible, they at the very least felt they had done their best to resurrect the truth by shining a light on the suffering and pain of the past.

This Fingerprints reaction remained strictly secret between the two of them. Sometimes Georgia wondered if this need for secrecy was merely childishness on her part; a hidden fear that if Elena or anyone else were involved that might destroy the fragile balance of belief and disbelief in what she and Peter sensed. Worse, did her fear stem from jealousy, a longing to cling to something special that she and Peter had shared during those long years when Elena was absent from their lives? Thankfully, although once Elena would have liked nothing better than to play an active role in Marsh & Daughter's cases, the years had brought wisdom to her (relatively) and she contented herself (usually) with publicising her role as a family member.

Now Georgia was aware that she had to face the fact that she hadn't been dreaming. Something had happened here, something terrible. Was it one of Percival's Maid of Kent's murders—perhaps Cecilia's?

'Those police cars at the pub car park—the fact they're still here suggests this is something out of the ordinary. I can hear voices now.' Peter turned his mobility scooter towards the track leading to where yesterday the two huge beech trees had been guarding the stage.

Georgia agreed. It wasn't usual for police to still be around at a scene such as this. The coroner or his officer might have come and gone long ago, his duty done, and any archaeologists too. The mere fact that the police were still here added weight to the remains not being an ancient sheep carcass. Forensic scientists and pathologists must be involved too. As they rounded a bend, this was confirmed. There were enough people standing around to suggest that the 'probably human' had been a formality on Will Whittan's part.

That, Georgia concluded, put paid to any theories that this was the grave of the maid of Kent. If these remains had been found tangled around the roots of this beech tree, they surely couldn't date back to a sixteenth-century murder such as Cecilia's as beeches don't live that long. The tree could be eighteenth century perhaps, she reasoned, then ruled that out too. There wouldn't be police from a modern force still lingering here if the bones were thought to be that old.

'This,' Peter said, drawing to a halt, 'appears to be as far as we can go.'

He was right. Along the bush-lined track ahead of them Georgia could see a group of half a dozen people and beyond them the sprawling buttresses and roots of the tree rearing up, but a police tape was stopping access to the scene. That clinched it. Not ancient bones. The police tape, although not curtaining off a huge area, was extensive enough to suggest that there might be evidence to be collected that could be of interest to the police. Which must mean that the bones must be thought to be relatively recent.

And that meant—

'It could be a crime scene,' Peter said soberly.

'Potentially, yes. Maybe not though. Do you know what the inn was used for during the war?' Georgia asked. Skeletons of fallen airmen, both Allied and German, were still occasionally found in Kent.

'No, but remember Bernie told us there'd been big trouble in the village in the past between two factions. Might be to do with that.' Peter frowned. 'I seem to remember the name Cobshaw cropping up when I was a child though. My parents talked about it. It's ringing a faint bell that I can't get to grips with.'

They could see Will Whittan striding towards them, so they'd obviously been spotted, Georgia realised. His tall sturdy figure and hand grip as he arrived were now familiar. The smile accompanying them was deceptive on occasion, but this didn't seem to be one of them.

'Not usual for a superintendent to inspect a few old bones at this stage, is it?' Peter enquired.

The smile continued. 'Fishing trip, Peter? I like to be sure. Your ringing me about the Maid of Kent yesterday and these bones popping up represent coincidence. Always a magnet, don't you think?' Without waiting for an answer, Will continued, 'They're human remains all right. The forensic archaeologist is on his way. We emailed a photo to the lab, he took one look and said he'd come and check out the bugs. Want a look yourselves? No problem over scene suits and shoes for this one, Georgia. But best not to risk this state-of-the-art contraption of yours, Peter.'

He was well used to this situation and shrugged, as Georgia followed Will through the barrier.

'We've had a tree surgeon in already, as well as the doc's verdict,' Will continued. 'The tree's two to three hundred years old but the bones are more recent. At least forty years or so, though. The bones weren't all together but it looks as though they could had been buried between two of the tree buttresses.'

Georgia steeled herself. She was well used to crime scenes, but they never failed to move her. This one, with the fallen bulk of the mighty beech-tree's trunk and its smaller roots pathetically waving in the breeze, was no exception. Around it were the now well-trodden May spring flowers, the anemones and some bluebells now past their prime.

'The other tree's unaffected,' Will continued. 'The tree surgeon guy says this one was probably brought down because of all the coppicing over there.' He pointed to woodland beyond the boundary fence which showed every sign of that from the piles of timber and exposed undergrowth where the trees had been chopped down. 'It left this beech too exposed—and down she came.'

Georgia knew enough about trees to know that copper beeches were rarely naturally planted, but cultivated by choice, which added weight to the theory that when this tree had started its life here, the Maid of Kent must have been in its glory days, either as an inn or perhaps, she wondered, a manor house. The latter might explain the tree's presence here as even as early as the eighteenth century when there were already plenty of commercial seedsmen to supply rich or not so rich landowners.

'Are you and Peter planning to give us a hand in this case to find out who this mystery man is?' Will asked, deadpan. 'I say mystery *man* because that's the view of our pathologist—the pelvis is different for a woman—amongst other indications. The uprooting hasn't dispersed the bones too much, and the sex is still clear in this case.'

'I'll check my diary to see if we can squeeze you in,' Georgia assured him. Taking the light side was one way of dealing with tragedy, past or present.

'Meet our mystery man, then.' The group surveying the site spread out giving Will room, with Georgia in his wake, to work his way through a now cleared short path between some of the roots. A few of these had been cut away together with small piles of the earth that had probably been partly covering the bones and any artefacts that might be linked to them.

She forced herself to ignore the quivers inside her and to take a professional look at what she could see in the loosened soil. It was harder than she had expected. As Will had said, the bones themselves weren't scattered to any great extent but she could see one dislodged limb flung out at an angle as if pleading for recognition amid the mass of small twigs and branches around it. There seemed to be a few shreds of clothing still with the bones although much of it, Will told her, had already been removed in evidence bags. One thing was clear to her: he didn't think these remains dated back to Cecilia's time *or* the eighteenth century.

'The coroner's going to email us a licence to remove the bones in view of the local interest,' Will told her. 'We don't want them disappearing overnight or any remaining booty pinched.'

'Was there any?'

'Some. No treasure trove though, or even smugglers' hoards. Remains of the clothing, and the disruption as the tree fell must have disturbed its location. Nothing too ancient there though. Looked like wool trousers, jacket, shirt and so on from a brief glance.'

'Shoes?' Georgia asked.

'Yes. Remains again but only one still by the foot, though again disruption could have caused that. There was a watch—a good one. Omega. Cuff-links and—' He grinned at her—'a sword of some kind.'

'*Sword*? Is that what killed him? she asked in amazement.

'That remains to be seen. No evidence on that so far. But our victim's unlikely just to have tripped over it, banged his head and fallen into a hole,' he continued more soberly. 'Also, it's significant that a lot of the locals have gathered to watch us at work. More than sheer curiosity would have attracted. Villagers have long memories, and this man doesn't seem to date back to the time of pistols at dawn.'

Georgia looked down to where the groups were gathering beyond the stage and the crime scene tape. Will was right and there were more people there now than when she and Peter had arrived. Word had spread and there must be at least forty-odd onlookers. Idle curiosity or was it more than that? Amongst the crowd she spotted Brenda Randall, whom she'd seen in the pub yesterday. She was standing next to the man Georgia identified as Dave Cook, Brenda's ex son-in-law, with whom Brenda was apparently at odds, so what was all that about?

Remembering Peter, Georgia guiltily hared back to where he was patiently waiting for her. 'Sorry to have taken so long,' she apologised.

Peter graciously waved this aside. 'I've remembered why the name Cobshaw cropped up in my youth as a mysterious sort of place. Rick—' he swallowed. Sometimes it was still hard for him to talk about his son—'mentioned it once too.'

'So why was that?'

'The missing knight,' Peter declared triumphantly, then obviously seeing her puzzled expression added crossly, 'The English language has a lot to answer for. Knight with a k, dear daughter. The case of the missing knight has never been solved. Nineteen fifties or early sixties, I recall.'

Georgia was with him now. 'Sir John Wilbourne?' she asked with interest. 'The famous actor? Rivalled Laurence Olivier and John Gielgud. The darling of the gods and of every woman in town, if I remember rightly. But what did he have to do with the Maid of Kent and Cobshaw?'

'That I don't recall. What I do recall is that somehow Cobshaw came into the story.'

Georgia racked her own memory. 'If you're implying the missing bones might be his, you're wrong. I remember reading about the John Wilbourne story and I'm sure it said he was in London when he disappeared.'

Peter frowned. 'It's coming back to me too. He lived there and I think you're right that he was last seen there too. I was only a child at the time but even then I had a nose for investigation,' he explained complacently. 'There was a big newspaper placard outside Mrs Jones's newsagent's shop in Haden Shaw—long gone of course—and it read: "Missing knight kidnapped?" It was the question mark that mystified me. Why didn't they know the answer?'

'Very precocious of you,' Georgia said straight-faced 'But how does Cobshaw come in?'

'I don't know whether it did. I didn't think to ask. I was only six years old.'

Fair enough. But Peter's parents, her grandparents, hadn't necessarily been talking about Cobshaw. Georgia braced herself to ask the vital question: 'Those Fingerprints yesterday—connected, do you think?'

Peter looked at her uncertainly. 'They could have been Rick's, remember. He often came here.'

'No, not his Fingerprints,' Georgia said gently. 'We've been through the worst of our grieving now. He wouldn't be signalling to us. He's at peace.'

'But someone isn't. The question is who?' he replied quietly.

Belatedly Georgia saw they had company descending on them. Brenda Randall was marching towards them with a purposeful look on her face. If she had taken the trouble to leave the village group and take the winding path up to collar them, she must have a very definite mission. Bearing in mind that according to Bernie she was the village historian, it wasn't hard to guess what that mission would be. An identity for the bones?

'You're Marsh & Daughter,' she informed them grandly as she reached them.

'We are,' Georgia admitted.

'You write those true crime books about Kentish murders. Are you planning to write one about us?' Brenda's gimlet eye swivelled to Peter.

'Do you think there's one asking to be written?' Peter replied politely.

'There most certainly is. Several in fact.'

'Excellent. Would one be based on today's discovery? Do you have any idea whose remains they could be?'

Surprisingly, Brenda looked disconcerted. 'No—that is, we cannot be sure of course. Until we know…. I mean Cecilia, our maid of Kent. They might not be though.' Then she regained her composure. 'The *true* story of Cecilia needs to be told. Hers is a story *well* worth recording and when this building is a professionally run hotel the visitors are going to be most interested in its history.'

'Is the hotel a certainty?' Georgia asked.

'It has to be. There is this quixotic notion that the community can buy and run it but there is no way that's practical. A historic hotel, however, would be of great benefit to the whole village.'

'Based only on Plantagenet heritage?' Georgia was becoming even more curious about this place. Even the pub's bar was heavily decorated with its medieval connections.

'Good gracious, no,' Brenda barked back. 'The hotel will most certainly not be Plantagenet-based. There is of course the mistaken belief that Cecilia was a Plantagenet. That's nonsense. Cecilia was a Tudor by birth and *owned* what is now called the Maid of Kent public house. When the hotel takes over that will be made quite clear. Meanwhile Percival FitzRichard will doubtless continue with his ridiculous story that Cecilia was born in my home, Cobshaw Cottage, and that she was the impoverished granddaughter of the Plantagenet Richard of Eastwell whom Percival foolishly claims lived in Cobshaw Cottage for many years. Then apparently she had the good fortune to marry a Randall and move into what is now the Maid of Kent. More nonsense on Percival's part. Cecilia's true heritage is that she is descended from Owen Tudor himself,' she announced, 'and was thus related to King Henry VII, the first of the Tudor monarchs.'

'That's a load of cobblers, Brenda,' Dave Cook said amiably, strolling up as Georgia was reeling from this onslaught. 'Cecilia was indeed the granddaughter of Richard of Eastwell and you know it. You just can't face the idea of her having lived in your house once.'

'What I *know*, Dave,' she retorted coolly, 'is that you are ignoring the facts of history. I trust that the sad events of today prove that this is a heritage site to be cherished and not to be ruined by football and drunken degenerates.'

Dave regarded her impassively, clearly used to such tirades. 'Get used to it, Brenda. This is meant to be community space. Used by everyone. Run by everyone for everyone. Nowadays no one wants to see only a few well-heeled folks wandering around here. It's *our* history too.'

'My dear man, have you any idea what *your* history involved?' she shot back at him.

'Course he hasn't.' Mick Buckley, Dave's companion in the pub, joined them, but the affability of yesterday was no longer on the agenda, or so Georgia judged from the look on his face. Not towards Dave anyway. Odd though, as he worked for the Randalls, Mick didn't seem very amicably disposed towards Brenda either, judging by the way he was deliberately ignoring her.

'This pub is the beating heart of the village, Mick,' Dave said levelly. 'If you rip it apart, the village will die.'

'There's such a thing as history,' Brenda retorted. 'The Maid of Kent inn was once Cobshaw Court before it became a common alehouse. It needs to return to its former glory.'

So she'd been right about its former use, Georgia thought, giving herself a mental pat on the back.

'History's for everyone, not just the rich, Brenda,' Dave said mildly.

'And what have you ever done for history, Dave?' Mick jeered.

'It seems to us as outsiders,' Peter hastily intervened, 'that history might indeed lie with those bones. Do either of you have any ideas on whose they might be?'

There was instant silence, which Brenda at last broke, somewhat uncertainly. 'I suppose it is just possible that they are Cecilia's.'

Dave Cook grinned. 'You can rule that out—unless Cecilia wore dark trousers. That's what I've just been told.'

Brenda managed a weak smile. 'Some tramp then.'

It didn't sound convincing, Georgia thought. What was Brenda really thinking? Tramps didn't leave swords around and tramps who met a natural death would not be neatly buried and forgotten, Georgia thought. And this silence was strange. The natural reaction to a situation like this would be morbid speculation on whose body this might be. And yet there seemed none. The village seemed to be waiting on events, and Brenda Randall, Dave Cook and Mick Buckley were keeping their speculations to themselves.

Georgia held her breath, noting that Peter was looking from one to the other of the warriors in this village battle. He too must be noting their silence and wondering what was *not* being said.

Dave Cook eventually spoke, still bent it seemed, on ignoring what had brought them all to this spot in the first place. 'You realise, don't you, Brenda, that the village is irretrievably split over this hotel idea of yours. Whether Percival FitzRichard finds his true Plantagenet or not, nothing is going to stop that now. The division will just become even deeper. It never healed when Joyce and I married, did it, not even when we divorced? No Tudor can marry a Planter. That's still the case, isn't it? Young Louis Sanders is making eyes at Sophy but he won't stand a chance. The Tudors and the Planters will see to that. We're still fighting, heading right back to those days our parents remembered. The dark days when reason forsook us. They warned us not to let them return, but you're helping bring them back, Brenda.'

This seemed to have shaken her for she stared at him for a moment or two before replying. 'You don't understand. How can we tell who is a true Plantagenet? And does it matter? But the Tudors—and yet…'

'How were the bones?' Luke was calling out from his lounger in their garden, as Georgia arrived late in the afternoon, intent on dumping her iPad in the summer house she used as a spill-over office.

His call startled her because he'd been masked by the tree he was sitting under. Luke was usually hard at work himself in his office in the oast-house, so the lounger was a departure from the norm to say the least. She had dropped Peter off at Haden Shaw and then made a beeline for Canterbury where she had had an appointment with her accountant followed by various fruitless missions, including a failed attempt to meet her stepdaughter-in-law Jill; she hadn't answered her phone or her mobile and was out when Georgia walked round to see if she was in the house or working in her garden. She wasn't to be found anywhere, it was now late afternoon, and Georgia could have done with some lazing in the sun herself.

'Work too much for you?' she called out crossly.

'I am working. I'm thinking,' he returned amicably.

'Then think Cobshaw,' came a shout. Peter appeared on his scooter around the corner of their house, looking extremely gleeful. She was taken by surprise partly because she hadn't heard his car arrive and partly because it wasn't like him to make an unplanned visit so what on earth had brought him here?

'Fee, fi, fo, fum,' Luke called out to him as he drove over to join them, 'do I sniff the smell of another Marsh & Daughter best-seller coming along?'

'Only a sniff at present,' Peter said, 'unless you want to publish a book on her ladyship, Cecilia, maid of Kent—I still don't know much about her yet. I could manage another one on Richard of Eastwell or the Plantagenet kings of England.'

'Not my line. Nor yours, I thought,' Luke replied. 'What about those bones though? They're not Plantagenets, are they?'

'Ninety-nine per cent sure they're not. That new book you think you can sniff is probably less royal. But no case *yet.*'

Luke sat up. 'Tell me more.'

'How about a tentative title of *The Case of the Missing Knight: Sir John Wilbourne*? I've been doing preliminary research.'

Georgia blinked. Peter had already made a start? He must have felt those Fingerprints strongly and she felt a familiar excitement beginning to pulse through her.

Luke looked interested. 'I remember hearing about that. But didn't it all happen in London? We only cover Kentish crimes.'

'On the night before, Saturday 22nd August,' Peter said complacently, 'Sir John Wilbourne was starring in *Romeo and Juliet* in an outdoor performance in the village of Cobshaw.' He paused for effect.

He achieved it. Georgia stared at him in momentary disbelief and even Luke, who usually took surprises in his stride, was taken aback. So that's why her grandparents had talked of Cobshaw in connection with the story of the missing knight, Georgia realised. 'Even so,' she pointed out, 'he must have gone back to London that night or at least in the morning, otherwise there would have been investigations made here. It would have been big news.' Nevertheless, Peter's story was odd. 'Why should a major star be performing in a village the size of Cobshaw?' she added, 'especially in an open air theatre with a fifty-fifty chance of rain?'

Peter beamed. 'I'm glad you asked me that. It did seem curious. But not quite so curious when I discovered that John Wilbourne was the nephew of Jacob Randall, then the owner of Cobshaw Hall. Georgia was speechless. One question immediately came to mind, but Luke forestalled her. She could tell even he was hooked.

'Why not hold the performance in the grounds of Cobshaw Hall then?' Luke asked.

'I'm *not* glad you asked me that, Luke,' Peter said. 'Because I don't know. But we know a lady who does, Brenda Randall, local historian and a member of the local elite.'

'Are you suggesting he disappeared from here, not London? Or worse—' yes, this must be it '—that he might have been murdered here if those bones are his?' Georgia asked incredulously. Surely Peter was going too fast.

31

'I am. There's a hitch though,' Peter said. 'He was seen in London the following day.'

'So why are you so excited then?' Luke wanted to know. 'Murder in Cobshaw seems to be ruled out.'

'Always worth investigating,' Peter said airily. 'He doesn't seem to have had a wife, so there was no one to report on whether or not he returned from Cobshaw. And there were only a couple of witnesses to his being in London the day after his Cobshaw performance.'

Luke lifted an eyebrow. 'The two murderers perhaps?'

'Could be.' Peter refused to be cornered. 'I'll look into it His solicitors applied for a presumption of death in the late sixties. There seems to have been a lot of gossip at the time as to whether he decided to vanish or whether someone helped him do it permanently. In the latter category suspicion fell on one of the cast, Edward Colduggan.'

'*The* Edward Colduggan?' Georgia's head was really spinning now.

'Indeed. Sir Edward Colduggan—who in 1959 was a rising young star in the same company as Sir John.'

Chapter Three

Everyone had heard of Edward Colduggan. Now in his mid to late eighties, he was still playing cameo parts on the stage, on TV and in films. One glory of the passing years, Georgia supposed, is that the scandals of colourful early lives tend to fade in significance in the public consciousness. And that was surely the case with Edward Colduggan. The drama of his divorce from Hollywood film star Lena Bright and subsequent brief marriage to Anna Feverel had provided the media with ample fodder for many years. His return to the British stage—successful though that had proved—had brought him back to the heights of fame for his classical roles. But that had been long after his appearance at Cobshaw. In 1959 he had been playing Mercutio to Sir John Wilbourne's Romeo and Laertes to his Hamlet. Why had he become a suspect behind Sir John's disappearance? Would ambition have driven him as far as murder?

With this tantalising query, Georgia was itching to push ahead but she had heard nothing from Peter although it was now Thursday, 23rd May, three weeks after the bones had been discovered. The only information that had filtered through from the coroner's inquest via Will Whittan was that the bones had added up to an almost complete skeleton, they were human and male, roughly forty to seventy years old. With natural causes ruled out, the verdict was that damage on the remains was consistent with a sharp blade. The sword? Georgia wondered.

She had plenty to do in her own office without chasing out to Haden Shaw to her father's home, not least arrangements for the concert, but nevertheless she was fretting over her unanswered phone messages and emails to him. Her antennae were hard at work over his silence. She knew he wouldn't keep major news to himself, but there was a distinct possibility that he might be pushing the boundaries of their joint understanding on such issues. Was he, for instance, still pestering poor Detective Superintendent Will Whittan?

In the end she could bear it no longer and drove over to Haden Shaw to demand answers. A mistake. No sooner had Georgia let herself in than she realised Peter was not there. The silence greeting her was unmistakable. Margaret now put in fewer hours as a carer, so not even she seemed to be present. She and Elena, Georgia had decided, must have an unspoken understanding that they would never publicly vent their joint suspicion of each other's motives and deeds. If they did, Peter would be the unenviable piggy in the middle.

This morning, although Peter was not present, Elena was. The inner door through to Elena's home next door (once Georgia's territory) flew open. Fond though Georgia was of her mother, she feared that this was going to be one of those rare occasions when Elena's curiosity about her daughter and ex-husband's joint business led her to overstep the agreed boundaries.

Fortunately not, although it was clear that Elena had something on her mind. Her neat and elegant dress sense always made Georgia feel like an awkward schoolgirl again, and today, with Elena immaculately clad in skin-tight trousers and a pale blue silk tunic, was no exception. That made it all the more difficult to carry out her plan.

'Darling,' Elena cried anxiously. 'Peter said I should telephone you as he hadn't time himself. I'm so glad you're here—there was no reply when I rang your landline and I can never find my mobile when I need it.'

'Nothing's wrong with him, is it?' Georgia asked sharply.

'Good heavens, no. I don't know where he is though. Do come in and I'll tell you what's happened.'

What was all this? Georgia followed her mother into the elegant living room that she hardly recognised as the same homely room she'd created when she had lived in this house. Peter's apparently urgent message must be about the Maid of Kent. Then she registered that Elena was looking genuinely distressed so it couldn't be work related. Her alarm grew.

'It's Jill.' Elena burst into tears. 'She's going back to the States and taking Rosie and Robbie with her.'

'*What?*' Georgia was aghast. 'Is Mark to blame for this?' Jill was American by birth and Mark and their children had dual nationality but it had never occurred to her—or to Luke—that his son would return to live in the States. Elena had bonded with Jill immediately when they met and she and Peter were very close to Mark's family.

'No, it's Jill's decision. She's leaving him. She says she's bored here.' Elena hiccupped. 'She can't find work, and although she writes the occasional article for magazines and so on, she says she needs to be fulfilled.'

Jill had been a university lecturer in English literature when she met and married Mark, but she had been in the UK so long now that it seemed incredible that she would want to leave. Jill's father was no longer alive and her mother paid visits (all too frequently for Georgia and Luke) to see her daughter and grandchildren here.

Georgia grappled with common sense. 'Rosie's at an age when she ought to have a say in it.'

That produced another flood of tears, in the midst of which Georgia heard Peter returning. 'Turn right,' she called out.

'News!' he cried gleefully as he reached them, but as he turned a practised eye on his sobbing wife he exchanged glances with Georgia. 'Ah, you've heard the other news, Georgia. Darling,' he addressed his wife, 'how about Georgia and I have a brief pow-wow and then we'll have a conference about Jill over lunch?'

No way would he get away with that, and Georgia for once was on Elena's side despite the fact that she was agog to hear what Peter had to say on the matter of Sir John Wilbourne. Jill's ultimatum was major news though. Georgia was aware that it would affect her more than Elena as it was Luke's family at the heart of it but nevertheless Elena's distress was real and had to be dealt with. The conference took longer than she'd hoped and ended—as usual—with Peter's promising to 'talk to Jill'. They all knew that this would lead nowhere but at least Elena was somewhat comforted.

Once established on neutral ground, in Peter's office, Georgia tried to concentrate on business. Or, she amended to herself, what *might* be business at the Maid of Kent pub. So far there was little activity.

'Will Whittan is the most stubborn chap I've ever met,' Peter complained. 'All I got from him was that whatever the weapon was, it was unlikely to have been that sword—it was one for stage combat, which makes me think we must be on the right track. The bones, as I texted you, are indeed human, but I had to force a confirmation out of him that they're at least fifty years old judging by the evidence from the clothes and the tree roots.'

'Nothing more than that?'

'No,' he replied somewhat grumpily. 'What's more, he just won't concede that they could be those of John Wilbourne; he's approaching it the long way around instead of going straight to following that line up. No, he wants to study in due course every document in the Kent police archive, as well as the Met's contributions before checking that angle. There's no talking yet about calling in the Serious Crime Directorate. All because he's still sticking with the fact that unless two people were lying, Sir John Wilbourne was alive and well in London on Sunday and Monday, 23rd and 24th August 1959. The remains could therefore be anyone's, he claims, especially as the sword is now irrelevant as a weapon. Nevertheless he does graciously grant there there's a faint possibility that we're on the right track.'

'DNA?' Georgia asked hopefully.

Peter looked at her scathingly, as if it were perfectly obvious that had been checked. 'No such luck. In due course, Will says. Costs money and in the meantime it's—'

'WPT,' Georgia finished for him. 'Wasting police time.'

'Quite. First hunting down blood relatives for blood samples, then the DNA costs and probably no distinct result at the end of it. It's almost sixty years ago that Sir John disappeared so I can see those bones heading for the back burner as regards our Will's attention.'

'Not for you though. You've already done some more work on it, haven't you?' She could always tell when he was treading dangerously close to breaking the rule of keeping her fully informed.

Peter had the grace to blush. 'Perhaps. Let's go then. Sir John Wilbourne, was forty-four years old when he disappeared on or shortly after 22nd August 1959.'

'Was the knighthood inherited or his own hard work?'

'The latter. Granted two years before his disappearance. He'd played every major part several times over in every major country and every major theatre, it seems. Nearly all classical, but occasionally he condescended to dip his toe into comedy and modern drama.'

So far nothing much, then. 'What else?' she demanded. '*Why* was Edward Colduggan suspected?'

'That's where it gets interesting. When the performance in Cobshaw was over, most of the cast, according to the press, went back to London with the scenery and props that Saturday night—possibly missing that one stage sword. Some stayed in the Maid of Kent overnight though and returned to London the next day.'

'Who stayed over?' Georgia pressed him. Assuming that these were indeed his remains, this would be a crucial factor, since that was the probable time he was killed if those witnesses who saw him in London were mistaken—or lying.

'Not yet known to us, save that one of them was Edward Colduggan.'

This was indeed getting interesting. 'But why was he suspected of being behind Sir John's disappearance? Why did the gossip start?' She'd seen some of Colduggan's performances in London in the past and plenty of them on screen recently and it was hard to connect her memories of a now ageing brilliant actor with the passionate youth he must have been in 1959.

'Who knows where gossip starts?' Peter said piously.

'It's usually where it ends that's interesting,' Georgia retorted. 'It could end in a red herring or the truth.'

'Either needs to be established on firm ground.'

'In that case,' she said, 'I have a question.'

'Rhetorical?'

'At the moment, yes. The same points as I made earlier. Sir John had relatives here in Cobshaw and would surely have paid a family visit to them. Otherwise, why bring the company to play Shakespeare in an obscure English village for only the one performance? And, as Luke pointed out, why hold it in the grounds of an old pub—especially a pub,' she added, 'that has a penchant for Plantagenet kings?

If the performance had been *Henry VI Parts One, Two and Three* I could understand it, but *Romeo and Juliet* seems somewhat off-beam, especially at Sir John's age.'

Peter stared at her. 'I'm glad that was a rhetorical question. It seems to me I'm losing my grip, Georgia. Put together, the oddness of it all could be our path ahead.'

'Born in 1915,' Georgia muttered to herself a few hours later, unable to get those bones off her mind, although ostensibly she was enjoying the late afternoon sun with Luke in their garden before supper. She'd stopped dignifying it with the name of dinner as its contents tended to be woefully pedestrian, at least during the working week. The glory of take-aways and ready meals loomed tantalisingly in front of her.

'Anyone I know?' Luke enquired politely.

Georgia laughed. 'Sorry. No. Just Sir John Wilbourne again.'

He sighed. 'I suppose he helps take your mind off what's going on in our family.'

He was right. Instant guilt for not reading his silent signals earlier. Georgia dithered, not wanting to tread on tender ground, but then decided the issue had to be faced. 'Are Jill and Mark really splitting up or do you think this a temporary hitch?'

'No idea,' Luke said gloomily. 'Madame Jill hasn't told us and if she's bothered to tell Mark, then he hasn't shared it with me. We, my dearest, are extraneous and so apparently is my son as far as Jill's concerned.'

'Rosie and Robbie aren't though. Do you know their views?'

'I know Rosie's, which is an unequivocal no, and I can guess Robbie's is the same. Rosie's been shouting it at me on her mobile most of the day as if I'm to blame for her mother's insistence on her crazy plan, and Robbie's been crying to make his view obvious too. I suppose as he's only eight he can't be blamed for not seeing both sides of the problem.'

'Do you? You called it a *crazy* plan.'

Luke managed a laugh. 'Caught out. Well, I can understand why Jill's frustrated. There she is, twiddling her thumbs—'

'She doesn't twiddle. There's masses going on in Canterbury and she's always dashing around somewhere, although I realise that that's not akin to her former academic work.'

'Do you think that's the only reason she wants to leave?' There was a note of hope in Luke's voice.

A dodgy one this. 'Pass.'

'Ah. But,' Luke added, 'in case you had this in mind as a solution to her problem, I don't want to publish academic books on my list, nor do I require Jill's assistance in running the firm. Much as I love Jill, I couldn't work with her.'

'You do with me,' Georgia pointed out.

Luke grinned. 'You a mere author. Me great big important publisher. Or, to be fair, sometimes you famous author and me unimportant publisher. It works,' he added, ducking as she chucked her notebook at him.

'I'll have another talk to her, shall I?' Georgia dreaded that, but it was worth the risk. Jill was charming, forceful and determined. Once she saw a path ahead, she took it no matter what obstacles lay on either side. Georgia loved her, but she also trod very gingerly where Jill was concerned—or had done so, until Mark had confided in her once that Jill found her, Georgia, intimidating. That was nonsense, of course.

Time to divert Luke, Georgia decided. He was brooding too much on the family problem and there was little they could do about it. After leaving Haden Shaw that morning she had spent an hour or two doing some preliminary research online about Sir John. There was a surprising amount to find despite his disappearance having been so long ago. Newspapers, theatre magazines and online sources provided plenty of material and there was even a fan club although from a quick glance at its website the most thriving section of it was entirely devoted to theories as to his present whereabouts. These ranged from his being in South Africa with Lord Lucan to drowning himself in the River Avon after bad reviews of his Othello.

Sir John had paid guest appearances at all the great national theatres, but his main career had been with the famous Bard of Avon Company attached to the West London Theatre. After his disappearance, the company had continued for a year or so, then disbanded, and the West London Theatre then hosted another company, managed by and starring, she noted, Edward Colduggan. That was before Hollywood claimed him, and his subsequent return to the UK as an international star.

After John Wilbourne's disappearance, Colduggan's stage career blossomed after his big breakthrough with his own Hamlet. No more secondary roles like Mercutio for him. Was there significance in this? Georgia wondered. *Romeo and Juliet* had not been in the Bard of Avon's 1959 London repertoire, though it had been the year before, so why had Sir John wanted a single performance of it at Cobshaw? His last stab at Romeo perhaps in view of his advancing age? That was possible.

She was still meditating on this question the next day. Peter had been vague to say the least as to the reason that it was so important for them to be at the Maid of Kent this Friday. Georgia had been all for following up the London end of the trail although it was true, she supposed, that this would be best done if and when it became a certainty that those were John Wilbourne's remains and better still when they could publicly say so. Meanwhile the more they learned about the Maid of Kent today meant they might learn more about its past.

'They're holding some kind of village meeting of the worthies there,' he told her. 'Percival FitzRichard called it and I gather that all the usual suspects will be present.'

'We're not suspects, I trust?' Georgia had a moment's fear that Peter was planning to play a leading role in whatever was going on but dismissed it. Even he would have the sense not to get involved in a dispute in a village like Cobshaw. It was small enough for any split to affect everyone there to some degree.

'No, but the issues affect us because of the concert,' Peter replied. 'Anyway, that's our excuse for going along.'

'What's the real reason?'

'Brenda Randall told me we should be there.'

Remembering Brenda's odd reactions last time there was a hullabaloo over the Maid of Kent's future, Georgia was intrigued. 'Why?'

'No idea, but we might find out.'

'Some kind of meeting' was an understatement, Georgia soon realised. The car park was full and she had to park in the lane nearly ending up in the ditch. The bar too was packed, which was fortunate as in the hubbub their arrival went almost unnoticed, even with Peter's mobility scooter which usually attracted attention. Dave Cook currently had the floor as they entered. His stalwart figure was squaring up to Mick Buckley accompanied by roars and boos from their audience. Amongst the crowd around them she could see Percival FitzRichard dancing like a crazed umpire trying to get a word in—which he finally managed.

'I'm not selling,' he screeched in a sudden lull. 'Plantagenets only. Understand that, you morons? You may be a Planter but you don't have a drop of Plantagenet blood in you, Dave, and nor do you, you Tudor peasant, Mick. And nor, as far as I know, has this hotel fellow, Howard Green.'

It was brave of him to bandy insults with someone of Mick's build, Georgia thought. Percival was buzzing around like a wasp stinging where the flesh was weakest and that could turn nasty. With Mike his status as Cobshaw Hall's manager was likely to be his weak spot.

Tony was pushing his way through the crowd looking very determined about supporting his wife in this uproar. 'Face facts, Percival,' he said. 'We've got to do something soon. This place is falling down. It needs money spent on it. Big money.'

'He's right, Dad,' Bernie cried from the bar.

'I know that, you cuckoo,' her father yelled at her. 'But we keep wasting time with all this chatter about community and hotels. Bollocks to the lot of you. This place needs someone with a drop of royal blood.'

Dave Cook's face was flushed. 'The Maid of Kent's already acting as a community centre, Percival. It's the only place we can all gather and I'm planning to keep it that way. We're not going to hand it over to a bunch of strangers coming here for fancy food and a gawp at the village yokels. Community, that's what we need, and we can raise the means to buy it.'

'That's a bloody joke,' Mick Buckley loomed large again. Cobshaw's never been a community and never will be. Planters and Tudors, that's what we were once and still are, and this is a place that needs a touch of the Tudors—they got things done, did the Tudors. Those Plantagenets were too busy fighting each other.'

Here they go again, Georgia thought, wondering whether this would lead anywhere other than a punch-up.

'Been reading your kiddies' schoolbooks again, Mick?' Dave retorted.

'You need millions poured into this place and not one of you has got a dime,' Mick sneered.

'There are ways of funding places like this,' Dave threw at him. 'Lottery funding for a start. They understand community projects like ours.'

'They understand money in the bank to run it as well. The Maid needs a hotel.'

'I don't want either of you,' Percival yelled. 'I'm only selling to a Plantagenet!'

'But you do need a buyer *now.*' Brenda's voice brought them to a sudden silence. Georgia had noticed her anxious face and she was speaking now with real urgency in her voice.

'That hotel friend of yours, Brenda,' Dave broke the silence that fell. 'This Howard Green. Is he a Tudor or a Plantagenet or neither? Time we heard a bit more about him, isn't it? Unless he's a Plantagenet, Percival here says he won't sell to him. So who is he? Are you hoping to get one of your Tudors in by the back door?'

'I have no need of back doors,' Brenda said hotly.

'I don't need surprises, I need a Plantagenet,' Percival snorted. 'And none of those Tudor lies that they're all descended from Plantagenets. I want a *real* Plantagenet.'

Dave made a valiant effort. 'It's not my place to speak out but you *do* need a buyer. The Maid of Kent needs restoration, whether it's a pub, hotel or community centre. So give over, you two. This is business. We need to sort out who's in the best position to buy this place and be quick about it. Some hotel chap we've never met or the local parish council you know. Certainty. That's what you really want, isn't it, Perce?'

'I told you what I really want,' Percival snarled.

'Mr Green will be arriving soon to put his proposition to you,' Brenda Randall told them anxiously. 'The only viable proposition.'

'What are you up to now?' Dave asked wearily, and Georgia was near enough to hear his muttered 'you crazy old bat' as he finished.

Unfortunately, Brenda must have good hearing because she retorted loudly enough to attract attention, some of it hostile. 'Not crazy at all, thank you, Dave. It's not for me to say, but you'll see this hotel offer is the best for Cobshaw. Its heritage must be preserved and Howard Green intends to do so.'

Mick Buckley nodded vigorously, somewhat to Georgia's surprise. Tudor or not, he hadn't seemed a fan of Brenda's. Georgia was all too well aware that the thirty or so other people at this meeting were following what was happening and already beginning to split into two factions. Restless and ready for action.

Just as Dave also seemed to be squaring up for battle, Tony came rushing in. 'Out,' he yelled. 'Finish this outside,' and he promptly began breaking up the hard core of fighters, which for a slightly built man was no mean feat.

Georgia speedily moved out of the way as he set about ushering them outside to continue their 'discussion', with Dave and Mick amongst them. Even Brenda Randall scuttled out, and Georgia sensed definite menace in the air. She could see Brenda needed moral support, strong-minded woman though she was, and Georgia hurried to catch up with her outside where the crowd was now gathering. As the crow flies, it might only be a short walk to Brenda's home, which Georgia guessed was on the Cobshaw Hall estate, but fortunately Brenda had chosen wisely in driving here.

'Sorry you have to leave, Brenda,' Georgia said intentionally loudly, and as Brenda looked undecided, she gave her a gentle push towards her car. The crowd was beginning to show signs of advancing on them.

'They don't understand,' Brenda said to her through the open window, once safely in the car. 'This community idea of theirs is fine talk, but not practical. And there is so much heritage to preserve—and yet there is…'

She shook her head in despair as her voice trailed off and she started the car. Then she added abruptly, 'I would like your father and yourself to come to my home where I can explain my dilemma. It's a matter of history.' She looked over her shoulder and when Georgia turned to see what had attracted her attention she realised with a lurch of fear that the crowd was already much closer. From the rising noise level and the definite menace on some of those faces, it was bent on confrontation.

'*Go*,' she urged Brenda.

But Brenda still hesitated. 'Do come tomorrow, Georgia. Let's say eleven o'clock.'

'*Go!*' This time Brenda started up and drove off.

Breathing a sigh of relief, Georgia walked back to the pub skirting the hostile group which was already breaking up. Trouble averted—for the moment, she thought thankfully.

As she rejoined Peter at the bar, Bernie came out from behind it.

'It's the first time that Brenda's claimed publicly that she's backing Howard Green despite Dad's stupid requirements over heritage,' Bernie said anxiously 'I don't like the sound of that one little bit. This hotel man is an outsider, not a Plantagenet or a Tudor. I think old Gerald Randall must be backing him too, as he's the reigning owner of Cobshaw Hall. His brother was Brenda's late husband Thomas. Gerald's a Tudor, though, which Dad says rules him out, however much Brenda tries to claim that the Tudors were partly descended from the Plantagenets too. Dad doesn't think that counts.'

'You're backing community ownership then?' Peter asked.

'Depends what they have in mind.' Bernie gave them a wink that mystified Georgia, but Bernie didn't seem disposed to explain.

Percival was on his way back to them, bristling with indignation. 'Ruddy Tudors,' he muttered. 'Still going on about their divine right to buy the place. Those Planters, they're good sorts, but they don't have a drop of true Plantagenet blood in them. Not like me,' he added complacently. 'I'm a FitzRichard. Descended from my father Montague, I go straight back to Teddy the Third himself. Know what Shakespeare said? "This sceptred isle, this throne of kings." Throne of *Plantagenet* Kings. No Tudors for him. No one but a Plantagenet can keep this place going. That's what my father told me, and that's what I intend to make happen.'

'Very well, Dad,' Bernie said firmly. 'I've had enough. I'm a true Plantagenet, aren't I? You're one, granddad was one, and I'm one. Tony and I will raise the funds, restore the place to a community centre, together with the Planters.'

Percival's jaw dropped and he was silent for a moment. Then: 'Girls don't count,' he roared.

'Where,' Peter muttered to Georgia, 'is this leading?'

This was crazy, Georgia thought. True, they were outsiders, but Percival seemed set on his own track where apparently daughters did not count. She could see that Tony was looking horrified over by the door and Bernie was fuming.

'Look at the deeds, Dad, and Grandad's will,' Bernie said crossly. 'I'll be bound that doesn't say it has to be a man. You keep going on about the Maid of Kent. About time it had a Mistress of Kent. Me.'

'Who's your money on?' Georgia asked Peter as they left. She felt exhausted as if she'd been taking part in the physical battle as well as the wrangling. She'd seen village feuds before and knew all too well that the rancour could linger for years but what was happening in Cobshaw seemed different. More than just a clash over who was to buy the pub. That row could be fixed one way or the other by the signing of a contract, but this enmity had the feel of something that had happened way back. Fanciful? Perhaps. But this village had roots as strong as those of that beech tree. Even so that storm had exposed its roots and in time that would cause its death. Georgia had an uncomfortable feeling that the storm over this village was gathering pace and the results could be disastrous.

'It's time we heard the case for the Tudors,' Peter replied.

'You've got your chance, then. Brenda would like to see us tomorrow,' Georgia said. 'She seemed very upset. We've got to remember though that this is nothing to do with our Fingerprints experience, which must surely be connected with that skeleton.' The few brief words she'd just had with Brenda on her way out of the pub made that clear. Which was odd as surely the battles inside couldn't have worried her that much.

'Who knows—Georgia! Look at this!' Peter waved his phone in front of her as she prepared to help him into her car.

'News hot off the press from Stour Valley Police,' he cried, 'with full permission for it to be broadcast. According to the DNA from a family member, the remains are indeed those of Sir John Wilbourne.'

Chapter Four

'Ready for it?' Peter slammed down the landline receiver and beamed at her as soon as Georgia arrived on Saturday morning. Bank holiday weekend though it was, he was hard at work in his office. 'That was the great Will Whittan himself.'

'Very much ready.' She could feel her familiar surge of energy. Even the familiar bookshelves around her, stacked untidily in a method understood only by Peter, seemed to be crying out for more Marsh & Daughter case books to join them. Now with a fair wind behind them they might be able to include in due course *The Case of the Missing Knight* and bring some kind of justice for John Wilbourne's terrible end.

'I take it we're now formally on the case from his point of view?' she added.

'We are, daughter, we are,' he assured her.

'A completely clear road ahead?'

'Just about.' Peter grimaced. 'Will again made it clear that this case wasn't top of his list, although as the Met has sent over the original files he said he might have a look at them right away.'

'Could that be because the press will be going to town with it?' Often a vital factor. 'It's quite a story, so were those witnesses who saw him in London later part of a cover-up or just mistaken?'

'Not necessarily either,' Peter pointed out complacently. 'Sir John could—theoretically I grant you—have been buried in Cobshaw at any time after his death if he was murdered in London and the body driven here after his death.'

'Accepted, but why would his murderer have risked doing that?' Georgia agreed. 'Anyway, at least we're going ahead with Will's half-blessing?'

'On the usual terms of reporting back to him.'

'Good,' she declared. 'So now that's clear, how did Sir John die if not by that sword found buried with him? Any comment from Will?'

'Only to confirm that the sword wasn't the weapon. The forensic lads took a look at the remnants of the clothes and they're still working on what might be blood stains for the DNA, whether the victim's or the aggressor's.'

Georgia thought this through. 'So we're probably back to a sharp-bladed knife of some kind as the probable murder weapon. Is Will going to keep us informed or do we have to badger him?'

'Ah.' Peter looked pensive. 'He's pre-empted us on that one. We're to have a liaison officer. One DI Jack Cotton. Will thinks highly of him.'

'That might be a mixed blessing.' Georgia could see pitfalls ahead. 'Are we tagged to him?'

Peter grinned. 'No, but we're honour-bound to play our cards honestly. That gives us leeway, don't you think? Still want to go ahead?'

Georgia wavered, then decided, 'Yes. Luke's really enthusiastic about this one. He told me that he'd seen John Wilbourne in one of those late fifties kitchen-sink dramas about angry young men and never forgot him.'

'A change from all his Hamlets and Romeos.'

'Nonsense,' Georgia shot back at him. 'Hamlet was the angry young man of his day.'

Peter snorted. 'Hardly. 'He's the ultimate man of inaction. The Laertes and Mercutios were the hotheads.'

'And Edward Colduggan played Mercutio in the 1959 production.'

'So he did. I'll look at some of his work on Netflix, including his Hollywood films. Maybe a few John Wilbournes too. And look up the Colduggan press coverage. It will give us a taste of what this case might be about.'

'Luke's already glued to Wilbourne performances,' Georgia remarked. 'One up to the Frost household. I've never known him so keen on a new project. And he won't be the only one wanting to know more about how and why our Sir John disappeared.'

Even as she spoke, Peter's mobile rang. After a moment or two as he listened, she could make an educated guess as who was calling. The press was already on to it.

'Press?' she asked, as he switched off.

'Yes. Cathy, from the *South East Post*. She's on the case already, egging us on. Wants an exclusive.'

'And so?' Cathy Bone, editor of the *Post*, was married to Peter's nephew.

'I hedged. Good job we're booked in to talk to Brenda Randall this morning. I wonder why she asked to see us?' Peter frowned. 'Another history lesson about Cecilia? We need to know what was going on in Cobshaw sixty years ago, not in the sixteenth century.'

'Sixty years ago *is* history,' Georgia pointed out. 'And clearly something was worrying her when we saw her yesterday. Now we're going to find out what.'

Cobshaw Cottage was an interesting address. As Georgia turned her Audi to enter the grounds of Cobshaw Hall, the huge gates, showing signs of rust, were standing open and beyond them was an impressively gravelled drive. It took a winding route, dividing at a point where Georgia could see in the distance an imposing red-brick late eighteenth-century or early nineteenth-century building—presumably Cobshaw Hall itself owned by Gerald Randall, Brenda's brother-in-law. From the impression she and Peter had picked up so far Gerald was of the same ilk as Percival—cranky, opinionated, possibly grumpy and probably about the same age. It followed, Georgia concluded, that if Gerald wanted to buy the Maid of Kent, he wouldn't stand a chance. Even his backing of the hotel plan must surely put that in jeopardy because of his Tudor ancestry.

Another fork in the drive took them past woodland and spacious open grazing land, which looked more extensive than Georgia had expected. The estate was giving the impression of having been founded by a wealthy owner on the way up in the social pecking order in the eighteenth century. Although under later ownership, wealth and status might have declined, it must still be a flourishing concern.

A twist in the track brought them unexpectedly to what was misleadingly called Cobshaw Cottage, Brenda's home. It was more modest than the Hall looked but was undoubtedly a large and highly desirable residence. It dated from an earlier period than the hall, with a ragstone base and timber beaming on the upper two storeys, and it was surrounded by a spacious garden fenced off from the arable land around it.

The track they were driving along had a three-foot high fence on either side, ending abruptly a short distance further along from Cobshaw Cottage and with a large white painted gate in the fencing across the track. Brenda Randall, clad informally in an elegantly cut tunic and trousers, welcomed them at the front door as they approached her 'cottage'. Her anxious face changed to signs of relief at seeing them—or so it seemed to Georgia. She escorted them round the outside of the building to a conservatory, solicitous of Peter's welfare as he negotiated the corners on his scooter. She ushered them inside via a ramp and was clearly eager to start the proceedings.

There was no doubt from the conservatory that Brenda was addicted to history. It was large, almost aspiring to be an orangery with jardinières and a modestly sized statue or two, and books and files were stored on bookshelves lining the house wall. A laptop adorned a business-like table at one end together with two elegant upright chairs, two cushioned loungers and plenty of room for Peter's scooter.

'You'll take coffee?' Brenda asked, obviously trying to be the archetypal hostess but finding it hard in her eagerness to begin talking on the subject so dear to her heart. She asked twice whether Peter took milk and when he said no, proceeded to pour some into his cup. Her mind was elsewhere and it wasn't hard to guess why.

'It is good of you to come,' she finally burst out, when cups and biscuits had been distributed, and after her Yorkshire terrier had paid his respects and been escorted back to another room. 'It is so important that you should be aware of Cobshaw's history. The news about poor John Wilbourne makes it all the more important that the Maid of Kent should become a hotel, and yet history is so uncertain in the amount of evidence it provides. Does one have a duty to the truth when it might not be the whole truth? Or even true at all? I really don't know quite what to do.'

To Georgia's relief, Peter took this one on. 'I always work on the principle that historians must view all the evidence available to reach their conclusions and base their theses on that. Often facts come without doubt attached, sometimes they do not.'

Brenda gazed at them, as if trying to absorb how this might apply in her case. 'One's sources, yes. In this case, impeccable. But should one do the right deed for the wrong reason, as did poor Becket? St Thomas had a well of course, one in the basement of the cathedral. And I read your book on the case of St Thomas's well on the Old Road to Canterbury. So interesting. Though that was a Plantagenet well, which makes it all the more difficult. You are historians in your way, aren't you?' she asked anxiously.

Georgia nodded gravely. 'We have to be with our job.' What was this talk of wells about? And why should they be deemed 'difficult'? she wondered.

'Yes indeed. Your book made me think…'

Peter broke in as Brenda's voice trailed off. 'Georgia and I found that an intriguing and successful case,' he said. 'As I'm sure Sir John Wilbourne's will be. Now that the police are officially investigating though, we're co-operating with them so anything you could tell us would be most valuable.'

His shop talk patter was a slight exaggeration, Georgia noted, mentally crossing her fingers, especially as Brenda looked uneasy.

'That might be difficult,' Brenda replied. 'The family is involved. I am only a Randall by marriage of course, but am treated as though it were my own.'

'As far as we've been able to check, it seems John Wilbourne was unmarried in 1959 and that he couldn't have been close to the Randall family here, as he was due to stay overnight at the Maid of Kent.'

Brenda frowned as though they hadn't done their homework—perhaps that was true Georgia thought, ruefully. 'I have little to say about Sir John. It is Cecilia who concerns me at present.'

Not helpful. Georgia tried again. 'But there might be a link between them in that the history of the Maid of Kent pub is an important factor in the hotel deal and Sir John's death has now been confirmed there. Both Cecilia and Sir John need to find justice.' She was aware of Peter's eyebrows mentally shooting up at this risky manoeuvre, but she was astonished to find it seemed to be working.

'Justice,' Brenda repeated. 'You're right. John deserves that. He was my late husband's and Gerald's step-brother,' she explained, 'much older than them as their father Jacob married twice. John's mother died quite young. John left the village as a young man and took his mother's maiden name.'

Why was that? Georgia wondered. Problems at home? 'Did he visit the family?' she asked.

Brenda hesitated. 'He paid the occasional visit, I believe.'

'You must have been very young in 1959,' Georgia said cautiously. Something strange here. 'Did you know him then?'

Brenda looked uneasy. 'I was at the 1959 performance of course. I did not marry my dear Thomas until 1963 but I was born in Cobshaw. My father was the doctor for this village and another one nearby. I had met John several times as a girl as he visited Cobshaw Hall on occasion to see his father and siblings and would come into the village. He was at least twenty years older than I was of course and he had been married for a short while.'

'Children?' Peter asked.

'No. His wife Elizabeth—a quiet little thing—left him long before he came here for that performance of *Romeo and Juliet*. A difficult life being married to an actor, I suspect.' Brenda gave a light nervous laugh.

'Did you see him to talk to before or after the performance?' Peter asked.

'Neither,' she replied sharply. 'They were far too busy with setting up the stage and adjusting microphones beforehand and packing up afterwards. John was surrounded by people who wanted to talk to him afterwards. I came straight home,' she added. 'I thought I might see him the next day, but I was told he had already left. But,' she added firmly, 'although John was born a Randall, that is really all there is to it. He did not stay at the Hall that night, nor did my late husband ever mention contact with him that evening.' She sat back in her chair, visibly relaxed. They'd get no further on that score, Georgia realised.

'When did the Randall family first come to Cobshaw Hall?' she asked to bridge the silence that followed.

This was a good move and Brenda responded enthusiastically. 'There have been Randalls in this area since at least the fifteenth century, and in the sixteenth century one of them married Cecilia who owned Cobshaw Court, now the Maid of Kent public house. A *Tudor*. Not a Plantagenet. The Randalls fell upon hard times but in 1817 they built the hall you see today. A Lieutenant William Randall was most helpful to the Duke of Wellington at the battle of Waterloo.'

'This beautiful home of yours is much older, surely, so was there a former building where Cobshaw Hall now stands?' Georgia asked, keeping to safe ground.

'No doubt,' Brenda said dismissively, much more confident now that she seemed to be on safer ground. 'My cottage is the more interesting of the two and dates back to the fifteenth century at least.'

'As does the Maid of Kent building,' Peter murmured.

'A most misleading name in historical terms,' Brenda cried out in indignation. 'As I have pointed out before, Cobshaw Court is the Maid of Kent's proper name and it belonged to the maid of Kent herself, Cecilia, whose father gifted it to her on her marriage to a Randall in 1542. As a Tudor she was related to King Henry VII and his son Henry VIII and through her father could trace her ancestry back to the Yorkists and also to the Lancastrians, thus unifying the two warring factions and becoming a legitimate heir to the throne after the death of Edward VI, the weakling son of Henry VIII.'

Brenda paused for breath, but not for long. She was still engrossed in the story to which she was so passionately committed. 'But Cecilia was murdered in cold blood in 1553 by fanatics,' she swept on, 'amid rumours that she might pursue her claim to the throne of England. This was a time when Lady Jane Grey had been imprisoned for that same reason by the Catholic Queen Mary.'

Don't raise the obvious point, Georgia told herself, but Peter immediately entered the battlefield: 'What about Mr FitzRichard's belief that Cecilia was descended from Richard of Eastwell and the Plantagenet line?

Brenda fired back. 'He is quite mistaken,' she said firmly. 'The slightest investigation and his whole argument crumbles. Or rather his father's argument. Montague FitzRichard was blind to all but his own ridiculous theories. He would go to any lengths to convince himself that he was descended from the Plantagenet line via the Yorkists—in other words from Richard III. I'm sure you agree that heritage must be preserved correctly. It is so important to ensure that the Maid of Kent building survives. It holds so many secrets.'

She seemed to be talking to herself as much as to them and Peter made a determined effort. 'Secrets such as what?'

'Perhaps even as to where Cecilia is buried, although the well is also a possibility, as she is recorded as loving to walk and read there. Nevertheless, she owned Cobshaw Court and that is where she was murdered, and thus is the more likely place for her burial.'

'Tony Beane agrees with that but can't find any trace of it.'

'Even Percival FitzRichard concedes that,' Brenda replied disdainfully, 'although he is under the delusion that Cecilia lived in this very cottage with her grandfather. I grant you that Richard of Eastwell who died in 1550 at Eastwell was a very real person, but as for this notion of Percival FitzRichard's that he lived a secluded married life in Cobshaw before he went to work for Sir Thomas Moyle for some years before his death, that is ridiculous. It is true that a secluded life was essential for Richard. Although the Tudors had rightfully claimed the throne they would not have tolerated a son of Richard III to challenge their claim, whether or not he was legitimately born as Percival so foolishly claims. But he did *not* live here.'

Whoa! Getting into marshy ground. Georgia risked stepping into it. 'Could there have been two maids of Kent called Cecilia perhaps, yours and Mr FitzRichard's?' She sank into the mud immediately.

'Emphatically not. There was just the one, and one alone.' Brenda was clearly shocked at this suggestion. 'However, part of the reason I asked you to visit me is to explain about the *well*. I wish there to be no doubt about this. The well belongs to the Randalls as we are descended from Cecilia and it is a vital part of Cobshaw's history. And you cannot investigate John Wilbourne's death without being aware of Cobshaw's heritage. Don't you agree?'

There was definitely something strange about this focus on wells. First, St Thomas's well, now this one. Georgia glanced at Peter who gave a vigorous nod. 'Everything we learn about Cobshaw might be valuable,' he told her diplomatically.

Brenda promptly took up the story again. 'In his later years, Richard Plantagenet had a well at *Eastwell* which is clearly marked on Ordnance Survey maps. As I told you, he did not live here, nor did he have anything to do with *our* well. It is *Cecilia's* own very special place, whatever Percival FitzRichard claims. In Cecilia's time the well was owned by the Randalls. She was then living in Cobshaw Court, now the Maid of Kent public house, but the well *still* belongs to the Randalls. Come with me.'

The last few words were a command, not a choice. At least they were going to see this famous well. If there was anything weird about it, Georgia thought, or ghosts of the past haunting it, at least they would have their own reactions to judge it by. Maybe Cecilia herself would make a ghostly appearance. With Peter safely manoeuvred out of the conservatory, they followed their hostess—now back in her element as history instructor in chief—back to the white gate Georgia had noticed on their arrival. It was a dark, gloomy spot because of the overhanging trees, and the wide area to which it gave entrance was surrounded by low fencing.

As they approached, Georgia could see a pond with a wall of Kentish ragstone about three feet high around it. In its centre was what seemed to be another small pond. It too had greyish white ragstone walls, which stuck out of the water by a foot or so. This, Georgia realised, must be the disputed well which according to Brenda Richard of Eastwell had nothing to do with. It was now totally surrounded by the larger pond, which had probably been converted from it and now boasted a water-lily or two. Perhaps that was Cecilia's doing if she did pop back in ghostly form to see her well every now and then.

Georgia hastily reproached herself. This was Brenda's pride and joy and so she and Peter should be taking this seriously.

'Cecilia's well,' Brenda said proudly, pointing to the pond's centre.

'Why is this area fenced off? For safety?' Georgia enquired after duly admiring it, although its age seemed to be its main attribute. At first sight despite the gloom there seemed nothing very sinister about it, even if it was a bone of contention for the village. It looked disappointingly ordinary after Brenda's build-up.

Brenda bristled. 'Because, unfortunately, although it belongs to the Randalls, it is viewed as communal property. The surrounding pond was added to it early in the Second World War, I believe, by the parish council. Cecilia's well draws water from the water table beneath as does the pond, although the latter draws it also from a diverted stream.'

'Why did the council decide to convert the well though?' Peter asked curiously.

'I'm told it foolishly decided to enlarge it for wildlife purposes, and a back-up in case of local fires. It seemed set on doing so. It ignored the fact that it was Randall land and our claim that the pond had covered ancient footpaths. Indeed it insisted that we permit access to the pond by creating new public paths on our land,' Brenda said bitterly. 'They had stupidly listened to Montague FitzRichard's false allegation that he owned the well and, as he was willing for the pond to be built around it and for it to be communal land, the council went ahead. Now both the council and Percival FitzRichard mistakenly consider they own it. I believe there is also another claimant to the land but there is no doubt that this is Cecilia's well, built on Randall land.'

'If the Randalls of today are descended from her, it follows she must have had children,' Peter pointed out.

'Indeed she did. Her son was nine years old and was fortunately spirited away by her husband before her enemies reached her. I should explain that although she was married and had taken his name of Randall she was still known as the maid of Kent because of her serenity and beauty.'

Georgia stared at the pond before her. An innocent enough sight now, surely, and yet it was the tangible evidence of the divisions in the village today, which probably had changed little from the times of Cecilia herself. The more she looked at it, however, the heavier the atmosphere seemed to be, almost threatening. Nonsense, she told herself. Pure imagination at work again.

And then Peter whispered to her, '*The doom has come upon me*, as the Lady of Shalott said. Cecilia's probably floating around in that pond.'

Today that didn't seem to be a joking matter, and Georgia made an effort to break the heavy silence. 'Isn't it strange that Cecilia's remains have never been found?'

'It is possible they are in the grounds of the Maid of Kent, but it is more probable they are somewhere in the building itself. Remember that she was assassinated by murderous agents of Queen Mary, nervous of Cecilia's claim to the throne. They would hardly respect the need for decent burial,' Brenda said firmly. 'Cecilia keeps her secrets to the last which is one of the reasons that the Maid of Kent public house must revert to the name of Cobshaw Court again by becoming a hotel. Heritage must be preserved.' Brenda fell abruptly silent, and there was an awkward pause.

Georgia glanced at Peter. She was adept at picking up his symptoms of restlessness. At the moment his body language seemed to be indicating that he thought they were slipping away from the point.

'Was John Wilbourne interested in Cecilia's story?' she promptly asked.

Brenda was instantly defensive again. 'He was. As he came here occasionally, he had even considered buying Cobshaw Cottage at one point. His father Jacob refused the offer, as he intended it for John's step-brother Thomas as Gerald was to inherit the Hall. Later Thomas of course became my husband. Gerald would now dearly love to see me out of the way so that Mick Buckley could move his large noisy family into it. Mick is *very* enthusiastic about that idea. I have refused to move, of course. It would be a betrayal of my late husband to do so.'

Peter ignored this new diversion. 'Did you *like* John Wilbourne?'

Brenda Randall stiffened. 'I have told you. I was only nineteen when he went missing and not yet married to Thomas,' she replied somewhat coolly. 'I hardly knew John. He and my father-in-law

Jacob did not always see eye to eye. John became famous of course. Thomas told me that John was inclined to remind the family of that.'

'And the reason for his not seeing eye to eye with his father?' Georgia noted that Brenda had avoided answering Peter's question. Surely a nineteen-year-old girl wouldn't have been immune to the presence of such a heartthrob as John Wilbourne?

Brenda brushed this aside. 'I've no idea. Probably a minor upset.'

Georgia could see Peter was longing to press further, but luckily he refrained. They needed allies at this stage, not enemies.

'John was a great actor,' Brenda added rapidly, as if to further dispel the notion of family disharmony.

'Even though you didn't speak to him after the performance, did you see him?'

'I really cannot recall. Nor can I see that it is relevant.'

Peter cheerfully ignored the put-down. 'Was he popular in the village?'

Brenda's reply was cryptic. 'Cobshaw, like all villages, has had its troubling times.'

'And feuds, it seems,' Peter commented. 'Do these Planter and Tudor factions I've been hearing about stem from Tudor times?'

'Sometimes, Mr Marsh,' Brenda retorted, 'for the good of the present it is wiser not to judge the past. I believe Percival FitzRichard will soon be regretting his insistence on delving into history. History does not always suit one's own convenience.'

Brenda Randall was becoming rattled, Georgia realised. Should she push on or hold back? Push on, she decided. It was too good an opportunity to relinquish. 'As you say though, we have a duty to historical truth. Should one throw away the key? Sometimes history can't be ignored.'

'In some cases, perhaps it is better thrown away,' Brenda blurted out. 'The war of course was a factor. Everyone suffered.'

Georgia blinked. Which war? In 1959—assuming that she was thinking of village history in John Wilbourne's day—the Second World War had been over for fourteen years. But Brenda said no more and was looking tired. As they turned to leave though, Brenda cried after them, 'I went home with my parents after the performance. Straightaway. Women did not frequent public houses then. You do realise that don't you?'

Georgia did. She also realised that Brenda had more to tell—but they weren't going to hear it now.

The Maid of Kent was where they were to sign the agreement letter, for the concert would surely be crowded today after the news about John Wilbourne. However, the good thing about public houses, Georgia reflected, is that one's reason for being there is seldom questioned. Going for a pint, loo stop, lunch or business would be routine but today the news of John Wilbourne's remains having been identified would surely be the topic under discussion there. It had been headline news on the local radio station.

She and Peter had expected to see quite a few people gathered in the bar, but they were wrong. Once more picking their way through the Plantagenet-festooned corridors they reached the main bar to find it empty save for Tony behind the bar with only Dave Cook and Geoff Sanders, grandfather of the young gardener Louis. He eyed them as suspiciously as he had on their first visit here, and it was left to Dave to invite them to join them. Geoff Sanders's arms were meaningfully folded conveying the message that they wouldn't get past him.

'Didn't take you long, did it?' Geoff opened proceedings after Peter had returned with Tony carrying drinks for them all.

'Remarkably quick service,' Peter blandly misunderstood.

'I knew you'd be along here. That actor bloke,' Geoff growled. 'Heard it on the news.'

'Do you remember him on that evening?' Georgia asked.

A pause. 'Nothing but a nipper, missus. What would I remember?'

Georgia caught a quick look of surprise on Dave's face. Dave couldn't be more than in his late fifties, so he would genuinely have been a toddler at most if present in 1959, but Geoff—like Percival FitzRichard—would have been twenty or more, hardly a nipper.

'A lot, I imagine,' Peter said firmly. 'Did you see the performance?'

'Might have done.' Geoff was not going to be co-operative. So much was clear. Why though? Georgia wondered.

'And might you have stayed on a while afterwards, had a drink or two?' Peter persevered.

'Might have done.'

Dave took a hand then. 'Look here, Geoff. Sooner or later you'll have to talk about it, because the police are going to come asking questions. What are you going to say then?'

'That I don't know nothing, Dave.' They stared at each other, until Geoff's eyes fell to the empty glass in his hand. Georgia took the hint and hurried to the bar for another pint.

'Like I said. I were a nipper,' Geoff continued without much enthusiasm. 'His death weren't nothing to do with me, Dave.'

'Bollocks. You and Perce here were in your mid-twenties when this actor fellow went missing,' Dave replied. 'You're getting all mixed up. It's best you speak out if you remember anything of what happened.'

'Village stuff. Not important,' Geoff muttered.

'Then tell them. Can't hurt, can it?'

'Nothing but a lot of fighting and moonshine. Yeah, I remember that play. *Romeo and Juliet*. A lot of fighting. But it didn't mean nothing,' Geoff rambled on. 'Always fights in villages.'

It might be a risk for her to enter the fray too prominently with someone of Geoff Sanders' generation, Georgia decided. As a woman he might feel obliged to answer her or shoot her down if she read him correctly. A meek subservience would be more fruitful. She was right.

'The Planters and the Tudors have always been at each other's throats, long as I can remember.' Geoff paused for a hacking cough and a swig of beer. 'Happened in my dad's time. Never talked about it much. But there was that great-uncle of yours, Dave. Always spoiling for a fight was Brian Cook. Those Buckleys too. That Sam, dad said. He was always spoiling for a fight. Had to happen in the end.'

'Always one in every family,' Dave said equably.

'My dad said the war coming along stopped half the village murdering the other half, 'cos they all had to join up for service.' Geoff was warming up now. 'And by the time they shook themselves down again after the war was over, it was all forgotten. Village picked itself up and on we went. The posh folk up at the hall, they let the workers do their fighting for them, like that Mick Buckley now.'

'That's old stuff, Geoff,' Dave stopped him. 'We're talking of 1959 now. Was there a set-to then as well?'

'Reckon there was. I was out courting a young lady over in the gardens. A rumpus going on there was, couple of them actors having a fight—'

'In the play or afterwards?' Peter broke in.

'After. They was prancing around with swords on the stage.'

Stage swords? 'Who were they?' Georgia asked. 'Could you see?'

'No I couldn't, missus. But if you're thinking that's how this John Wilbourne fellow got killed, you'd be wrong. They all gave up after a while and my young lady having given me the time of day I was watching as the two gents went back to the pub together. One of them was still waving his sword about, he was. Them in the pub had spilled out to see what was going on. It was mostly those actor blokes in there. We locals had left them to it until this fancy fighting started. Afterwards the posh blokes went back inside with the Tudors and we Planters stayed out here. Don't like me mentioning Planters and Tudors, do you, Dave?'

'Not now the future of the village is at stake, Geoff. But that's to do with hotel versus community centres, not Planters and Tudors.'

''Course it is. Those Tudor Randalls want one thing, the Planters another. Daft idea, a community centre.'

'What's daft about that?' Dave bristled. 'Rather have a hotel, would you, Geoff? They'd hire their own gardeners, you know. Dig the gardens up into tennis courts and swimming baths. No more vegetable gardens. No jobs either. They wouldn't want you and Louis around.'

Geoff Sanders remained silent for a moment or two, then he said slowly, 'I know that, Dave. For all my talk, I'm with you. There's always trouble when the Planters and the Tudors fall out. It were bad when it happened, my dad said. Before the war that was.'

'What did happen?' Georgia dared to ask, as Dave stayed silent, and at that moment Tony Beane came out to collect their glasses.

'Talking about those bones, are you?' he asked cheerfully. 'Good for business that. We've had a lot of folk in this morning wanting to hear any gory details. Percival's dad Montague always reckoned it was one of the actors knocked John Wilbourne off.'

'Did he have one in mind?' Georgia asked.

'No idea. Ask Percival. They were all drunk from what he told us and there was a bit of a shindy.'

'Accident then?' commented Peter in his 'not particularly interested' voice. 'Is that how John Wilbourne died?'

'Accident?' Geoff snarled. 'In Cobshaw? Nah. It was one of them Tudors done it.'

Chapter Five

'Cobshaw,' Peter remarked as they left the bar, 'is a troubled village. It's split down the middle for reasons not yet fully understood. Brenda is equally troubled for reasons unknown. Fair summary, so far?'

'Agreed.' Georgia remembered both Brenda's anxious eyes and the atmosphere in the pub. 'Probably neither has anything to do with John Wilbourne, but who knows?'

Their business over the concert concluded, she was relieved that they could now leave. They were heading for the outdoor theatre, even though Peter pointed out it might still be a crime scene. This case had to be settled by August, so that it wouldn't spoil the concert. Rick deserved that. With that deadline, Georgia almost regretted they had taken on the Wilbourne case. There was no going back now though, and she could imagine what Rick would have said if they dropped it. 'You're my big sister,' he'd say, grinning at her. 'Lead on.' And that is what she would do.

'Someone must know,' Peter replied, turning his scooter towards the fallen tree. There it lay, its huge bulk sprawled pathetically along the rear pathway. The crime scene tape was still up, but the police were gone. They weren't alone here though. Studying the place where John Wilbourne's remains had been found was Percival FitzRichard.

Since they'd first seen it, the earth had been well turned over for quite a large area, but it was still chilling to think of this abandoned piece of ground as the resting place of one of the great actors of the twentieth century. There would surely be an interment service for him. Would the Randalls be making the decision over that?

Percival seemed oblivious to their arrival and it needed Peter's cry of 'Hey there!' to startle him into turning towards them aggressively. Nothing unusual about that. Maybe he thought they were Tudor supporters, Georgia guessed.

'Looking for more bones, are you?' he yelled at them. 'It was nothing to do with me.'

'It', Georgia assumed, referred to John Wilbourne's death. 'Were you here for that whole evening?' she asked.

'Can't say. Might have been. Might not.'

'You don't think this of much importance?' Peter enquired. 'The police will be questioning you for what you remember about it.'

Oddly enough this worked—except not in their favour. 'Police?' he screamed at them. 'With all I've got on my mind? I'm offered a fortune for this old dump and what happens? There's my own daughter without a penny to her name saying she'll buy it. Her husband thinks she's cuckoo, but she's a Plantagenet all right and the other chap won't be. Tony hasn't a penny to his name either, so he sees the sense of selling the pub to this Howard Green fellow. Son of Paul Green, he is, who owns a chain of hotels all over England. What do I do, eh?'

'Wait and see what happens,' Peter said practically. 'Nowadays property deals aren't handed over promptly on a nice neat cheque to be popped into the bank. They take time to go through the contract stage. Any surveyor is going to have a field day with this building.'

'You hinting I say yes to both of them?' Percival demanded. 'How the blazes could I get away with that?'

'Say the crime scene is delaying your response,' Georgia suggested.

'What's the point? Reckon a Plantagenet billionaire will turn up at this concert of yours?' Percival said cuttingly.

'No,' Georgia replied, wondering just how she and Peter had become caught up in this village feud, 'but there might be wealthy people in the audience who could donate to the community centre fund.'

Another glare. 'I don't want a damned community to take it over, Bernie or no Bernie. I want to be shot of it.'

'But I understood your father decreed that a Plantagenet *must* take it over.'

'There we go again, round and round the mulberry bush. Yes, he did. It's in his will. He was a stickler for the family. Went off like a stick of dynamite if you didn't obey orders.'

'Perhaps the Plantagenet clause was the only way of keeping it in the family? Does Bernie have children?' Georgia asked.

'Two in New Zealand and not going to budge to run a tumbledown pub in Kent, UK.'

She remembered seeing a photograph of Montague FitzRichard in the bar. A starchy looking man in a smart jacket and tie glaring down from the walls as though determined to keep an eye on his successors. What would he have made of all these plans for his cherished Maid of Kent? She made a determined effort to switch the subject back to their case.

'Your father was running the pub during that *Romeo and Juliet* performance in 1959 and we're told that John Wilbourne stayed overnight that evening.'

Percival looked at them guardedly. 'Maybe. Several of them did.'

'You don't remember John Wilbourne in particular?'

'Drunk, the lot of them,' Percival continued, oblivious to her question. 'Whole village was here, especially the ladies. They all rushed over here to see him. Like another blinking Rudolph Valentino, he was. Most of them went after the show but some of the men stayed around to drink. But there was a bit of trouble. Best forget about them. Those days are over.'

'What trouble?' Peter asked.

Percival looked shifty. 'My dad sorted it out. I wasn't there.'

Peter pressed on. 'We know Sir Edward Colduggan was one of those who stayed over.'

'May have been,' Percival muttered. 'I don't talk about those days much. Not now my dad's gone.'

Peter tried another tack. 'Do you have brothers or sisters, Mr FitzRichard?'

He must have hit the right button for Percival's eyes lit up. 'Sister. My dad married twice, first Elspeth, then my mum Agnes who died ten years back. My sister's a step.'

'She lives here?' Georgia asked.

She must have put a foot wrong as Percival didn't reply. He was no longer the irascible old man who yelled and screamed. He seemed to be looking back into a kaleidoscope of memories.

'Was she at the 1959 performance?' Peter persevered.

At last Percival spoke, very softly, almost as though he were living in the past. 'The day of the fête it was. She was beautiful, my lovely sister. Before the show, that was. There she was. Spun out of sunshine was my Serena. I'll be as happy as the day is long, she said. Just you wait, little Percy. Where are you going? I asked her. Where dreams go, over the hills and far away, she said, but I won't leave you, little Percy.'

'And did she?' Georgia asked quietly.

He still seemed lost in the past, but he answered her. 'She died in the war did my Serena. Blue eyes she had and hair as golden as the corn in the fields.'

Georgia could see a tear trickling down his face, but then he was Percival Fitz Richard, pub owner again, glaring at them.

'What am I going to do, eh?'

He could only have been a child when Serena died, but now he was back in the twenty-first century with all its problems. 'The Maid of Kent will survive one way or another,' Georgia assured him. 'It always has.'

Percival ignored this. 'Armageddon,' he muttered darkly. 'Beware the harbingers of doom.'

'Doom will come all too quickly if we don't make some progress with this case,' Peter said crossly on the drive back to his office.

'I agree.' So far all their efforts had not pointed them to a clear path forward. 'Did it strike you that there was something odd about what Percival told us?' she asked Peter. 'Why hark back to a pre-war fête?'

'Maybe because there was one in 1959 too. But more importantly there was no mention of any trouble between the Planters and the Tudors then.'

'Put it in the Tobdot list,' Georgia said. That was useful shorthand for 'to be done tomorrow'.

Peter laughed. 'Remember the way you got Tobdot mixed up with Toblerone chocolate when you were small? And Rick, too.' He fell silent. 'This concert,' he said after a while, 'is it a good idea? It's proving complicated.'

'Yes, it is,' she said firmly. 'The John Wilbourne case will be over by then.'

'Name one good reason for thinking so.'

'Lots of them.' Georgia paused, thinking frantically but failing to come up with even one. 'It has to be though, because the concert can't take place if there are still masses of question marks surrounding the case *and* we both know that we sensed Fingerprints there. Injustice. We can't just leave that on one side. Besides, I've got the guest list ready.'

'Not convincing but hopeful.' Peter looked happier to her relief. 'Let's have a go at Suspects Anonymous if you've got time.'

This programme had years ago been the brainchild of Peter's nephew Charlie Bone. It allowed them to feed the research material they'd gathered for their cold cases into the database, then sit back and see what the programme made of it. This produced interesting—though occasionally ludicrous—results as to where they should look for their 'Burglar Bills', which was how they referred to their possible suspects. Over the years the database had been updated to keep pace with the advent of DNA and other breakthroughs as far as their police contacts could share the information with them—and that was in return for the information that the Marshes had independently rooted out.

Suspects Anonymous would hardly pass legal scrutiny but was often a great starting point, and on occasion it had thrown up accurate possibilities amongst the suspects. That remained to be proven on this case, but its main offering for a Burglar Bill so far—and naturally enough at this stage—was Edward Colduggan, now Sir Edward. They had emailed him some days ago but frustratingly he had refused to see them.

'It's probably just a press overdose,' Georgia had reasoned. 'It's short-sighted of him if so, since he'll have the press pursuing him whether he likes it or not.'

'Why don't you try telephoning him?' Peter had suggested. 'He might not be so rude to you as he would to me.'

She had her doubts, but Peter was right. The voice at the other end of the line, recognisable from numerous TV programmes and films, was courteous but firm. No interview. It hadn't been a fruitless call however, as he had provided them with the telephone number of Roberta Watts, a vaguely familiar name that needed a little prompting from Colduggan to place her. According to the press, there had been two witnesses who had claimed to see Sir John Wilbourne in London the day after the performance. One was unnamed, but the other had been Rowena Watts. Even more interesting was the fact that she had played Juliet to John Wilbourne's Romeo.

The M25 had been in a surprisingly good mood today, Georgia rejoiced, as they drove along it on their way to Putney on Tuesday. The long weekend's bank holiday traffic was over, and there were no accidents, no breakdowns, and no roadworks to speak of. What more could one ask? They'd been lucky in that Rowena Watts was both available and surprisingly eager to talk to them. Peter's light scooter was no problem for her either. Remarkable.

'Sir Edward must have had a word with her,' Peter commented.

'Nonsense. It's my professional telephone expertise,' Georgia joked. But she too wondered what the reason might be.

Flinders, Rowena Watt's home, proved easy to find. It was a large Edwardian house in a Putney side street, set back from the road and with a sizeable front garden.

'Do come in.' The deep resonant voice of Rowena Watts welcomed them with a charm that spoke of years of professional practice rather than any enthusiasm for their company. No, Georgia decided she was being unfair. This wasn't going to be easy for Miss (Mrs? she wondered) Watts, so she was entitled to be wary of them. It didn't necessarily mean she'd anything to hide. She would be in her eighties now, Georgia calculated, but the lively eyes, skilful make-up and short curly hair that suggested ageing but couldn't be termed grey made it clear that her acting career was far from over. This was one very determined lady. She must have made a very determined Juliet too.

She ushered them with Peter's scooter into a room adjacent to the hallway. It was cleverly adorned with sufficient photographs and drawings to remind visitors of her profession but not so many that it could be considered brash. A tray of tea and biscuits—the latter clearly from Fortnum & Mason—awaited them. Tall, slender and lively, it was easy for Georgia to picture Rowena Watts as a young impulsive Juliet, even though the eyes that had once adoringly fixed on her Romeo John Wilbourne now had a steeliness in them, and carefully concealed wrinkles replaced the blushing cheeks of girlhood. And perhaps, given his heartthrob reputation the adoration had not been just for Romeo but for John himself.

'I can show you some photographs of the production,' she told them, 'although I'm sure you'll want to know—as does every journalist in town—' A light laugh—'why I gave an eye witness account of seeing poor John in London when we now have to assume that he died after the performance that night. Murdered. Quite terrible. Of course, with his being missing for so long, we had all feared that he was dead but to have it confirmed is still quite shocking. Poor, poor, John.'

For all her lamentations there was a gleam in Rowena's eyes, Georgia noticed. That did indeed suggest that for her the discovery of his bones meant more to her than merely closing a chapter, and that explained her immediate agreement to this interview. This was the actor speaking, not the woman.

'It is indeed sad,' Peter said amiably.

Playing the fish gently was always his way of dealing with such situations. Georgia's tactic of facing steel with steel wasn't always successful although, come to that, neither was Peter's. But was this a fish that could be easily caught? she wondered

'I understand you're working with the police on poor John's case and that there might be a book about it if your enquiries uncover the truth,' Rowena said.

'That's always our goal,' Peter said.

'Then I must give you all the help I can.'

And yourself publicity, Georgia thought meanly, then reproached herself for prejudging. Even so, there was a certain false graciousness about Rowena Watts that might be staged.

'Let me tell you what happened that night,' Rowena began earnestly. 'Now that it seems John did not leave for London the following morning, that naturally throws a question mark over who else stayed and so I have been trying to recall what happened. Most of the cast and crew returned to London that night with the scenery and so forth but a few of us stayed over. It was a long way to come from London just for the one performance and John was far from popular for insisting on it. We understood he had been brought up locally but there must have been a problem because he chose to stay in the pub and not at the ancestral mansion.'

A well-rehearsed speech, Georgia decided, as Rowena paused for a moment.

'We were all naturally on a high after the performance,' she continued. 'It takes time to unwind from the passion of Juliet to one's humble self—and this was even more the case, or so it seemed to me, as there was already tension between some of the cast. A row broke out between John and Edward after the performance and to the villagers' great amusement they went rushing back to the stage for a mock duel. So there was Romeo challenging Mercutio which is hardly how Shakespeare conceived his plot.'

Her light laugh grated on Georgia, but she steeled herself again not to prejudice the issue. The facts were the facts, regardless of how they were presented. Her job was to determine whether they *were* facts.

'Can you remember what the row was about?' Peter asked. 'There must have been a big age difference between them. Sir John was forty-four but Colduggan must have been much younger.'

'Twenty-four, I believe. John was the leading actor of course, and the manager of our company in true Victorian style. We had a nominal director, but John was de facto in command. John was, I fear, too old to play Romeo and yet he was set on doing so. It was an example of his naughtily holding poor Eddie Colduggan back.' Another light laugh.

'Was that fair?' This was intriguing, Georgia thought. No wonder there was animosity between them if so, and no wonder suspicion had fallen on him after John Wilbourne's disappearance, especially as Rowena's tone of voice suggested that her sympathies might not lie with Edward Colduggan.

'It was,' Rowena answered immediately. 'True, Edward was a good player in the making but he wasn't then at the stage where he could expect to be handed the major parts on a plate. Even then he was limited. Hamlet—never. Othello, Macbeth—no, the idea was ridiculous, though Eddie saw it differently. In my view, he is far from his best in those roles. He has a much lighter touch.' She made this sound distinctly the lesser achievement.

'What happened to the company after Sir John's disappearance?' Peter asked.

'It survived but not for long. The West London Theatre was a separate company to the Bard of Avon, which John had controlled. That made it simpler, and when John disappeared we carried on for a while with understudies and programme changes, but Eddie, who took John's roles, was no adequate substitute for him. One by one we went our separate ways, and the West of London Theatre was no longer the home of decent theatre. All that history lost.'

'Was John's wife in the company?' Georgia asked.

Rowena looked surprised. 'Good heavens, no. His marriage had ended well before my time. I heard she had left him long since. I believe her name was Elizabeth and that she remarried. She was not in the acting profession, and John's heart was in the theatre, not sitting beside home fires. Edward Colduggan was a different matter, as you no doubt know. His addiction to Hollywood betrays the fact that his heart was not then as devoted to the theatre as John's so often seemed to be. Yet he is so convinced that it was, poor man, and indeed that it still is.'

A pause (with a glance perhaps to see how her audience was reacting, Georgia suspected). 'It came to a head that night,' Rowena continued. 'A battlefield for them both. Dear John had given Eddie every chance he could, short of awarding him the major parts for which he was not yet suited. Hence the duel—they pretended it was light-hearted, but it wasn't for all they used the stage swords. I heard Eddie accusing John of having upstaged him in Mercutio's big speech. "O! then, I see Queen Mab hath been with you." Nonsense, of course. John was never spiteful.'

'You watched the duel?' Peter asked.

'Very little of it. I was talking to one of the villagers. The duel took place on the stage I recall, not where according to the press dear John's body has now been found. I remember the duel's end however, for the publican came out in a fury and broke it up.'

'Who was winning?' Georgia asked, thinking it could be relevant.

'I can't recall,' Rowena replied. 'There were other onlookers though and afterwards the crowd dispersed either back to the pub or presumably to their homes. I looked for John in the pub but saw nothing of him. I retired to my room there while everyone concentrated on getting drunk, and I was told that several of the cast slept in the bar overnight. If so, they had all gone when I came down for breakfast, and there was no sign of John. I asked where he was and the landlord said he hadn't seen him so either he was sleeping it off or he had already left, presumably by train.'

'Did you travel back that way too?' Georgia asked. Rowena's speech was too polished not to have been rehearsed, she concluded.

'Yes. I was anxious to get back to London because Eddie and I were booked to go to John's flat on the Sunday evening to discuss the autumn programme. When I arrived however, I was surprised to see John—as I then thought—being borne away in a taxi. He was sitting in the passenger seat next to the driver and as he was wearing a very distinctive Homburg hat with a feather, I presumed of course it was him. John had one just like it. I presumed that John had forgotten our arrangement. It wasn't the first time that had happened. Eddie, it turned out later, had still been sleeping it off in the pub. After he woke up he left Kent that morning. He managed to get himself back to London and duly arrived at John's flat to be told he wasn't there. Typical Eddie.' She shrugged.

So that was the 'evidence' behind at least one of the witnesses' stories.

'Do you have your own theory about what happened to John?' Peter asked.

'I couldn't presume to say,' Rowena replied quickly. 'Masses of stories flew around but they gradually died away. None of them held water. I remember one thesis was that he had eloped with Barbara Hutton, the Woolworths heiress. I married and continued my career—Watts is my maiden and professional name. Now that I know what did happen to him, I weep for him, even after all these years. That is why,' she concluded, 'I agreed to see you. I must know what happened to him.'

'An impassioned final speech from the leading lady?' Peter asked as Georgia drove them back to Kent. 'Or genuine? Or,' he added fairly, 'both?'

'Very good actor,' Georgia said briefly.

'Smile and smile and be a villain?' Peter queried

Georgia considered this. 'Pass,' she said at last. 'I'd like to know more about the script she's working from if that was an act. A weak story about seeing him in London, but so weak it could be true. There was a certain vagueness in detail, over and above what one might expect from passing years.'

'Agreed. Not fond of Edward Colduggan, is she?' Peter commented.

'No. I'd say that of the two she fancied John Wilbourne.' Aware that this visit had taken longer than expected, she added, 'Could you give Luke a call to say we're on the way back?'

'Will do.' Peter promptly picked up his mobile.

But she could hear Luke talking for longer than a mere thank-you, and Peter's face changed.

'What's happened?' she asked sharply as he put the phone down with a sober face.

'Luke asked if we ever bothered to pick up messages. Our new liaison DI Cotton wants us to ring him urgently. He wanted to know whether we'd met one of the villagers at Cobshaw. A Brenda Randall. She's been found dead—circumstances suspicious.'

Chapter Six

Judging by the few vehicles still parked along the side of the track when Georgia arrived at Cobshaw in the now fading light, it was clear that most of the police work must already have taken place at the crime scene. That was a relief. She had never come to terms with having to stand around with the pitiful victim's body still present while scene of crime officers methodically went about their business. The police trained themselves to put aside personal reactions as far as possible, but she had never mastered that skill. As Peter had been in the force before being paralysed, he usually managed to distance himself, but this evening she was here alone.

That was made even worse because the as yet unknown DI Cotton had given them the gruesome information that Brenda's body had been found in the pond surrounding the old well, which had been so special to her. On her way here, Georgia had tried to ignore the images this had thrown up in her mind, missing Peter's company. Was it coincidence that Brenda had died here? This was the place that for some in the village at least had a reputation for being sinister. And now it was indeed sinister.

Peter had driven back to Haden Shaw disgruntled at not being able to come with her—as though it were her fault that he had faithfully promised Elena that they could go together to 'have a word' with Jill about the wisdom of her future plans. Apparently, Georgia thought resignedly, the presence of Luke and herself had not been required.

'Supper?' Luke had asked plaintively as she rushed inside Medlars for a quick word after Peter had left in his own car.

'Over to you,' she'd had to say, At least, if need be, Luke could cook something for himself even though strictly speaking it had been her turn to cook dinner.

She could just about see that the crime scene tape surrounded the whole fenced-in area including the pond by which two or three people were standing and the track leading to Cobshaw Cottage. Thankfully, as far as she could tell as she drew nearer she was right in thinking Brenda's body was no longer there. From Will Whittan's information, relayed by DI Cotton, it appeared that an accident could be ruled out—and surely suicide too especially given where the body was found?

Only three days earlier Brenda had been here, anxious to impart as much of Cobshaw's history as she could to Peter and herself. For Brenda, Georgia reflected, history meant more than local squabbling over differing opinions. Something had been worrying her very much in the present, however—and now she was dead. Was there a connection? Or had the worry been over something trivial?

Someone at last spotted her, as she reached the gate. A young man with a shock of dark hair who, despite his casual demeanour, she instantly recognised as being in the police force.

'Show's over for tonight, madam,' he announced offhandedly as he strolled over to the entry point.

'Georgia Marsh,' she introduced herself. 'We had a phone call from DI Cotton.'

He shrugged. 'Procedural error. Sorry. I was expecting a guy in a wheelchair.'

'The said guy in a wheelchair is as mad as hell that he's booked elsewhere for tonight,' she returned tartly. 'I'm his partner and daughter.'

'Ah, Marsh & Daughter.' A tone of appeasement this time. 'Sorry. Let's start again. DI Jack Cotton on liaison service. I gather you're both in on it?'

'We're an investigative partnership.' Georgia picked up the signals that he wasn't too happy about his task, so it was best to get it sorted right away.

'No problem. But we're not here tonight liaising about old bones. This is a separate case, so you're an onlooker only. Right?'

'So you've already decided the cases aren't linked?' Whoops! Keep a lid on the situation, Georgia belatedly instructed herself. 'I'm not leaping to any conclusions, because I've only just arrived. But it's a coincidence, isn't it? A small village like this, the remains of a famous person missing for almost sixty years are found and the village historian who was present at the time he vanished is found dead. When I saw her on Saturday she seemed to be a very worried lady.'

This at least won her an appraising look. 'Weird, but coincidences happen, Georgia. I've already been told that this village is split in two and this woman was at the forefront of some campaign or other.' His eyes were fixed on her. Was he waiting for her to contradict him?

Impasse. Georgia drew a deep breath. Marsh & Daughter's best chance of solving the case of Sir John Wilbourne required co-operation and the likelihood of that would diminish fast if she didn't save the situation now. She adopted a grave and earnest expression.

'Look, as our liaison officer, why don't you tell me what happened here and if there's no link to the John Wilbourne case we can get out of your hair. But if there is the possibility of a link you might need to know what Marsh & Daughter learned from Brenda Randall and other sources. I take it this *is* your case?' she asked belatedly.

That must have jolted him, because he shot back at her, 'I'm SIO, yes. Are you planning to breathe down my neck?'

Careful here. Deep breath needed. This probably explained his wariness about Marsh & Daughter, especially if he was only newly promoted. 'Standing a respectful distance behind, but present,' she replied. 'As will my father, Peter.'

A pause. 'Fair enough,' he replied to her relief, although it was clearly a reluctant concession. 'But if there's a conflict of interest, I'm SIO and *not* your liaison officer.'

'Accepted. Now,' Georgia said firmly, 'could you outline exactly how Mrs Randall was found and is it known yet how she died?' She had to steel herself, remembering this was a woman she'd been talking to very recently and would have liked to have known better. 'I assume,' she added, 'that it wasn't an accident or suicide?'

'Not unless she strangled herself and jumped into the pond.'

The horror of this nearly overcame her.

The pond was constructed around the old well in the centre,' she managed to say, pulling herself together, aware that DI Cotton was watching for her reaction. One sign of displaying her disapproval of his offhand attitude, no matter the reason for that, and she would be lost. 'Any clues as to why her murderer pushed her in?' she asked.

He shrugged. 'Maybe not to be found so quickly?'

It was a weak retort and he obviously realised it. 'No reason to climb in voluntarily. Saving her cat perhaps.' Even weaker, but he made up for it. 'Want a look? We're more or less finished here.' He pointed to the pile of scene shoes as he opened the gate. 'No need for the suit.'

'Thank you.'

'Be my guest.'

Georgia walked up the path to the pond where a small group was now gathered. One of the men, a sergeant whom she remembered as a constable during Marsh and Daughter's last case, greeted her cheerfully to her satisfaction, as it helped her street cred with the indifferent DI Cotton. She tried not to think of the last visit she and Peter had paid here with Brenda, who was then so proud of Cecilia and her Tudor heritage.

The pond looked peaceful now with its gently moving water lilies, but it didn't take much imagination to picture the scene as it must have been earlier—nor to how it might have gained a dark and forbidding reputation. There was a goldfish streaking through the water and, sickened, Georgia turned away, thinking of Brenda's body with its sightless eyes in there with it. A woman she had known. Georgia struggled with herself. That could come later, and for now she needed her professional face.

'Manually strangled?' she asked.

'No, silk scarf. Now bagged up.'

'Her own?'

'Probably. We're guessing the victim could have been feeding those fish when her assailant came up, strangled her and tipped her in.'

'Why though?' Georgia asked again, with as much detachment as she could. 'She'd have been a heavy weight. Was there a blow to the head too?'

'A possibility.' A trifle more respect from his lordship now. 'Could have been caused when she was tipped in or she was hit before being strangled. The path report will tell us. Estimated time of death late yesterday evening.'

Georgia tried to imagine the scene, but there were too many gaps. Why had Brenda Randall come here at night-time? An odd time to feed the fish or to meet someone or show the well to someone as she had to Peter and herself. 'Any evidence of fish food?' she asked.

'Not yet. Might be some amongst the samples taken. No empty

bags around or in the victim's pockets. She was wearing an old fisherman's type smock.'

'May I ask who found her?' Tread gently, she told herself. No crossing boundaries. 'Her great-niece, Sophy. She came round here because she couldn't find Mrs Randall at home or in the garden and the dog was barking. Some chap was due to visit earlier and Sophy came to see if she was okay because Mrs Randall had been complaining that this fellow had been pestering her about her moving out so that he could take her house over.' He gestured towards Cobshaw Cottage.

'Probably Mick Buckley,' Georgia told him, relishing the opportunity to pass on information to this young know-it-all. 'He works for Gerald Randall who owns Cobshaw Hall on this estate and presumably rented the Cottage to Brenda Randall, but she refused to move.'

'Unhappy campers around, eh?' DI Cotton observed. 'Thanks. Still,' he counterattacked, 'it doesn't look as though your old bones are going to get much of a look-in with local issues rearing their heads.'

'Every village has issues over which there are different strong opinions,' Georgia fenced. 'But they rarely lead to murder.' From what she and Peter had seen though, Cobshaw might be the exception.

'In my book today takes precedence over 1959.'

'You recognise the date,' Georgia commented lightly. 'So you must have some interest in the old bones you referred to?'

Yet another shrug. 'Interest, but not in respect of my current case.'

What to make of DI Cotton? His off-handedness wasn't necessarily a sign of his indifference. It could well be the opposite, especially if she was right that he was only recently promoted. She wondered what Peter was going to make of him. At a guess, their liaison might be short-lived. What did Will Whittan see in Jack Cotton that made him think that she and Peter could work alongside him? she wondered.

Ambition? Skill? Dedication? More than that? Will understood Marsh and Daughter's needs almost as well as those of the police, but he would also know that the latter's had to come first.

The next morning, everyone in Cobshaw seemed to be fighting to get into the Maid of Kent. Georgia dubiously eyed the crowds mustering round the main door. It was hardly surprising. The victim was a woman whom they all knew well and she had met a terrible end.

'Good morning, Your Majesty,' Peter muttered as he negotiated his scooter into the side entrance and greeted the young Richard II staring nervously down from his painted throne on the wall at this intruder sailing past him.

If His Majesty replied, Georgia couldn't hear him as they continued along the Plantagenet royal route.

'Odd there aren't any pictures or articles about Richard of Eastwell,' Georgia remarked, glancing up at the poster of Laurence Olivier encouraging the troops as Henry V.

'Our good friend Percival said something about Richard's Room but we haven't been privileged to see it yet. Perhaps that features him.'

As if on cue, Percival flew out from his sanctum with his usual familiar 'welcome'. 'You here again?'

Either he had first class hearing for his age or he had a spyhole in the wall, Georgia decided.

'As customers only this time,' Peter explained.

Percival grunted. 'Takes a murder to bring them out in force.' Then he had the grace to change tack. 'And it's bad news about Brenda. Very bad news. Randall or not, she was a fine woman was Brenda. We don't want murders in Cobshaw and especially not hers.'

'You told us this pub had lots of murders in its time and that's not counting John Wilbourne's,' Peter observed. 'Including in Tudor times with Cecilia herself.'

'That was then.' Percival snapped, clearly objecting to the word Tudor in connection with the pub's origins. 'It's different when it's now. Hear that racket?'

They could. The noise level was going up.

'All piling the blame on each other.' Percival snorted. 'Even his blinking lordship Gerald Randall has stirred his stumps to patronise us today.'

'Any of this blame justified?' Peter enquired. 'What do you think happened, Mr FitzRichard?'

'I never think out loud,' Percival informed them seriously. 'Best not to in a pub. And especially when murder's involved. How d'you know who you're speaking to, eh? You tell me that.'

Georgia couldn't. She agreed with him, especially in a village the size of Cobshaw.

'Are the police still around?' Peter asked.

'Not round here,' Percival replied with relish. 'Set up shop in Cobshaw Hall they have. Trust them Tudors to appoint themselves on the side of the righteous. Never trust these Tudors, my dad said. They're no good, none of them. Brenda wasn't a Randall. She just stupidly went and married one of them. And she was killed on public land, not those Randalls' property.'

'Do you think this murder results from the old trouble between the Planters and Tudors?' Peter prodded.

'Could be. And I don't want them fighting it out here in *my* pub, turning my Brenda's murder into a battle over this hotel business. It's still *my* property and no one seems to remember that. I'll be off if it's all the same to you.' With this abrupt mood change, he disappeared into his sanctum.

My Brenda? Georgia noted. Interesting. He hadn't indicated any great friendship with her before.

That must have struck Peter too. 'Bit of a Cheshire Cat, isn't he?' he remarked. 'Now you see me, now you don't. Only he doesn't grin as much. I sense he was genuinely fond of Brenda for all his feud with the Tudors.'

The bar proved to be as crowded as predicted, and both men and women had turned out today. Any expectation of harmony in the circumstances was doomed. A heated argument was clearly in progress centre stage.

The table where Brenda had been sitting on their first visit was now occupied by the taciturn Geoff Sanders and his grandson Louis. Dave Cook was in the heart of the argument and so was Mick Buckley. On the far side of the room Georgia could see another elderly man sitting giving a distinct appearance of aloofness as though he were doing the pub a favour by his presence. At last! This could surely be none other than Gerald Randall himself. The head Tudor, forced to appear at a Plantagenet pub from lack of an alternative. Where Geoff was bristling and defensive, Gerald looked calmly detached although a gleam in his eye suggested that trouble might be in store. Perhaps he was right, Georgia thought, for Percival had reappeared pushing his way past them to the bar and over through the crowd to reach his bête noir.

'Come to have a pint with the peasants?' Percival greeted him loudly, taking a seat with him uninvited.

Not the way to address someone who had just lost a member of his family in terrible circumstances, Georgia thought, appalled. But it seemed to be normal practice because Gerald merely stared at Percival as he replied:

'I wouldn't say you were a peasant, FitzRichard. Merely an upstart.'

Dave Cook must have anticipated impending trouble for he pushed through the crowd to join them. 'Not today, you two. We've had a murder in our midst and respect's due. By everyone.'

That sobered them, and although the air bristled with hostility, there was at least silence from everyone present. There followed a few awkward moments, then people turned to the bar and began to break into smaller groups. To Georgia's surprise, with the crisis temporarily over, Dave Cook joined Gerald Randall rather than returning to his own group—the Planters presumably?—in the central area. Perhaps this was intentional, a sign of temporary unity, although that suggested that the Tudors might have won this first move in a metaphorical game of chess.

Dave looked over to them. 'Come and join us,' he called out. A big honour in pub etiquette, as both she and Peter appreciated. 'Peter and Georgia Marsh,' Dave introduced them to Gerald Randall as the barman brought their drinks over.

'I've heard about you,' Gerald said. He sounded quite jovial, to Georgia's surprise. 'You're writers. Quick off the mark, aren't you? My sister-in-law only died on Monday night.'

'And our sympathy to you for that,' Peter returned. Her father had a knack of speedily adjusting to situations, Georgia acknowledged, whereas she veered the other way. 'We're here,' Peter added, 'because the police might need to talk to us.'

This explanation earned him only a rebuff. 'They've all the information they need,' Gerald said grandly. 'My granddaughter was very attached to my sister-in-law. It was she who found her.'

'We met Sophy briefly with Louis Sanders,' Georgia said incautiously.

Gerald Randall's calm aloofness promptly vanished. 'What was she doing with that scoundrel?' he barked.

'Hold it, Gerald,' Dave said promptly. 'They're friends, that's all.'

'*Friends*? He's a good-for-nothing,' Gerald spluttered. 'A Planter like you, Dave. You Planters killed Brenda because she stood up for our rights over the well and was all for saving this dump of a pub by turning it into a first-class hotel.'

He'd gone too far. Dave stood up, slowly and deliberately. 'Enough, Gerald. What would the Planters gain by killing her?'

'A lot. Her support would have clinched the deal. Howard Green is about to visit Cobshaw to settle the matter. Brenda told me there was a surprise in store for you all. She was a clever woman and a great historian. She was going to make a convincing argument over the heritage issue. As Green has no Plantagenet blood and your daughter, Percival, hasn't got a penny to her name, it'll be a case of the best man wins, and that's Howard Green. You've got as much Plantagenet blood in you as a stick insect, Dave. What this village needs is someone like Green to bring some prosperity to this place, not have it turned into a run-down community centre with the walls tumbling down around it.'

'If this fellow Green isn't of the blood,' Percival galloped into the fray, 'I can't sell it to him and that's that. It goes to Bernie.'

'Who hasn't the money to restore it,' Gerald said coolly.

'We plan to rival anything this Howard Green offers,' Dave said evenly. 'We've plans for raising major gifts.'

'Yeah?' Mick Buckley marched over to join in. 'Like a couple of tenners in the donation box?'

Louis too must have heard what was going on for he left his grandfather and marched over to join the battle as well. 'Sucking up to the Tudors again, Mick? Where's your community spirit?' he shouted at him. 'Forgotten, is it, now you're going to move into Brenda's house?'

Mick, purple-faced, lunged at him, but was caught by Dave just in time.

'None of your business, young man,' Gerald shouted. 'And keep away from my granddaughter. Is that clear? She's not for the likes of you.'

Mistake, Georgia thought. His clear disdain would only enrage Louis further.

'Nothing to do with you, Mr Randall,' Louis yelled back. 'Days of you Tudors are over. Sophy can do what she likes because she's over eighteen. And what Cobshaw needs is a referendum on what everyone wants for this pub, hotel versus community centre.'

'No point,' Percival snarled. 'It's my pub. My Bernie's a clever one. She'll find the cash herself. None of your hotels *or* community centres.'

'Time to go,' Peter whispered to Georgia. 'We're in a foreign land here. Nothing to do with John Wilbourne.'

'And,' Georgia pointed out, 'little or nothing to do with Brenda Randall.'

'There you're on shakier ground. I'd say Brenda had a great deal to do with one if not both subjects.'

She was about to reply when Percival stood up to make another declaration: 'You can all leave referendums and Tudors out of it,' he yelled. 'The pub has to go to a Plantagenet and that's that.'

'Depends on whether you find one with the cash,' Gerald drawled. 'Asked Tony about this, have you?'

'Asked him what?'

'Considering his options, is he? He might do well out of the Green deal.'

'Nothing to do with him. He's not the Plantagenet, Bernie is.'

The battle was still in progress as Peter manoeuvred his way to the exit door and Georgia breathed a sigh of relief. 'The path to sanity,' she declared.

'Where,' Peter asked half an hour later, 'does this leave our concert?'

They had stopped on the hillside overlooking the grass terraces of the theatre. Here there was a small area of uneven paving stones with a few determined love-in-the mist growing up in their cracks. It was a peaceful spot though and a great deal more relaxing than the Maid of Kent bar.

Georgia shared Peter's gloom. This concert might have been a mistake. It was already the end of May, only two and a half months before the performance. How could they even envisage holding it now that it was overshadowed by the discovery of Sir John Wilbourne's remains and now by a very current murder case in which the victim was known to them? Add to that, the fighting over the future of the pub and the outlook was indeed disturbing. Time was fast vanishing before 17th August.

'Do you think,' she began slowly, 'that there's the ghost of a chance that Brenda's death was due not to the fuss over the Maid of Kent but—'

'Our investigation?' Peter finished for her. 'Could be. Everyone seems economical with the truth. Including Brenda Randall. But why? We're investigating a crime that happened sixty years ago. Do we go ahead and hope the Battle of Bosworth doesn't break out in the meantime?'

Georgia took a risk. 'What would Rick's answer be?'

'We both know that.' Peter sighed. 'He'd say go right ahead.'

Chapter Seven

'Are Marsh & Daughter at home?'

To Georgia's amazement, Sophy Randall was standing on the doorstep, looking very nervous, despite her bravado. The plan for a long and hopefully uninterrupted discussion with Peter in his office after yesterday's hullabaloo rapidly changed as she took in Sophy's obvious distress. The shock of finding her great-aunt's body must have been immense and that was only two days ago.

'Sorry just to turn up like this,' Sophy said jerkily, 'but that policeman—Jack Cotton—said I should talk to you. I thought I might chicken out on the way so I didn't call first.' She managed a weak smile.

'I'm glad you didn't chicken out,' Georgia said sincerely. Jack Cotton suggested it? Why? Sophy was clearly deeply affected by Brenda's death, and Georgia was surprised at how much she herself was shaken. Terrible though it had been, she had not expected it to tug on her emotions to this extent. The death seemed so unfair. Brenda must have stood in someone's way, because she surely couldn't have actively offended someone to the point of murder. Added to that was the coincidence of her murder being so close to the discovery of John Wilbourne's bones, which had provided fate with one of its funny little ways of packaging things together. If not coincidence, then there might be an as yet undiscovered link between the two. Was Jack Cotton taking that into account and that was why he had suggested Sophy should come here?

'We didn't have a chance to offer our condolences earlier,' Peter said sympathetically to Sophy. 'You must have been close to her.'

'I was.' Sophy sank into one of the two comfortable armchairs. 'She was brilliant. Really kind and warm-hearted but she wouldn't let it show very often.' There was a glint of tears.

'Why was that?' Peter asked. 'There's usually a reason.'

Sophy thought about this. 'No idea,' she replied at last, 'unless she was disappointed in love. But that would have been decades ago.'

'Love in her marriage?'

'Great-uncle Tom was a dry old stick—or so the family all thought until he pranced into greener fields in the comely shape of a young blonde. Brenda stayed with him, but it could have been what threw her into history with a capital H. But why would anyone kill her in that awful way?' Sophy burst out. 'Just tossing her into that pond. She really loved that place.' Her lips trembled and Georgia reached out a comforting hand.

'Why did DI Cotton suggest you come to see us?' Georgia asked. 'He knows that primarily we're investigating the death of John Wilbourne.'

'That's why. The message he's getting from his boss is that Brenda was killed over this hotel business and perhaps that's right. There are a lot of vested interests heating up. So Jack Cotton listened to me but told me to talk to you. He said you had other ideas.'

Was that to his credit, Georgia wondered, or simply to offload on Peter and herself any concerns Sophy might have? 'Brenda seemed very stressed out when we met her. Do you know why or if it might have had anything to do with her death, even if that seems unlikely?'

'Nothing concrete. I wish I did,' Sophy replied. 'Brenda's death was horrible, *horrible*, and I want her murderer found. We've been taking care of her dog and every time he barks I feel he's getting at me for taking her away from him. So I've been trying to think it through. The hotel business is one line for a motive, but I think it's just possible that her murder was connected to the John Wilbourne you mentioned. I've been working it out,' Sophy added eagerly. 'He was step-brother to Great-uncle Tom, who wasn't married to Brenda in 1959 and I don't think John Wilbourne was married then either. So it could have been a Romeo and Juliet situation between John and Brenda, couldn't it? John was a Randall, so suppose Brenda's family were Planters. It would have been just as with Louis and me. Cobshaw hasn't changed.'

'That's a real possibility,' Georgia agreed when Sophy came to a halt. She'd had the same thought earlier. 'Is the situation with you and Louis deadlocked?'

Sophy seized on this. 'Yes. Bonkers, isn't it, in this day and age? Grandfather getting all wound up because I want to marry a Planter. Big deal.'

'Are the Planters and Tudors still really as fiercely at odds as they seem?'

'Oh, believe me, they are. As a child I was threatened with "the Planters will get you".' She shrugged. 'For the Randalls, the Planters are a dark cloud over the village that never passes over. How and when it all began, I've no idea. Grandfather Gerald keeps ominously mum on the subject and so do my parents. They're lucky. They're still travelling the world to escape this place, but they had this weird idea I needed my education here. Wrong. Glad they did though, because I met Louis.'

'Is the feud between the FitzRichards and the Randalls part of the Planters and Tudors split or is it a separate issue?' Peter asked curiously.

'More or less the same, but I don't think it's ever been defined that way. When it erupts though it gets personal. Dave Cook usually leads for the Planters and Mick Buckley for the Tudors though I'm pretty sure that Mick came from strong Planter stock way back. But he's been solidly Tudor for a long while. He won't broadcast it too loudly, but now he's getting his heart's desire by moving into Cobshaw Cottage. It belongs to Granddad Gerald so as soon as Mick heard that he was off to Granddad like a shot. Didn't take long, did it? But as to *my* heart's desire, here I am, a Tudor, in love with a Planter. Great, isn't it? Ironic that John Wilbourne's last dramatic performance was in *Romeo and Juliet* playing Romeo, perhaps with his personal Juliet watching him in the audience. But rest assured, I've no intention of stabbing or poisoning myself and nor has Louis. We're merely going to stalk out of the Randalls' life—we don't fit into that.'

Georgia smiled. 'You're over eighteen, aren't you?'

'Well over. I'm twenty-two, graduated from uni last summer and working in Canterbury. It's Louis who's reluctant to leave Cobshaw, otherwise we'd go and wash dishes in London in order to be together.'

'But why does he rule that out?'

Sophy grimaced. 'Louis's convinced he's honour-bound to stay here. He graduated in garden design the year before me but feels he has to work locally so he can keep an eye on his grandad. He does landscaping work to keep the wolf from the door but basically he looks after the Maid of Kent's grounds for his grandfather's sake.'

'Why's Geoff Sanders so personally attached to them?' Peter asked curiously.

'He says it's all about the gardens dear Cecilia tended over four centuries ago and how he wants to restore them properly. But if you imagine the hotel plan could fit in nicely with that, forget it. The hotel would doubtless want swimming pools, tennis courts and so on, and to hell with anything that's in their way. So the Sanders are firmly wedded to the community plan through which everyone would have access to the gardens.'

'And Louis's parents? Can't they take care of Geoff?'

'Like mine. Shaken the Cobshaw dust off their feet and gone their separate ways, leaving Louis to uphold the honour of the Planters under direction from Dave Cook.'

'Who'll win the battle for the pub, do you think?'

Sophy considered this. 'The field's wide open, in my view, with Bernie and Tony in the picture. Not that Tony would stand in the way of an easier life. Anything that paves the way for keeping his Porsche immaculate would please him plus a healthier bank account. Howard Green still has to play his full hand, though. He's made an offer but Percival is dithering. If Brenda knew anything that affected that issue, we'll never know now.'

'Would your grandfather know what was worrying her or even Geoff Sanders?'

'Not my grandfather, and as for Geoff—well, I expect you've met him in the Maid of Kent. Getting anything out of him is hopeless. I like him, but it's hard to get through to the man I remember as a kid.'

'He seemed to remember 1959 and the play though,' Peter said.

'You're right. He remembers some things if he chooses to. But every so often he'll stop what he's saying to inform you that the past is always with us. Nothing but dark hints though. The village will have to atone, secrets can't be hidden for ever etcetera. That sort of thing.'

'Is that just an old man rambling on or could it be more than that?' Georgia felt a sudden surge of excitement and she could see Peter's interest stirring. Take it step by step, she warned herself—and then promptly forgot this sage advice. 'He certainly remembers the play and so there might have been something about that which was also troubling your aunt? If so, have you any idea at all what it could have been about?'

'Not a clue,' Sophy said simply. 'And if I ask him he'll clam up. That means there could be nothing to it or it could be the whole story of John Wilbourne or where dear old Cecilia is buried.'

'My money would be on John Wilbourne,' Peter said, glancing at Georgia.

Fingerprints, Georgia thought instantly, remembering their first reaction to the Maid of Kent stage. There was no evidence of Geoff Sanders' connection with the Wilbourne death, but it was possible.

'You could help us with something else, Sophy,' she said. 'Percival FitzRichard mentioned a village fête. Is or was that an annual event? Do you know if there was one before the 1959 performance?'

'Afraid I can't help. I've heard there used to be fêtes, but I've no idea when they stopped. Someone said the war, but before or after I don't know. But beware. Brenda always said that Percival had a head full of moonbeams, as she put it. Hardly surprising. She thought his father Montague put them there. He was a real autocrat, apparently, crazy about ancestry, heritage and the Plantagenets of course. He created Richard's Room, as Percival calls it, for studying the Plantagenets and Richard of Eastwell in particular. Montague was the reason Brenda became interested in history. Montague would talk about them to her, she told me. And talk and talk and talk. Yet Brenda supported the hotel plan because of its Tudor heritage not Plantagenet. Weird, isn't it? That might be, I suppose, because the hotel was somehow connected with an old love—who could,' Sophy ended triumphantly, 'in theory have been John Wilbourne.'

Old love? The more Georgia thought about this, the more likely it seemed. It had been clear Brenda had a yen for him, but not necessarily that she was in love with him. 'Did she talk about him to you?' she asked hopefully.

'Not that I remember—not until these last few days when she was really jittery. Don't know why.' She managed a smile. 'Over to you.'

'You can't get in there. For some reason my crazy father-in-law's locked himself inside.' Tony told them glumly, when Peter and Georgia reached the Maid of Kent.

'It's time we saw Richard's Room,' Peter had decided after Sophy had left. 'Let's bone up on those Plantagenets.'

'Do we need to do that urgently?' Georgia had asked cautiously. 'We're not players in the hotel game.'

'No, but we're watching it from the sidelines and it helps to know the rules. Richard's Room might help.'

So it might, Georgia had thought, but now they were here it looked like a wasted journey.

'Bernie's the only one who might get Percival out, but she's in town today,' Tony continued. 'It's Brenda Randall's death that's upset him. He's not usually this bad. The police probably got his goat too. He won't speak to anyone.'

'Not even if we told him we want to learn about Richard of Eastwell?' Georgia asked hopefully.

'He can always say no.' Tony's voice was not encouraging. Still, he led them round via the corridors they already knew and then took a branch in it that they had previously bypassed. It ended in a forbidding-looking heavy door.

Dungeons? Georgia wondered. She wouldn't rule it out in this labyrinthine building.

'Visitors, Percival!' Tony yelled.

'Get lost, the lot of you,' came the muffled reply.

A second appeal got the same response, but as Peter was beginning to turn his scooter around the door flew open and Percival stood on the threshold, red-faced and clearly furious. His eyes were red-rimmed though, Georgia noticed. Almost as if he had been crying.

'Oh, it's you,' he snarled. 'Come in if you must. Not you, Tony. Get back to the bar.'

Tony took this pleasantry in his stride, obviously used to this reception, because he obeyed with a mere 'Thanks for the welcome, Percival.'

The good thing about speaking to eccentrics was that some latitude could be allowed, Georgia reckoned, which was useful in dealing with the Percivals of this world. It was a struggle to manoeuvre the scooter inside and it was an even greater challenge once in there, despite her efforts to help. The room resembled a huge storage place with only one definable narrow path through. There was now no sign of Percival anywhere, so where had he disappeared to?

They looked around in stunned amazement. Low-ceilinged, glimpses of a hearth and chimney on one side and of a window overlooking a garden on another. An eccentric's room to say the least, full of goodness knows what. The passageway lined with large stone statues, waxworks, piles of files and books led to—what? A high pile of storage boxes, with the only light in the room edging its way through more statues and boxes on what must be a window on the right. From the doorway it seemed the passageway came to an abrupt end but taking a step or two forward Georgia could see it made a sharp turn towards the window, somewhere near which, she guessed, Percival must be waiting.

'Careful!' Peter called sharply as she backed into the collection on the left to allow room for him to advance at least a little way along the path.

She instinctively turned towards him, only to find a huge medieval knight lunging towards her, almost ceiling height and complete with an all too real arming sword withdrawn from its sheath. This one at a guess was a waxwork but whatever it was, it was realistic enough to make her stumble over an iron trunk with the biggest locks she'd ever seen.

'Who is this gentleman greeting us?' Peter shouted out to the still absent Percival. 'Richard of Eastwell?'

'Don't be daft.' It was Percival's voice yelling from the direction of the window and shortly he emerged at the end of the path. 'He's over there,' he snarled, pointing towards the wall with the chimney behind the knight.

Peter promptly tried to twist the buggy as Georgia managed to edge her way through to the far wall to the open hearth. Next to one side of it on a plastered section of the wall was a large mural that must be at least a metre wide and roughly as tall as she was. It depicted a robed figure placing a crown on the head of a seated youth in what could be the artist's idea of Westminster Abbey. Next to the mural, on the low stone seating running part of the wall from the inner corner towards the huge hearth, was another sculpted figure. Clad apparently in medieval peasant's garb, he was sitting huddled, studying a book with his right hand and the other arm resting on the stone at his side. No prizes for guessing who he was, nor probably the boy in the mural, Georgia thought.

'You may address him as Your Majesty King Richard the Fourth,' Percival announced smugly, having advanced along the path to keep an eye on her.

She braced herself for more Plantagenet history.

'We gather you have proof that Richard of Eastwell was legitimate,' Peter asked him mildly from the doorway. This was not an ideal room for scooters. 'He's usually considered one of Richard III's illegitimate sons.'

Percival eyed him balefully. 'He was *legitimate*. Plenty of evidence for that. He wrote his own autobiography. Never read it myself, it disappeared centuries ago. But the Eastwell family knew all right.' He glared at them. 'What more proof do you want?'

Quite a lot, Georgia thought, remembering Bernie's offhand outline of Richard of Eastwell's story, but Percival was not waiting for any reply.

'I'll give you some anyway,' he continued grandly. 'Richard III had a secret marriage before he publicly married Anne Neville,' he informed them. 'They'd got friendly long before that. Or the secret marriage could have been with someone else,' he conceded. 'Anyway, Richard of Eastwell was the result. *Legitimate!* That's why he had to hide away. Those Tudors would have had him on the execution block if they could have laid their murderous hands on him, he being the rightful king. He trained as a mason, came down to Kent and hid himself away. His granddaughter Cecilia lived with him until she married a Randall. But that didn't make Richard a Tudor any more than it did Cecilia. They were both Plantagenets. He got too interested in his grandpa-in-law's history though, so Richard scooted off to work for Sir Thomas Moyle down the road in Eastwell thinking he'd be safer there, in case the word got around on who he was. Those Tudors would still be after his blood, him being the rightful king so his son-in-law might get tempted. The Tudors got Cecilia in the end though. Murdered her. But they didn't get her child. He was a Plantagenet all right, and that's my ancestor,' he concluded proudly, his eyes by now wet with tears of emotion.

'Brenda seems to have thought that Cecilia owned the Maid of Kent, or Cobham Court as she called it. And that she was a Tudor,' Georgia said. Nothing like putting one's head in the lions' mouth.

'She was wrong,' Percival whipped back, almost indulgently. 'I said to her, I know I'm right. But she would have it her way. And that's why she died. Brenda always was stubborn.' They were treated to the familiar glare again. 'I loved that woman. She was a stunner. She was going to marry me. Her father, being the village doctor, weren't a Tudor, more like a Planter. Then old Tom Randall came along, a blinking Tudor.'

Tread carefully, Georgia told herself. They were getting into deep water here. Peter had less reserve.

'That was after 1959 though. Were you courting her then?' he asked matter-of-factly.

No stopping Percival now. 'Star-struck she was about that Wilbourne fellow. There was a group of them students she went around with; they went up to London to see all the Bard of Avon Company shows. Even had special t-shirts made for them, with stuff like 'I Love John' on them and there was a rival group with 'I love Edward' all over them. Edward Colduggan that is. When my Brenda heard they were coming down to Cobshaw nothing could hold her back.'

'Do you know *why* they were coming here?' Georgia asked. 'Did you see her at all that evening?'

She was ignored. 'Wild horses wouldn't drag her away,' Percival said gloomily. 'She came rushing in to say that Edward and John were going to have a fencing duel and wasn't that fun. Off she went like a medieval lady thinking the duel was all over her.'

'And was it?'

'No way. It was artistic rivalry, my dad said.'

'They both came back to the pub afterwards though, and yet one of the stage swords was found where he was buried,' Georgia said.

Percival blinked. 'If you're thinking that's what killed him it must have been Banquo's ghost done it. Anyway, I saw Edward Colduggan waving his sword back in the pub after that duel of theirs.'

There would have been plenty of knives of one sort or another available in the pub within easy reach of any of the villagers as well as the cast and staff, Georgia reasoned, and possibly knives at the theatre itself if the backstage staff were still active at that point.

'Did you watch the duel?' she asked. At least Percival seemed in co-operative mood.

'Perhaps I did,' came the answer. 'Some of it. The end anyway. My dad came out and broke it up. I was having a few words with one of those Tudors most of the time. Old John Wilbourne was winning. It wasn't much of a duel, as Colduggan was half drunk already. Swine, he was, that Winbourne. Broke my Brenda's heart.'

'Who do you think killed her?' Peter asked quietly.

Percival looked surprised. 'Them Randalls,' he growled. 'Them Tudors in the past killed more women than Bluebeard, with their Anne Boleyns and Catherine Howards. All to protect themselves and keep the Tudor line going. Tudors? You talk to Geoff Sanders—and Mick Buckley who's a Tudor when it suits him. That's the Buckleys all over.'

'We're going round in circles,' Peter said in frustration after they left. 'That didn't advance us much. Georgia, there's a heart beating at the centre of this Wilbourne case that we haven't yet found. Don't you agree?'

'Reluctantly, yes.'

'Granted it's sixty years ago,' he continued, 'but there are enough people around to give us clues to reaching it if only they would come clean. We aren't getting the full story, even from Percival. We know John Wilbourne survived the duel, so what happened after that to bring him back to where his bones were found—assuming that he *was* killed there or nearby? The stage perhaps. A knife is the probable cause of death, but we've no idea what kind of knife.'

Peter stopped his scooter as they passed the entrance to the walled garden on their way to the outdoor theatre. 'I can see Louis in there. A non-partisan witness, thanks be.'

He promptly turned the scooter and headed through the brick wall's archway at such a pace Georgia was almost running to keep up. Louis was now disappearing towards the greenhouse, which like the pub was in sad need of attention, but he paused to poke around in the pit outside, looking up without much surprise as they arrived.

'They used to grow pineapples in this pit,' he commented. 'Not now. No time.'

'If the Maid of Kent becomes a hotel, they might use it,' Georgia said innocently, then felt mean as she saw his face darken.

'Won't be a hotel. It's going to be a community centre.'

'If so, would the gardens still be maintained?'

'I'll come to some arrangement with Dave. Sell the produce maybe. Run a community shop.'

'Let's hope that's not pie in the sky,' Peter said seriously.

Louis took this in good part. 'Pie's on the plate ready for the eating. You'll see. Bernie will get the place on its feet once we get grants to do the place up. Tony's not too happy about it but he'll go along with it. Got to. It's heritage.'

'The Tudors and the Planters have different ideas on what that heritage is,' Georgia said.

Louis groaned. 'You're here about what happened in 1959, aren't you? I reckon that's village heritage too. I don't know anything about it but I think my granddad does. Won't talk fully about it though. All he says is no one can be free in Cobshaw until all the dead bodies are dug up. I always thought he was talking rubbish, but now those have been found and Brenda's been murdered I'm not so sure.'

Peter went very still. 'Hasn't he ever explained what he means by that?'

'No. He's just burbling on about stuff his father told him. Just repeats it or trots out, "Then the war came".'

Chapter Eight

Until all the dead bodies are dug up. Was he just harking back to Cecilia again? And which war? The two world wars or further back? Anything seemed possible in Cobshaw, divided over the centuries and still fighting. And Percival and Geoff Sanders had talked of trouble as though it were closer to home than deaths in centuries past, but Georgia wasn't convinced that they were thinking of John Wilbourne or even Cecilia.

Georgia had planned to work in Haden Shaw today, concentrating on Suspects Anonymous, plus returning to the Maid of Kent in the hope of reconstructing what they knew so far about what happened after the performance. Doing so on the actual site might produce new ideas.

Tomorrow, Saturday, would be the first of June, which brought August's concert uncomfortably close. Elena was already deeply involved with dealing with queries over the invitations. With Josephine Mantreau and Lucien Marques performing, the audience would be a sizeable one even though it was a private event. At present though Georgia found it hard to reconcile enthusiasm for the concert with their knowledge of John Wilbourne's last performance there.

She was just about to set out for Haden Shaw when her mobile rang.

'I've had our esteemed liaison officer on the line,' Peter began without preamble.

'News?' she asked hopefully. 'They've made an arrest for Brenda's murder?'

'Nothing so dramatic. Press briefing in Cobshaw village hall. Even though it's not directly connected to our case, I think I'll go. Want to join me?'

So much for Suspects Anonymous and her planned solitary mission to the Maid of Kent. It occurred to her that Peter didn't sound that enthusiastic about the briefing. Sure enough: 'There's a drawback,' he admitted.

'Not good. Tell me.'

'I'd promised to take Elena and Jill out to lunch, so they'll have to come with me to Cobshaw. It's going to be a family lunch at the Maid of Kent.'

Great. Her plan was scuppered. Peter was breaking Marsh & Daughter rules about not mixing business with pleasure, but she bit back her protest, aware that she was being childish. There was nothing to be done. It was spilt milk.

'Just this once, Georgia,' he added in appeal. 'It could be all right. You and I can go to the briefing and then have lunch all together at the pub afterwards.'

She knew that Elena had been pleading with him to have yet another talk with Jill. Far from abandoning her plans to leave the country, Jill now seemed to be firming them up, preferably without poor Mark but definitely with Rosie and Robbie. Some kind of family conference was needed, so it might as well be today. Peter explained that having given his reason for wanting to call the lunch off, Elena had immediately broken in with 'Splendid, darling. You can drive us all there.' True, Elena had probably spoken without thinking it through, but Georgia's plans for today looked a lost cause.

She gritted her teeth, still struggling to be rational over this hiccup. Once more, however, she was swept back to a childhood brightened by her fun-loving mother, whose high spirits had entranced her but made her feel unimportant in her company. Fortunately, there was nothing much secret about today's briefing at Cobshaw. Every local newspaper for miles around plus half the national press would be descending on the village to hear the latest about Brenda Randall's death—and for the press the story of the missing Sir John would be trailing behind it. Not only journalists but most of Cobshaw's residents would be glued to the scene too. There was no help for it, she told Peter. But in for a penny, in for a pound. She would stay with Elena and Jill at the pub while Peter went to the briefing alone. He could join them for lunch afterwards.

When she arrived at the Maid of Kent, however, Elena and Jill were already established with Peter still with them. He was looking miserable perched between them. He hated being a position where he couldn't rule the roost and that was definitely the case here.

Elena jumped up to kiss her. 'Darling, it's so exciting. That press briefing you're going to must have set tongues wagging. We've seen so many cars heading to the village hall.'

There weren't many at the Maid of Kent, Georgia had noticed. The village hall was in the centre of the village, a twenty-minute walk from the Maid of Kent, and that's where all the cars must be parked. There was no sign of Bernie, but Tony was at the bar, and she could see Dave Cook sitting there with Percival. There were only half a dozen other people here, one of them a stranger at the far side of the pub looking happily ensconced with a newspaper and what looked like a burger and a half pint of bitter.

'Peter said he'd go to this briefing alone,' Elena chatted on. 'But I've persuaded him to stay here with us instead. As I pointed out, darling, I'm sure you two already know so much about that lady's death that you wouldn't hear anything new.'

Peter's eyes didn't meet Georgia's as she forced herself to count to ten—and then extended it to twenty.

Jill intervened after a glance at Peter. 'I've a better idea, Elena. Why don't you and I go to the briefing with Peter? Peter said you had plans of your own, Georgia, but we can all meet up for lunch here.'

Georgia did indeed have plans and clutched at this chance to carry out her mission after all. 'Yes, that's a great idea,' she said gratefully.

She had always got on well with Jill—despite the present deadlock over her future. Jill was six foot tall, very purposeful and exuded her American charm of gracefully conveying the conviction that she was always right. Which, to be fair, Jill usually was—except in this current crisis.

'You can tell us about the case on the way there, Peter.' Elena checked herself. 'Not in detail, of course. I know you and Georgia can't talk about your work. Such a shame. This case of John Wilbourne is so interesting, for Jill especially.'

'Why's that, Elena?' Georgia asked casually. *Damn*. She'd fallen into the trap. Another minute and family business would be the order of the day.

Jill tried to rescue her. 'Elena's too kind, Georgia. English Literature is my field, and I guess this old inn has tales to tell. It's places like this that bring history to life.'

Georgia breathed again. 'Like Canterbury.' A flat-footed comment to say the least, considering Jill currently lived there amid the city's many wonders.

'Sure, but Cobshaw is timeless. It's stopped in mid track, you know?

Canterbury keeps its treasures from pre-Roman times right through to St Augustine and up to your modern Banksys. Cobshaw's a different matter. It's kind of stuck in a time warp. Bernie has been telling me about this Cecilia maid of Kent lady and the way Bernie talks makes it sound like the lady's still around.' Jill grinned at Georgia. 'Some story to take back to the States, though. Sorry, Georgia,' she added belatedly, 'should have kept away from that.'

Too late. 'You're still planning to leave?' Elena adopted her hurt voice.

Jill looked serious. 'We all have to follow our own stars, Elena. Mark has his, I have mine, and the kids are yet to find theirs. If I give them a fair taste of American life as well as life in Canterbury, they have a choice.'

Stay silent, Georgia decided. Just nod sympathetically. This isn't the time.

Jill must have noticed Peter's expression though. She broke off, saying brightly, 'We'll see you back here for lunch then, Georgia.'

'Enjoy the Plantagenet tour,' Georgia called, as Jill and Elena set off to follow Peter's exit route through the corridors. She remained where she was, relaxing. Family tensions, she thought, had a place all of their own on the anxiety scale. She looked around the bar as a few more people had gathered including Dave Cook. The stranger she had first noticed was still glued to his newspaper, the burger abandoned by his side. She couldn't blame him. The cuisine here was not rated highly.

Dave had obviously come in to pick up Percival, as they set off together with Percival casting his usual glare at her. Nothing personal, she now realised, merely an objection to seeing anyone in his pub who wasn't a practising Plantagenet.

Seeing Tony still behind the bar, she went over to order a quick coffee. She had enough time for that given that she'd be on her own for over an hour at least.

'Bernie's left for the briefing,' Tony told her. 'So if you're wanting lunch you're stuck with me.' He grinned at her.

'Aren't you interested in the briefing?' she asked.

'Sure, but I'm not a Cobshaw native so although Brenda's death was a shock, I don't take it personally. Not too good knowing there's a murderer about the place, though. I don't see a passing vagrant strangling her then pushing the poor woman over the wall into the pond.'

Georgia shivered. The images were all too clear. Brenda had been killed during the late evening although not found until the next day. In the meantime, the milkman had probably left her milk on the doorstep, phones had gone unanswered, newspapers had been delivered—everyone oblivious to what had happened the previous evening.

'Has to be someone local,' Tony continued. 'Plenty of folk round her had it in for the Tudors and she was an obstinate old thing.'

'Is that what the Tudors believe? That it was the Planters killed her?' she asked incredulously.

''Course they'd think that. This place seems empty without her though.'

'She wanted the deal to go through.'

He gave her a curious look, handing over the coffee she'd ordered. 'All the Tudors do. But the Maid of Kent's set to be a community centre.'

'The well was dear to her heart too. What about that?' Georgia forced herself to ask. 'Brenda told me it was disputed territory though it seems the Randall claim isn't affected by her death.'

'It's disputed all right. If those Tudors have their way and this becomes a hotel, they'll claim the well too. No doubt about it. They'll have the money to make it a damn sight more special than it looks now. It would become a tourist attraction.'

'What about Percival's claim then?' Georgia asked.

Tony shrugged. 'Percival claims the well was on common land

in the days when Cecilia and her granddad Richard used it. It was then acquired in the eighteenth century by the owners of what's now the Maid of Kent and its grounds. Montague FitzRichard therefore owned the well but he allowed it to become common land again.'

'And what do the Randalls claim?'

'They maintain that it was Cecilia's favourite spot and that the well was on land she owned after she inherited Cobshaw Court which her Randall husband inherited.'

'So both sides could claim it as a tourist attraction,' Georgia reasoned, 'but if Howard Green takes over he would have to negotiate with the Randalls.'

'Maybe.' He paused. 'Bernie's got plans for it too.'

'And you?'

He shrugged. 'Where Bernie goes, I go. Sorry, but I'll have to go to start lunches shortly—and then I'm going for a spin in the Porsche. That will have the hotel guests goggling if the hotel deal goes through.' He glanced up. 'Good. Jimmy's here. I'll get going.'

Georgia sipped her coffee as the lanky young man she'd seen there once or twice before arrived to take over the bar. The coffee tasted bitter, almost undrinkable, but that might be because she was beginning to feel emotionally trapped in the Maid of Kent. The oppressively low ceilings made her conscious of how much strife this bar had seen over the years. In 1959 it had been packed with villagers and cast crammed in here late at night, drinking, drinking... Centuries earlier it had been a home overrun by rioters, resulting in Cecilia's murder and since then so much must have happened, good and bad, that had never been recorded. The house seemed almost to be crying out to her, overburdened by its secrets.

Her head began to ache and so she abandoned the coffee. She needed fresh air and made for the nearest door—the one that took her along the Plantagenet-lined corridors. They at least had nothing to do with the horror of Brenda's death, she thought gratefully. Even so she was reminded that murder a-plenty had hit these people: whether victims or perpetrators, Richard II, Edward II, Richard III, even King John. These staring faces all had their secrets, as though defying her to guess them. Past Henry V looking so smug on his horse, past Henry VI, so pious as he stared back at her, and lastly past Richard II, scared out his wits. Concentrate, Georgia told herself. Where is the maid of Kent buried? No, think about what happened here in 1959. She tried, but the only answer was a suffocating silence.

Outside she felt she could breathe again and began to walk through the gardens towards the theatre as she regained her composure. No sign of Louis or anybody else today. Everyone must still be ensconced inside the village hall, including both her parents. For the umpteenth time she wondered why she still felt so torn over Elena? She loved her, no doubt about that, but at times she didn't *like* her one little bit. Which predominated? The first of course. When the chips were down, she was a child again, falling down the steps into their garden, rushing to her mother for comfort or bewildered by the world in general and looking for guidance. Did she get it? She tried hard to remember but nothing came back to her. Was she selfish in wanting to keep Marsh & Daughter to Peter and herself and not giving in to Elena's eager attempts to be involved? From a practical point of view there was no way they could share their work with her. Elena was a chatterbox and her idea of discretion was not theirs. Nevertheless, Georgia realised she had to face the possibility that it was selfishness, not reason, that made her insist on keeping her own ground intact.

There were times when the years of separation from her mother just fell away. When Elena had lived in France, visits to and from her were infrequent and she had seemed a different person to the one Georgia remembered so clearly from her childhood. Once back in England though that Elena had vanished and the years slipped away. Georgia could remember her parents together with Rick at their side. She was in no doubt that Elena's grief over his loss was just as constant as hers and Peter's, despite the time that had passed, and yet they each mourned separately, secreting the pain away in the midst of the thousand and one other thoughts and emotions that dominated everyday life.

When she had first come to these gardens with Rick, Georgia remembered, they had walked along this same path, but then there were roses and now those rose bushes had vanished, leaving only the spreading greenery of shrubs. 'Then there were roses,' she repeated to herself. But there were weeds in the past too, which she chose not to remember. If Rick were suddenly to appear with his infectious laugh, he would think she was crazy to reach back into the past at all. He'd be egging Peter and her on, cross that he wasn't here to enjoy his own memorial concert with the girl he had loved so much and the boy whose life he had saved.

She realised that her steps were taking her towards the higher ground behind the stage, not far from where Sir John Wilbourne's remains had been found. No crime scene now. The ground had been levelled, the roots of the fallen trees cut back and the trunk partly chopped.

Looking down, she was surprised to see someone sitting plumb in the middle of the stage on what looked like a portable seat of the kind lugged round stately homes by those with tired legs. It appeared to be an old man, although whoever it was had his back to her and she couldn't recognise him from this distance. He was sitting upright, straight-backed, completely alone. Why there? Why pick this spot? she wondered.

Curious, she hesitated on what to do. His bearing didn't suggest he would welcome company, so the polite thing to do would be to retreat and walk away. The almost polite thing to do would be to saunter down past him and wish him good day. The downright impolite thing to do would be to stop and question him. And the last of these, she decided, was what she would do. Probably he would merely turn out to be an elderly villager taking the sun.

'Lovely morning,' she greeted him cheerily as she walked down the path to the stage and drew near him—close but not too close.

He looked round at her with a look of mild surprise, which seemed somewhat false as he must have been aware of her approach.

'I agree,' he said.

The deep resonant voice struck an instant chord. She'd heard it before. And she'd seen that face, only not in Cobshaw. A very familiar face—or was she imagining that? No, she wasn't. One quick glance as she drew nearer left her in no doubt.

Colduggan she realised. Sir Edward Colduggan himself, *here* for some reason. Presumably he had come for the press briefing, so why was he sitting here?

'Sir Edward?' she asked. He looked more aged off the screen than on it and despite his frequent appearances on TV and in films, age might be taking its toll.

More mild surprise greeted her, again obviously assumed. He must be used to fans approaching him, so Georgia pushed ahead, rejoicing at this unexpected offering from fate. She had nothing to lose except if, having turned down a request for an interview once, he replied with a few choice words indicating that she could get lost.

'Georgia Marsh,' she introduced herself.

'Marsh? I recall that name,' he said quietly. 'Forgive my not rising. Age has its liabilities. Wisdom arrives but agility tiptoes out of the door. Marsh & Daughter, I believe. You, I take it, are the daughter?'

'I am.'

'And I refused to see you. Did you follow my suggestion that you speak to Rowena Watts?'

'You did refuse, Sir Edward, and we did speak to her.'

'Delightful and famous,' he murmured. 'Did you know that's the meaning of the name Rowena? How very appropriate. And now you will wish to interrogate me on that ever-fascinating subject, the past.' He sounded weary rather than annoyed, which was a good sign although his comment on Rowena mystified her somewhat.

'Of course I would like to,' she replied, 'but it's unfair of me to pounce on you and expect you to change your mind, much as I would welcome it. Did you come here for the press briefing?' That was a safe enough question, whether or not the briefing was going to be relevant to John Wilbourne. It seemed unlikely.

He smiled. 'I admit it sparked my curiosity. The name Randall rang a bell, and the events of my last visit are naturally much in my mind after the unexpected discovery of John Wilbourne's remains. However, curiosity is easily satisfied at my age. Not for me peering through train windows wondering why well-built ladies walk through fields in gloves.'

'But you miss so much if you don't,' Georgia instantly replied, picking up the reference to Frances Cornford's poem.

He looked at her steadily. 'No doubt the well-built lady the poet noticed wearing gloves was merely allergic to ripened wheat or nettles. My own story might be equally disappointing. Should my train now steam onwards and bid you farewell?'

'I hope not. This is your stage, Sir Edward, and I'm hoping you'll take the leading role and talk to me.' Could she keep this up? she thought desperately.

'Perhaps. All the world's a stage. But, more prosaically, I have to remain here until my chauffeur comes to fetch me.'

Safe ground. 'Ah, the gentleman reading the *Daily Mail in* the bar?'

'Your detective skills are finely honed, Miss Marsh. Or should it be Mrs Frost?'

So he had done some homework on Marsh & Daughter. That was encouraging. 'Today, it's merely Georgia,' she replied. 'Why did you really decide not to go to the press briefing?'

'I chose to recall that night instead.'

Georgia was very still. Don't push it, she warned herself. 'And have you?' She made that sound casual, but he was not deceived.

'Miss Marsh, pray take this blanket my chauffeur insisted I brought with me and take your place on this grassy stage of mine.'

'Thank you.' Don't say anything more, she thought as she obediently did as he asked. Let him take the lead.

'I am Patience sitting on a monument, as far as that night is concerned,' he informed her. 'It is a blank.'

Still playing games then. She was the one who needed Patience, she thought wryly. She scrabbled in her mind to place the quotation, aware that if she failed this test he would politely end the conversation—if that's what it was. She grabbed at the answer, hoping she was right, '*Twelfth Night*, my lord.'

'But not a blank for the same reason as Viola.'

Which, if she remembered correctly, was unspoken love. What if not that, though? Was he telling her the night Sir John Wilbourne died after the performance was a blank? If so, this was not promising. Start with a neutral question, she decided.

'Did the play go well that evening?' she asked.

She suspected Sir Edward was shrewd enough to see through this manoeuvre, because his lips twitched slightly before he replied.

'Excellently,' he replied. 'Georgia, it was almost as though he *knew* that was his last appearance on stage. He was superb. He spoke with a fire that warmed and inspired the entire cast. In my big speech as Mercutio I felt that warmth. Rowena felt it too. Naturally though, given her relationship with John she was in a special position to shine.'

'Relationship?' Georgia was aware she was being played like a fish on a hook but this was too good an opportunity to miss.

'John was, shall we say, inclined to favour his leading ladies. By the time I joined the company, his marriage was long over and young ladies such as Rowena were all too eager to accept such favours. Let me be clear, though, John was no predator. Whether his heart followed his physical appetite I cannot say. But he most certainly was not gay. And, as you have no doubt studied my life story you will be well aware that neither was I. That night the cast was inspired and I was highly satisfied with my own performance. I have to confess I never felt comfortable playing Romeo myself after John's disappearance. It seemed to me that I would be diminishing his performance in some way, unable to match the heights to which he took it. It was as though he were standing there like Banquo's ghost, admonishing me for playing his role so badly. My Orlando was much praised hereafter, but never my Romeo.'

'Perhaps he felt Romeo was his best role and that's why he chose it for his return to his home village. Was that the only occasion he had brought the company to Cobshaw?'

'To my knowledge, yes. He did of course have local connections, and I believe brought the company he was then working with here on one occasion at least before the war.'

'Did he play Romeo then?'

'I've no idea, and looking back I don't think that it was his favourite role anyway. He much preferred Benedict. Nevertheless, playing opposite Rowena that last evening he was brilliant.'

This was her opening. 'I understand you stayed here overnight,' Georgia said.

'I did. I am not wholly blank on that matter. I returned to London early the next day, hence the suspicion that floated around London that I had something to do with John's disappearance. Now it seems probable that John never left Cobshaw. Murdered. Perhaps an accidental killing.' He paused, then added, 'He was at odds with his family, I recall. I understand that his remains were found quite close to this stage which is surprising if his death were the result of a dispute with his killer, relative or not. Why would he have returned to the stage or this area of the grounds at all—especially,' he paused, 'after he and I had had that ridiculous duel here?'

'After which duel we I understand that you both returned to the pub.'

'Ah. I am relieved to hear that I am thereby removed from your list of suspects, Miss Marsh.'

Not quite, she thought to herself. 'We never have one,' she replied lightly. 'We wait on events.' It was true enough and there was no need to explain that Suspects Anonymous was their faithful—if sometimes unreliable—aid in this respect.

'Another blank then. My own blank concerning that evening is chiefly about what happened after John and I returned to the pub bar after that duel. There was, I'm told, much drinking, so it's hardly surprising that my mind is a blank. When I awoke the next morning, it remained blank, although I recall the events of the morning still. The publican whose name was Montague FitzRichard, I'm told—my dear, what a name—insisted on showing me around the inn. He told me that all my comrades had already left for London and I assumed that John was with them. I have met his son Percival today, or rather re-met as I recall him from that earlier occasion. He was a lad a few years younger than me then, but the father was a giant of a man, in nature if not in stature. The king of the village, or perhaps more accurately the Napoleon of the village. The villagers seemed to be split between those who loved him and those who hated him.'

'Weren't you surprised when you returned to London and didn't see Sir John there? I believe you had a meeting arranged with him?'

'Not at first. The publican thought all our party had left, but I discovered several members of the cast were still around and so I travelled back with them. I arrived for our scheduled meeting that evening—it was a Sunday of course—to find no John, only Rowena who had, she informed me, seen John driving off in a taxi. John was inclined to be forgetful of such minor matters as meetings and so she returned to her home. As I then did myself. I had no concern at that stage. It was not an urgent meeting and we were due to meet at the theatre on the Tuesday—we were between productions but rehearsals were due to begin. When he did not appear on the Tuesday, we rang friends and hospitals in vain and finally informed the police of John's disappearance. But it seems that Rowena was wrong about having seen John in that taxi and I had assumed she was right. And now it seems that anyone present that fateful Saturday evening might have been guilty of his murder. Including of course myself.'

He had been leaning forward in his earnestness to convey his message but now he sank back in the chair looking, Georgia thought, pleased with himself. He had hurled the ball back into her court with a vengeance and he was fully aware of it. He had the air of one who had delivered Hamlet's 'To Be or Not to Be' soliloquy to great applause.

She grasped the nettle. 'In theory, you're right, Sir Edward, but the police—'

'Quite,' he interrupted, not a whit disturbed. 'I have hitherto refused to see either your local police or Scotland Yard. I shall now be obliged to do so and confess that I have no memory of that evening after that foolish duel.'

'But you have talked to me.'

'In person you are not as formidable as your voice on our telephone call suggested.'

Formidable? Take care, she warned herself. Keep it light. 'Does talking about it blur memories of those days?'

'Ingenious, Georgia, and perhaps true, because that might explain the obstinate blank in my mind, and yet that does not render talking invalid. Now I suppose I must now sit upon the ground and tell sad stories of the death of kings, like poor King Richard, only mine are to the police.'

Back to Shakespeare again, she thought. Still, this sounded more hopeful. 'Do you remember anything in particular about that duel with John Wilbourne?'

'Nothing of import. I played Mercutio and thus I only recall my duel with Tybalt. Did I challenge John or he me?'

'I don't know. All we've been told,' Georgia explained, 'is that there was a stage sword found near his remains, though of course that can't have been the murder weapon.'

'Only one sword? Why? And it is odd that it was found with his remains. I do recall, however, that our duel took place on this stage. Incidentally, did your informant know who won our duel?'

'It seems to have been interrupted and you both went back to the pub.' Weak, Georgia, she told herself. Edward Colduggan was winning this present duel and he knew it.

'I do so hope I was winning, but I trust that the duel wasn't responsible for the suspicion cast in my direction by the theatre world after John's disappearance. Quite uncalled for, although I fear John and I were not always on the best of terms. John had a touch of Henry Irving about him; there was little move towards an egalitarian company when it came to casting or press interviews.'

Still winning. She decided not to tackle the issue of what he recalled of that evening in the Maid of Kent. It would have to remain a blank, unless he chose to raise it again… Move on to more general ground.

'What puzzles me,' she plunged in, 'is why Sir John wanted to come all this way for just one performance, even though he was Cobshaw born and bred. An expensive venture for the company, wasn't it?'

'I was a mere up and coming young actor. One did not enquire too far into the actions of management. And John of course was management as well as the leading player.'

'I was told, though, that you took over the company when Sir John died.'

'Ah, dear Rowena, our diligent memoirist. She probably conveyed that information to you. Not that there's anything secret about it. I ran the company for a short while, during which my own career flourished having emerged from John's shadow.' He paused. 'You look surprised, Georgia. I should explain that I both admired and loved John Wilbourne. We all loved him. That aside, there was a professional clash between John and myself at the time of his disappearance. Romeo, for instance. How ridiculous for John, then well over forty years of age, to play a teenage boy—especially since Rowena, our passionate Juliet, was a mere youngster of twenty. Had he played Mercutio the age difference would not have been noticed, but by playing Romeo it stood out.'

'His family must have been in the audience,' Georgia pointed out, 'so he would naturally want to play the lead.'

'Perhaps, although he also played the part elsewhere that season. Nevertheless, he did not have an easy childhood, I fear. I recall his parents had separated and John all too often had to stay with Gerald's father—Jacob, I believe. He was, I understand, not an easy man to get on with and John seemed anxious to show him what a success he had made of his life. He was the boy made good. Even so, playing Romeo at forty-four was not a clever way to prove that.'

He paused. 'Georgia, I believe I'm beginning to remember more about that duel. My duel with Tybalt on stage stands out clearly but that later one is arising again in my memory. I challenged John to a duel after he made some trifling joke that I was the ideal Mercutio but could never play Romeo. That, after he had upstaged me that evening, either by accident or deliberately. I wasn't serious about the duel, but he insisted it should take place on the stage where according to him I had falsely accused him of the crime of upstaging. When we reached the stage, I recall that he seized a couple of swords that the departed stagehands must have overlooked and we proceeded to brandish our weapons to dramatic effect. It was attracting attention, though, and I do remember the publican intervening to break it up. I remember also that John cast his sword down in disgust but I still clutched mine as we returned to the pub, escorted it seemed by most of the village. The rest of the evening is still a blank, I regret to say. I woke up in a bed I couldn't recall getting into. I was still fully dressed.'

He broke off. 'I believe someone wishes to speak to you, Georgia.'

'Hi, Georgia!'

She whirled round to see Jill hurrying towards them.

'I'd gotten tired of that briefing so I said I'd see them back at the Maid of Kent. May I join you?' She glanced at Edward Colduggan and her face changed.

'Your Hamlet,' she began without ado. No screaming with delight from Jill. She just accepted his presence as normal, sat down beside Georgia and got down to brass tacks.

'Sir Edward, I watched your Hamlet on video, and I'm puzzled by your interpretation. Tell me, do you still maintain that "To Be or Not To Be" is not about suicide?'

'I do, Mrs er....'

'Frost,' Jill supplied. 'Georgia's my step mother-in-law.'

He smiled. 'Not, I trust, of the Snow White ilk?'

Georgia laughed. 'I seldom hand out poisoned apples.'

But Sir Edward's attention was not on her. He was intent on Jill. 'Hamlet is a young man furious with himself because he wants to be a man of action and he's not done anything towards achieving that. He wishes to take up arms against a sea of troubles, not kill himself.' Having thrown down the gauntlet, Sir Edward sat back and awaited her comments.

Jill leapt on this. 'Not a bit of it,' she said fervently. 'He just wants out but is fearful of the dreams. He doesn't care a hoot about anything else.'

Georgia quietly left them too it, still arguing. Jill was settling down nicely for the battle.

Chapter Nine

Never be surprised at how quickly a situation can change. The golden rule in any investigation. Against the odds, Georgia felt she could now deal with Sir Edward Colduggan. It was the family lunch ahead that was the challenge. She was bursting to tell Peter about her encounter with Edward Colduggan, but with Elena there her lips must be sealed, even though Jill had been fully occupied with him when she left.

When she reached the bar a reprieve awaited her. Peter arrived alone, over half an hour late, with no sign of Elena. Tony, Peter told her, had steered him through the corridors, treating him en route to a chat about Porsche 356SCs plus the soaring costs of repairs to the pub and then had insisted on a detour to admire it in its converted stable home. There Tony had treated him to a debate on whether or not the hotel deal would go through quickly enough for him to go ahead with a pricey down-to-bare-metal restoration of the Porsche. It was vital, he maintained, that this took place before the end of the rally season.

'I don't know what kind of financial arrangements they have with Percival at present,' Peter concluded, 'but I presume every penny they have goes into keeping the Maid of Kent from falling down.'

'That must mean an awful lot of pennies,' Georgia commented.

'Now tell me what's happened to Elena. I know where Jill is—or was.'

'Your mother abandoned my humble wagon for a chauffeured car to Canterbury which also contained, to my understandable surprise, Sir Edward Colduggan and Jill. I gather you weren't included in this remarkable expedition to a Michelin-starred restaurant. Did you know about this?' Peter enquired.

The stranger with the *Daily Mail* had disappeared from the bar and so her guess that he was Sir Edward's chauffeur had been right. Her guilty relief at hearing Peter's news, however, was tempered with slight annoyance at their own exclusion from this expedition.

'Yes and no.'

'No, will do. You'd have to explain a yes, but Colduggan can wait,' Peter told her. 'I've other news. The Maid of Kent is soon to be blessed by a visit from none other than Howard Green. He's lunching with Percival, the latter in a foul temper.'

'The great Howard himself?' This was certainly interesting news—though not to be compared with her own which she was bursting to tell Peter, but that would have to wait a little while.

'The very same. Son of the MD of Paul Green Country Hotels, whom I left chatting to Will Whittan and DI Cotton in the village hall.'

'Are they all lunching here?

'If so, we're not invited. But we are meeting Howard at 2.30 pm. Bernie and Tony will be there too, as well as Percival. Apparently all of them would like us to be present. I suspect the reason for this unexpected bonhomie is that they want witnesses if the hotel deal is on the table. We are classed as being independent.'

'But why are you so eager we should go?' Georgia asked. 'Mere curiosity?'

Peter looked perplexed. 'I'm not sure. But this is the village that probably had the same problems back in John Wilbourne's day. It does mean we're doomed—guess what?—to sausage and chips for lunch though.'

'Delightful.'

That was the word Sir Edward Colduggan had used about Rowena, Georgia reflected, as Peter studied the menu. Now was the time to tell him all about that, and yet her initial eagerness had subsided. Peter might not be best pleased at hearing this second-hand. She braced herself. 'Now I can tell you *my* news.'

This took some time to relate and it was nearly 2.30 before they had both finished lunch and she had done justice to the whole story of her meeting with Sir Edward. There had been remarkably few 'buts' from Peter as she did so, which was gracious of him. He preferred listening to potential evidence first-hand. Lunch had been a slow process, with only Jimmy left in charge. Very tough on the young barman, Georgia thought, considering the numbers of people streaming back from the village hall.

The meeting room was on the first floor, to which there was a lift—amazingly for the Maid of Kent. In days of yore this room must have been a splendid bedchamber, Georgia guessed. The table had seen better days but at least the room wasn't plastered with Plantagenets. The wood panelling could be seen to good effect and it was superb. There was, inevitably, an old painting of a saintly looking young woman who might be Cecilia, probably painted a century or two after her death, and another of a gallant young man who might be Richard of Eastwell, also definitely not painted by a contemporary of his.

There was no sign of either Will Whittan or Jack Cotton, which confirmed this meeting must clearly be solely about the hotel deal. Even so, Georgia hoped, something might emerge that might link to Brenda's death or even John Wilbourne's. Looking round the table, she could see that Bernie was set for battle with an apprehensive Tony at her side. Thankfully she and Peter were mere onlookers. Percival looked ready for battle, which did not bode well for a peaceful discussion ahead. The star of the show, Howard Green, looked in his late forties and seemed a typical suave businessman pretending to be a countryman at heart, wearing a smart sports jacket with no tie. His whole bearing gave the impression of the outsider marching in with a solution to all their problems. If that was the image he was trying to put over, he was succeeding, Georgia decided. He was summing them up with a practised eye.

'My agents,' Percival announced loftily, introducing Peter and Georgia.

Peter returned a bland smile. *Agents*? What, Georgia wondered uneasily, was expected of them in this role? So much for their being independent witnesses.

'Excellent,' Howard Green smiled, clearly not believing Percival. Georgia awarded him full marks for that. He had done his homework before he arrived. 'Then I trust you have decided to accept my offer,' Howard continued briskly.

'Not yet,' Percival snarled. 'Bernie here has made me an offer. She and Tony will be paying me something so they can take over the place now without waiting for me to kick the bucket.'

Howard Green must have been forewarned, Georgia thought, for he didn't blink at this. On the contrary he merely looked mildly surprised. Suspicious, surely? 'Weigh that against a million pounds in your bank account as soon as you sign with us.'

'But we will preserve the heritage of the property,' Bernie retorted.

'As we will when we convert it into the Cobshaw Country Hotel,' Howard Green replied. He looked so relaxed he clearly believed that his was a done deal, Georgia thought. Even more suspicious. 'I'm told,' he added, turning to Peter and Georgia, 'that you saw Mrs Randall not long before her tragic death. As I'm sure you know, she was devoted to the history of Cobshaw. She differed from you, Mr FitzRichard, in that she believed in the inn's Tudor heritage, not Plantagenet, and she backed my offer wholeheartedly. Having met her, I am sure she had given due recognition to all sides of the argument. That is the great strength of my offer. Guests will be presented with all the evidence about Cecilia, both Plantagenet and Tudor. The well of course, which we are negotiating with Mr Randall to purchase, is a good example of how both historical theories can be accommodated, tragic though it is that Mrs Randall lost her life there.'

So that was his plan. Pleasing everyone. Was Percival going to fall for this? Georgia held her breath. She looked round the table. Percival looked flabbergasted, Bernie furious, and Tony obviously at pains to stay calm.

'But the well is a problem,' Tony pointed out to Georgia's relief. 'The parish council is convinced that the village owns it and the Randall estate that it does.'

Howard had an answer for that—of a sort. 'Our solicitors are handling that matter. There is strong evidence that it is Randall property, but we will of course bear in mind that Cecilia is an icon for both the Tudors and the Plantagenets,' he said smoothly. 'The hotel will have rooms named for both dynasties. I understand there is a Richard's Room here,' he added, almost too casually. 'We will create a Cecilia's Room, an Owen Tudor Room, a Richard III room and so on—perfect. The two sides united.' He paused, then said to Bernie, 'Your offer, Mrs Beane, would incur you and your husband into enormous expense in restoring this place. I do beg of you to consider that.'

Georgia held her breath, waiting for Percival to erupt, but he seemed to be biding his time.

'What do you say to that, Bernie?' Tony asked anxiously. His role was clearly to smooth troubled waters—whichever way the negotiations went.

'I say no,' Bernie replied sharply. 'We are Plantagenets, the Maid of Kent can only be sold to a Plantagenet and Paul Green Country Hotels is hardly Plantagenet by birth, is it? And as for the well, we don't accept the argument that there's any doubt about Cecilia's origins. She grew up in Cobshaw Cottage, then married and lived here. She was a *Plantagenet* and the well is on common ground. And regarding restoration, Dave Cook wants to turn this into a community centre and Tony and I will be working with him. We'll be applying for a lottery grant first of all.'

'And what if you don't get one?' Howard pre-empted Percival's growing agitation. 'You'd have lost over a million pounds, Mr FitzRichard, and still have an unrestored building on your hands.'

That did it. Percival exploded. 'Look here,' he burst out, 'I can't sell to you, Green, and that's final. The deeds say I can only sell the property to someone with Plantagenet blood.'

'The legality of that being binding beyond the first conveyance of title is doubtful,' Howard replied calmly.

'Whether it is or not, that's what my ancestors wanted and that's what they'll get,' Percival snarled. 'Plantagenet blood it's got to be.'

Howard sighed. 'I had been hoping not to bring personal details into this business transaction, but I see I have no option. My dear sir, I *do* have Plantagenet blood in my veins.'

Nothing like a bombshell for changing the situation. Georgia was flabbergasted, and even Peter looked taken aback. This claim was clearly news to everyone here—so perhaps it was just a gambit in Howard Green's skilful manoeuvring and had no foundation in fact.

Percival recovered first. 'That's what all the Tudors say when they're in a tight corner,' he retorted.

'No, Mr FitzRichard. I really do have Plantagenet blood. You and I are related. My grandmother was your sister Serena.'

'And that is that,' Peter observed, 'as John said about his Wellington boots.'

'The poem to which that belongs was called "Happiness",' Georgia replied, still bemused by the turn the meeting had taken. 'And I don't see much of that around, except for Howard Green.' Percival had been white with shock, demanding details from Howard Green. Tony had kept his composure, but Bernie was trembling as Howard assured them that he would be providing them with evidence of his claim.

'But,' Georgia continued as they reached the car park, 'Howard Green's story can't be true because I can't believe Brenda would have been backing him if she'd known he was a Plantagenet.'

'Perhaps,' Peter pointed out, 'she did find out. Remember how agitated she appeared? This could have been the reason.'

'You mean—' Georgia stared at him. 'A motive for her murder? Surely not. Theoretically perhaps—but we're only talking about the sale of one old pub.'

Peter shrugged. 'A pub with a past—don't rule it out, Georgia. If I were Bernie, though, I'd be on my computer right now delving into family history. Fortunately, Tony looked as if it was all in a day's work, which is good. He's the practical one.'

'Except where old Porsches are concerned,' Georgia pointed out. 'I grant you though that if Brenda discovered the truth about Howard's ancestry, she died conveniently quickly for the hotel deal to win the battle.'

'All's fair in love and business,' Peter said wryly.

'Not in Cobshaw.'

'Green must have known right from the beginning what a card he held in his hands. There's little doubt the sale to Paul Green Country Hotels will go through now. Interesting that he didn't declare his ancestry to Percival earlier,' Peter ruminated. 'Probably to keep Brenda on his side.'

'And to avoid its leaking out to the Randalls,' Georgia suggested. 'He still needs their support, though, because the hotel plan is opposed by the Dave Cook brigade and the contract isn't yet signed. Howard's in a good position but Percival can still pull out so he needs to tread a fine line between Tudors and Plantagenets. He needs to keep the Tudors happy. If the Randalls withdraw their support the balloon could still go up, as it certainly would have done if Brenda had still been alive. Howard Green has the money, but the Randalls have influence and for luxury hotels that counts in all sorts of ways. Publicity for one thing.'

'True,' Peter agreed, 'For all Howard Green talks about having both Plantagenet and Tudor room names, it wouldn't work on bigger issues. Tudors would win hands down for attracting visitors and tourists. Cecilia was related to Henry VIII, had a claim on the throne, owned Cobshaw Court and was then murdered in case she became another Lady Jane Grey. That would tick more tourist boxes than Cecilia, granddaughter of an illegitimate son of Richard III, who married an unknown Randall and was murdered for her remote relationship to a long dead Plantagenet monarch.'

'History can be very awkward,' Georgia agreed, straightfaced. 'But weighing it all up, I'm not totally convinced Howard Green would have had reason to *murder* Brenda because she had discovered his Plantagenet blood. He looks tough enough just to ride roughshod over her wishes and probably Gerald Randall's too.'

Peter groaned. 'Do remember that we're only here to investigate the death of John Wilbourne.'

'The two deaths could be linked,' she maintained obstinately, although she had no idea how.

'True, but there's not the slightest evidence they are.' Peter said emphatically. 'As you said earlier, Cobshaw is fundamentally the same village it was in 1959.' Game, set and match—she hoped.

News travels fast. Peter had arranged to meet Dave Cook the next morning, by which time it was clear that the information that Howard Green was Percival FitzRichard's sister's grandchild had not only reached Dave, but the whole village. Dave lived with his wife in a neat modern house on a small estate behind Cobshaw High Street—the *only* modern estate in the village as far as Georgia could see. Cobshaw otherwise still looked the same as it must have done in Cecilia's time, a picturesque village of timber-framed medieval houses and quaint alleyways. For some lucky reason, it had so far at least escaped the eye of property developers and even this small development of a dozen or so houses was neatly landscaped and masked by trees. On its doorstep, preceding the estate by a hundred years or so, was the village hall, a nineteenth century addition from the looks of it. This fortunately boasted a small car park.

'Bad news,' Dave said cheerfully, having conducted them into his garden. 'Still, I reckon Bernie and us Planters are still in with a chance now. Even if this chap does have Plantagenet blood in his veins, Percival could still decide to sell it to Bernie. We peasants have survived over the centuries and we're going to this time.'

Optimistic, Georgia thought, given that grants take time to turn into available capital. 'Did you know Percival's sister?' she asked.

Dave laughed. 'Before my time. She was long gone, and neither Percival nor his dad ever talked about her. I knew them all right but not her.'

'So this Serena wasn't around in 1959?'

'Nor was I much—born in '62. My granddad would have done though he died young.'

'Percival mentioned her being at a village fête,' Peter said.

'No fêtes in my time. No talk of them either. My dad was at that play in '59 though. He always had a bee in his bonnet about the Randalls of course.'

'Over anything in particular?'

'Don't recall,' Dave said. 'He used to ramble on—he's passed on now. But the whole of Cobshaw was there, including I expect all those who found something to complain about afterwards.'

'So far no one seems to remember anything very helpful,' Peter observed.

'That's Cobshaw for you. Keeps itself to itself, including Planters and Tudors.'

'We still don't know how that feud come about in the first place,' Georgia pointed out. 'Bernie thought it went back to Cecilia's time, but that doesn't explain what the core problem is between them more recently. Do you know?'

'No idea,' Dave told them cheerfully. 'The Randalls were always the Tudor bogey men to me as a kid, and Dad got the same story from his parents. That was only because his great-uncle Brian went missing in the war. He was a navy regular, home on leave when the war broke out, but he never turned up at his ship. My gran didn't find that out till later so she passed the story on to Dad that the Tudor bogey man had got him. There were always bogey men around then to frighten kids into behaving properly or into going to sleep. Years back it was Napoleon. For Planters it was the Tudors and still is,' he grinned.

'You feel the Tudors are bogeys today??'

'Nope. I'm not made that way. That's why I'm chair of the parish council. I'm a Planter by birth, but I can see things clear. On the whole, I get on fine with Mick Buckley. He gets on with us Planters if he wants to but puts on a show of being Tudor because he works for the Randalls. Have a word with him though. See what he thinks of the news about our Howard and the Plantagenets.' Dave chuckled. 'And if he tells you that the pond and well belong to the Tudor bogey men, remind him the parish council paid for building that pond. I don't know why we bothered. We still cling to it as if it's Cobshaw's greatest treasure, but half the village won't go near it. Almost as if they're frightened of it. Last year some of the kids tried a Halloween stunt with ghosts and ghouls marching up there, but once they got wind of it the oldies soon put paid to that.'

Frightened? Not Brenda. For her, Georgia thought, it had been a place that Cecilia had loved and that meant Brenda valued it highly. No ghouls for her—until she had met one.

Strike while the iron is hot, Peter decided. The news about Howard Green being a Plantagenet's grandson might or might not have any relevance to their case, but the Planters versus Tudors feud was clearly raging as strongly in 1959 as now. The Buckleys, like the Cooks, had been living in Cobshaw for a long time, and the more Peter and she knew about these long-established families the better, Georgia agreed.

Saturday morning or not, they were redirected to Mick Buckley's office by his wife, who, judging by the packing cases visible inside their hallway was already engaged in house moving preparations. Georgia drove along the road skirting the Hall to what had obviously once been the stables and workshop area for the Hall. Mick's office had been converted from one of the stables, and inside was a mix of the old and the new. Mick was seated behind a solid-looking desk.

'Doing the rounds, are you?' he asked, eyeing them without enthusiasm. 'Heard you were down at Dave's earlier. Is it John Wilbourne or Brenda you're here about? Like to help if I can.'

The smirk on his face told a different story. Like to help? Georgia thought. He wouldn't help a zebra over a crossing. Looking jovial was merely his stock in trade.

'Both,' Peter said firmly. 'You can't have known John Wilbourne, but you must have known Brenda Randall well.'

Mick eyed him narrowly, obviously trying to sum up whether this idle comment was intended as a slur. If so, he dismissed it. 'Course I did. Moving into her cottage, aren't I? Why not? We'll wait till after the funeral though. The rent's good. Shame about Brenda though, poor old soul.' He looked genuinely troubled, Georgia was surprised to see. 'I saw you both heading for the old pond with her. Get the lecture about it?'

'We did. It's community-owned, we're told,' she replied, forcing herself not to think of the next time she had seen that pond.

'So the Planters say. It's Randall property by rights, but even that's complicated. You want my old grandfather Sam for that, but he's long gone. If you look at the old tithe maps, you'll see it's all part and parcel of Long Acre Field.'

'Seriously?' Surely Mick wasn't going to claim that he owned the well?

'You could say that. The Buckley family moved down from Scotland in the late nineteenth century in search of a better living. Lots of farmers settled in Kent then. We bought a few fields and did okay until the war came along and the depression. So we mostly sold out to the Randalls and my family managed the land for them. That's why we're Tudor supporters. That's life. We hung on to one field for a while though and a strip of it gives access to the well and pond so the village could have access to them, either to use the well or just gawp at it. When the well was converted into a pond, some of the pond covered the Buckley strip of land, and by then we'd sold the rest of the field to Jacob Randall. But we didn't sell that strip and that's why the Planters still think that pond is common land.' He stopped for a moment, and then added almost reluctantly, 'I don't know what the fuss is about. It's a creepy old place, if you ask me.'

Georgia agreed. 'We heard the parish council did pay for the wall round the pond and so presumably for the pond itself.'

He grinned. 'Been talking to Dave, haven't you? Parish council is all Planters, see? Sometimes they let a Randall on but not often. Just let the well situation be, we've always thought, but now Howard Green's come along things might turn nasty as to who owns it. Still, it's this Wilbourne chap you're interested in. You've come to the wrong generation for that. You want my dad's. But he never remembered much about that play, not that he told me anyway. He did talk about having had a skinful after watching that duel. Our Percival was a gallant young man in those days, and he told me once he'd been having a ding-dong with Gerald Randall in the pub. My granddad Sam never talked about it, either, and he's long gone.' Mick leaned back in his chair looking as though he'd scored a point.

'Quite a few in Cobshaw never talk about it,' Peter commented. 'Unusual, isn't it? Would your father remember Serena FitzRichard, Percival's sister, for example?'

'Nah. My granddad would, but he's dead and my dad died way back. The name don't mean anything to me. She wasn't around in my time.'

Yet another blank. 'How about village fêtes?' Georgia asked. 'Percival mentioned her being at one.'

'Must be going back a bit then. Ask old Geoff Sanders about that. If he likes the look of you, he'll tell you a story all right, half of it made up.' He sniggered, as though he couldn't care less. But she noticed there was a look of relief on his face as they left.

At least this time Geoff Sanders didn't have his arms crossed against his chest repelling all advances—perhaps because he was sitting in his own home. His small cottage in Love Lane, leading off the High Street, looked as though it had once been part of a large medieval Wealden house. As with the Maid of Kent, some of its original beams and plasterwork had been replaced over time. A few of the cottages were set back from the road, but Georgia could see Geoff sitting on a bench outside his front door half hidden by the display in front of him. Small or not, it adhered to the traditional cottage garden with a mixture of flowers, herbs and even vegetables. It was a mass of June colour.

'You again?' Geoff grunted as he hobbled in front of them, leading the way round the cottage to his larger garden at the rear. This too was full of colour. No sign of Louis today. 'Mick Buckley send you, did he? Full of himself as usual? He's going to grab Mrs Randall's cottage and her not yet in her grave. What are you always wanting to talk to me for, anyway? The war? Want to know whether I knew Vera Lynn?'

'Yes,' Peter said simply. 'Also, can you tell us anything more about that performance of *Romeo and Juliet* with John Wilbourne?'

'When would that have been?'

He was playing for time just to annoy them. ''Fifty-nine. John Wilbourne's theatre company,' Peter replied briskly.

'Ah,' he said reflectively. 'That the time I met that lady?'

No playing his game. They waited. Sure enough, it worked. 'Fell for that Juliet,' he announced. 'I was a youngster then.'

Silence again. This wasn't looking hopeful. 'You're a Shakespeare admirer?' Georgia persevered.

'Who's he when he's at home? All I admired was her big boobs hanging out of her dress when she leaned over the balcony. Took a real fancy to her, I did.'

Well, at least he was talking, she thought hopefully. Peter then took over. 'You told us you'd seen Sir John and Edward Colduggan walking back to the pub after that duel, and you went too.'

'You bet I did,' Geoff said with relish. 'Might have made a grab for that Juliet. But she was fawning over John Wilbourne and then the other woman comes in and picks a fight with her.'

'Two women?' Peter picked up sharply.

Geoff was clearly calculating what to reply to this—if at all. To Georgia's relief he continued. 'Couldn't stop them once they got going. Mr FitzRichard, old Monty to us, threw 'em out of the pub for all it was Brenda Parsons, as she was then, the doctor's daughter. Having a row with that Juliet, claws out they were. Us men had a bet on who'd win, but Brenda Parsons was a tough one and she wasn't going to let no London fancy lady have the man she was after. Well, that Juliet was a tough one too, so as soon as they were thrown out they were on the grass tearing each other's hair out, till old Monty came roaring out and heaved them apart. He couldn't bar Juliet coming back into the pub because she was staying there, but Brenda Parsons got an earful and packed off home for all she was the doctor's daughter.'

So much for Brenda having told them she went straight home after the performance, Georgia thought. Geoff's story had the ring of truth about it. It seemed passions were running high not only amongst the cast but amongst the audience too. Rowena hadn't mentioned this fight either, and she surely couldn't have forgotten such a dramatic encounter. Did Rowena and Brenda feel embarrassed afterwards? Did guilt linger on one side or the other? And did this have any relevance to John Wilbourne's death?

'Was John Wilbourne watching?' Peter asked.

Geoff shrugged. 'Couldn't be sure, mate. I saw him having words with Sam Buckley while the cat fight was going on and after it finished we Planters went off and left the posh actors to get drunk inside. Colduggan was already plastered by then.'

'What did you all think when you heard John Wilbourne was missing?'

'Nothing, mate. He'd gone, that's all. The papers said he was back home in London safe and sound the next day. They was wrong, eh?'

'You must have talked about that amongst yourselves,' Georgia said.

'Folks don't talk much round here, missus. Best way, ain't it? My dad told me that when he was a youngster it were like that too. Same with my grandad. You worked for the Planters or the Randalls so when this matter over John Wilbourne having gone missing came up, we'd nothing to say, being Planters. Like over the Buckleys and Cooks. Them Buckleys always were Tudors. Never got on with the Cooks. That Sam Buckley he were a real devil. I remember him. A Tudor and cosying up to the Randalls, but as thick as thieves with Montague at the old Maid too. Now there's Mick working for the Tudors and here we are split down the middle like we always was. Like over that pond. Never knew what it was all about, but my dad said least said soonest mended. So we button up when folk like you come along. Like you.'

'So why talk now?' Peter asked reasonably.

Geoff glared at him. 'Because Dave said to.'

Why was that? Georgia instantly wondered. Because if they gave the appearance of co-operation, she and Peter would be satisfied and go away? No chance, if so.

'What about earlier times?' Peter asked. 'The fête that Percival told us about. His sister Serena was there. Did the Planters and Tudors clash at that?'

Geoff's eyes shifted away from them. 'Like I said. Nothing to tell you. I was only a nipper.'

'So you told us when we met you earlier in the Maid of Kent,' Peter said amiably, 'but nippers have parents and pick up a lot from them.'

This riled him. 'I was a kid of six or so at that fête,' he growled.

'And Serena was there,' Peter repeated. 'Was she married?'

'No idea, mate.'

'What happened to her?' Peter pressed on.

'Probably went off in the war—lots of girls did. GI brides we called them. Off to America with menfolk they hardly knew.'

'Wouldn't she keep in touch if so?'

'Look, mister,' Geoff fired up. 'Leave her out of this. Them Buckleys are troublemakers. Always have been. All's fair in love and war, as my dad used to say. Anyway, Percival don't like talking of her.'

'But it was he who told us about her,' Georgia replied calmly. 'He was clearly very fond of her. He said she was dancing at the fête he mentioned, and that must have been before she left for the war and later died. So—'

But she'd driven him too far.

'Thirty-nine,' he howled. 'Week or two before war broke out. Look, missus, I don't know nothing. No one in Cobshaw knows about it. We don't look back, not in Cobshaw.'

That wasn't the impression Georgia had.

'So there we are,' Georgia related what they'd learned to Luke on her return. Sitting in a garden at dusk with the birds chirping and flowers blooming it was easier to see things in perspective. 'Goodness knows why he became so worked up. Maybe it was just because he doesn't like talking about his sister, but it sounded as though there was more to it than that. That there is something the whole village knows about but we don't. We're not getting the full story about anything, it seems to me, including this Serena.'

'At least she couldn't have been murdered here. She left home and died in the war, so Percival told you, Luke observed. 'And your case—dare I say, *our* case, considering I'm to be the publisher—involves 1959 so why dream up dramatic scenarios for twenty years or more before that? There's no link so far back, unless I'm missing something.'

Trust Luke to pick on the salient point. She and Peter had now talked to various prominent people in the village all of whom came from Cobshaw families of long standing. All of them had seemed willing to talk to some extent and yet she still felt they were fighting their way through dense undergrowth with no clear path. They had the ingredients of their 1959 case but nothing to mix them with.'

Luke laughed when she told him this. 'How about chopping your way through that undergrowth? And tell me the ingredients.'

She took this up immediately. 'Four lines of enquiry. Suspects, if you like. One: we have a rising young actor driven to despair because he wasn't getting the good roles. Two: We possibly have two women scorned: Brenda and Rowena Watts. Evidence flimsy but there. Three: Randall family dispute resulting in John Wilbourne leaving home. Four: John Wilbourne was seen talking to Sam Buckley after the duel with Edward Colduggan.'

Luke considered this. 'Which of the overall ingredients is the most likely to fit the scenario?'

'The Buckleys?'

'Possibly, but they could be a dead end. There's a bigger one.'

'Which is?' she asked cautiously.

'As I understand your case at present, the Plantagenets have had their say but so far only Brenda Randall has given the Tudors' version with a brief input from Sophy and perhaps Mick Buckley. What about the Tudor family, especially its big cheese?'

Georgia gazed at him. 'Luke,' she said, 'did I ever tell you you're the publisher of my dreams?'

'In that case, I'll reduce the royalties,' he answered amiably.

Chapter Ten

The path to the Tudors lay not through Gerald but Sophy. Peter was sure of that and Georgia agreed. 'Percival is quite enough to deal with,' Peter said. 'We don't want to battle with another eccentric.' True, they had only caught glimpses so far of Gerald Randall, but their first impressions had not boded well.

Sophy on the other hand was very willing to talk about Randall family history if it helped the enquiry into Brenda's death. She had been sufficiently convinced of that to suggest they join her on the Monday morning at Cobshaw Cottage where she was engaged in preliminary house-clearing. In the hall was a pile of box files.

'No trusting in computers for Brenda,' Sophy told her ruefully. 'Jenny, Mick's wife, is only too eager to help,' she continued. 'Isn't that sweet of her? She's even graciously offered to keep the antique furniture, Dresden china and first editions if it saves me bother.'

Georgia pulled a face. 'I hope you turned the offer down?'

'I did, to her disappointment.'

The corridors here were too narrow for Peter's scooter, so Georgia was taking the opportunity to speak to Sophy alone, while Peter was making his own way round to the conservatory—with the help of Brenda's dog who was clearly delighted to be back in home territory.

The interior of Cobshaw Cottage did not disappoint, and Georgia was glad of the opportunity to see it, as she and Peter had remained in the conservatory on their visit to Brenda. Though well maintained, there had been little modernisation inside Cobshaw Cottage. Narrow staircases creaked, overhead beams greeted her stolidly at every turn, and the rooms she glimpsed as they passed by had retained their medieval size with, as far as she could see, one or two doorways which if not original were at least in keeping with the age of the property. Even the conservatory achieved that, resembling a tiny version of an 18th century orangery. As they reached it, Georgia could see Peter waiting patiently together with the dog.

'Hope you don't mind Owen,' Sophy said, patting the dog. 'Named after Owen Tudor himself, the granddad of the royal Tudor gang.'

'And worthy of his heritage,' Peter said gravely.

'You wanted to know about the Randalls,' Sophy continued. 'I've sorted out a few things for you to look through—some photos of the play and one or two of the family. Not too good of the play because of the light of course, and there's a family tree which goes back to the year dot—or more specifically to sixteenth-century Cecilia and fifteenth-century Owen harking back to Edward III in the fourteenth.'

'Just for the moment,' Peter said gravely, 'your great-grandfather Jacob would do as an ancestor. At a guess, he would have been roughly the same age as Percival FitzRichard's father Montague.'

'And here he is. Jacob himself.' Sophy flourished a black and white photo in the air. 'You'll see Granddad's papa looks just as much of a firecracker as Montague.'

'Not Planters and Tudors but Capulets and Montagues then,' Georgia joked. 'As in *Romeo and Juliet*. Very appropriate.'

Sophy shuddered. 'Don't remind me. Louis and I were thinking about leaving right now, but sorting out his grandfather is still a sticking point.'

'Does he want to remain with him to mount a defence of the Maid of Kent gardens if the hotel plan goes through?' Peter asked.

'That too. But now that Howard Green has revealed his true colours as a Plantagenet under a Tudor mask, the field's wide open on the hotel plan. My poor aunt. She would never have allied herself to him if she'd known about his Granny Serena.'

But if Brenda *had* discovered it, Georgia thought, had she gone straight to Howard Green for a showdown? Had she warned him she'd have to tell Gerald which would put paid to their supporting the hotel plan?

Sophy fell silent and Georgia asked sympathetically, 'The funeral?'

'Not yet. The police are still on the case, but I want to do what I can over that, so if this John Wilbourne investigation is connected I've persuaded my grandfather to meet you. I should break it to you,' she said awkwardly, 'that you're booked in more or less straightaway at the Hall. I'd better warn you that you might receive more of a lecture on the glories of the Tudors than a chat about Sir John, but poor old Grandpa's genuinely worried. He's heard the Howard Green news of course, so now he's imagining the new Maid of Kent hotel being packed with coachloads of Planter vandals rushing in and waving battleaxes rather than behaving like civilised Tudors.'

'Civilised? You jest, I assume?' Peter commented mockingly.

Sophy giggled. 'I do. There's another reason you might be glad to meet him though. Grandpa has a new house guest.'

'Who's that? Georgia asked warily.

'Cobshaw Hall is to be honoured with the presence of Sir Edward Colduggan, though I doubt if he'll be here as early as this morning.'

'Good grief! How did that happen?' Peter asked incredulously.

'Apparently through someone called Jill.'

Georgia did a mental doubletake. This could be *their* Jill. If so, she must have gone into action to ensure that her 'Hamlet' didn't escape too soon. But did she know Gerald Randall? All too possibly. Jill, with her energy and charm, was at the centre of the Canterbury arts world.

'I'll have to leave you to the mercies of my granddad,' Sophy added. 'Too much to do here and where Great-Aunt Brenda's concerned I need some space in all senses.'

As she and Peter approached the Hall, Georgia realised that it was not as rundown as she had thought when they'd passed it on their way to Mick's office. True, it needed sprucing up. Weeds had encroached on the gravel, the paintwork on the huge Georgian windows looked overdue for renewal and the paving stones and porch were grey rather than white. But the sheer majesty of the building with its vast portico over-rode all those defects. It seemed almost an insult to the Randall heritage that the bell was a mere humdrum electric affair. The heavy door seemed reluctant to open when the bell was answered, although behind it was not the traditional majestic butler but Gerald Randall himself.

Amidst the high ceilings and spacious grandeur of Cobshaw Hall he appeared smaller than he had when they had seen him in the Maid of Kent and he wasn't as mobile as Percival still was. But the beard gave him a stateliness which Percival lacked and unlike his rival he looked delighted to see them. A contrast to the impression Georgia had gained of him in the Maid of Kent bar or even from Sophy.

'You're the writing johnnies,' he greeted them cheerfully. 'Jolly good. Come along in. That thing you're on, electric is it? Pip-pip. Bring it in. How about the morning room?'

Peter was the first to recover from this onslaught of Bertie Wooster geniality. 'Splendid,' he replied cordially.

'Jolly good. The flowers in there are dying and the newspaper didn't arrive today but we'll manage, we'll manage, won't we?'

'We will, thank you,' Georgia assured him gravely.

The morning room, full of elegant if somewhat battered eighteenth-century furniture, was adorned with prints of hunting scenes, chiefly the familiar Surtees pictures.

Gerald noticed her looking at them. 'Jorrocks' jaunts and jollies, eh? Can't beat 'em. Not too fashionable today. Hunting's changed. See why too. All fun for the horses but not for the fox. Still, these prints are part of the old tradition, what? I do my hunting in other ways.'

'What are they?' Peter enquired with interest. It was clear that he was taking to Gerald Randall.

'Hunting murderers.'

Georgia blinked as Gerald sat benignly gazing at them. Perhaps she'd been wrong in thinking he wasn't going to be as eccentric as Percival.

'Always fancied myself as a bit of sleuth,' he continued. 'That's why I suggested you came along this morning. I can give you a helping hand over these murders of ours.'

'Excellent,' Peter managed to say.

Faced with this crazy situation, what would his game plan be now? Georgia wondered, noting Gerald's 'murders of *ours*'. She'd leave that up to Peter for the moment, although whether they'd ever get round to talking about John Wilbourne was doubtful.

'Good to have you aboard,' Peter continued cordially. 'Your sister-in-law's death must be an enormous sadness and I can understand your wanting to help in that respect. You used the word sleuth, though, so is it crime fiction that interests you?'

'Good lord no. The real thing. Plenty of it round Cobshaw. The police didn't want to know my theories about Brenda's death and they said they'd get back to me over John's remains. It's been over forty-eight hours now and they haven't done either. So I'm coming right to you. You're the local sleuths—got a bit of a name for it, haven't you?'

'Thank you,' Peter replied solemnly. 'You must have been here in 1959 when John Wilbourne died too, and we're told he was a Randall.'

Good move, Georgia silently congratulated him. Seize the opportunity.

'Of a sort,' Gerald conceded. 'The rotten apple in the family. Brought disgrace on it.'

Disgrace? Georgia seized on this intriguing word in connection with John Wilbourne. She'd have to pursue this herself as Peter was holding back for some reason. 'You must have known him well,' she began.

'Know him? Indeed I did. He was my half-brother. Ran off to be an actor of all things, then popped back to show us how well he was doing. Doing well? Prancing around in *Romeo and Juliet*? Pah! Letting the family down. My father told me there was woman trouble too. As I said, he was a disgrace to the family.'

'His wife Elizabeth?' Georgia asked.

'Never knew the whole story behind that. Met her one or twice when he deigned to visit us, but there was no sign of her long before his coming down in '59 for that play. Had a way with women, did John. Even Brenda set her cap at him. She wasn't married to Thomas then, of course.'

'Percival FitzRichard was keen on Brenda too, so he can't have been pleased if she took a fancy to John.'

'That twerp FitzRichard? As if she'd look twice at him. Mad he was, even in those days. He and his dad. Old Montague was even dottier than he was.'

Perhaps Gerald wasn't the best judge of that. Georgia avoided Peter's eye as her mouth twitched.

'Both Planters. They're all the same,' Gerald continued blithely. 'Brenda used to say the warring factions in Cobshaw were just like those Capulets and Montagues in that blasted play, but she was wrong. We're Tudors, as I said. Civilised.'

'But as a sleuth,' Peter said innocently, 'it must strike you that it was Sir Edward and John who wanted to fight after the performance, not Percival. Why was that?'

Gerald shrugged. 'More woman trouble. Percival—ridiculous name—and I were having a sparring match in the snug but came out when we heard the fuss over a duel.'

'Was it over the girl who played Juliet, Rowena Watt?'

He looked surprised. 'Must have been, or they wouldn't have been fighting.'

Georgia gave up. Gerald was not cut out to rival Poirot.

'Anyway,' he continued, blind to his audience's reaction, 'everyone was outside watching that duel, and back we came into the bar. Everyone was plastered. That actor fellow Colduggan was under the table. Didn't budge even when old Montague threw them out.'

'Threw who out?' Georgia asked politely. This was probably the same as Geoff Sanders' story, but from a Tudor viewpoint.

'Rowena Watts and Brenda,' Gerald said impatiently. 'Brenda couldn't stand that woman though they must have got matey enough later. She rang us here at the Hall wanting Brenda's phone number.'

Georgia was instantly alert. 'Was that recently?'

'Couple of days before Brenda died. Anyway, then they started fighting again outside but Montague sent Brenda packing back home, and the other woman back to her room in the pub. John must have made himself scarce afterwards. I must have left then so that's that. Evidence concluded.'

Peter cleared his throat. 'So as a fellow sleuth,' he began, 'where does that lead you as to who killed your half-brother?'

Gerald beamed. 'Glad you asked me that. I'll tell you where it leads me. Straight to Colduggan. There, what do you think of that?'

'Proof?' Peter asked politely. 'But you told us he was under the table. Literally?'

'Cunning move that,' Gerald said approvingly. 'He was faking it. But it stands to reason. *Cui bono,* as the old Romans said, eh? Who profited by John's death? Sir Eddie Colduggan of course. He might have lost the duel but by murdering him he gets to run the company. Then he can have his pick of roles and women, including Rowena Watts if he wants her. Case concluded.'

'Motive granted, then,' Peter diplomatically agreed. 'Opportunity?'

'Plenty.' Gerald waved a lordly hand. 'As I said, he only pretended to pass out in the pub. After we'd all left, he grabbed a knife, sneaked out, followed old John and challenged him to another duel, and hey presto.'

'Did he dig a hole for the body?'

'Eh?' Gerald bore a look of don't-bother-me-with-daft-questions. 'Could have done, could have done. Killed him on that pathway and dug a hole—wait a bit: he must have had an accomplice.'

'Who would that be?' Georgia asked meekly.

'Look here,' Gerald complained, 'I can't work out every detail myself. There were plenty of stage crew, cast, villagers and so on around. Now I come to think of it, my deduction is that the accomplice was that Rowena woman. She had it in for John that night because he'd been chasing Brenda. Or, maybe she was really stuck on Colduggan and wanted John out of the way. Anyway,' he added, 'it's you two who'll have to explore the details, but Colduggan's your man all right—and that Rowena was his stooge.'

'You did say that Rowena had been sent to her room by Montague FitzRichard,' Georgia said gently.

'Trifles, trifles, you can sort that out.' Another wave of the hand from Gerald. 'But it was Colduggan, you can count on it, so that's why I invited him here to the Hall for you to tackle him,' he added triumphantly. 'No escaping justice for him. I'll give you a ring when he's a sitting duck for you to arrest.'

Whoops. Georgia saw pitfalls ahead. Change of subject required. It was clear that Peter agreed as he immediately said, 'Sophy mentioned that someone called Jill had brought you together with Sir Edward. Would that be Jill Frost?'

'That's the name. I met her at a party of some sort. She told me Colduggan was looking for somewhere to stay. Best to have the suspect on the spot, I thought. So here he is. I gather Jill's a Tudor by inclination.'

Don't get side-tracked by this red herring, Georgia warned herself. 'We know her. She's neutral,' she replied. 'And she could have played no part in Brenda's death so—'

'Pretty obvious who did,' Gerald cut in with great satisfaction.

'Who did you have in mind?' Peter asked with interest.

Gerald stared at him in amazement. 'Howard Green of course. He's a traitor. Turned Plantagenet, hasn't he? Comes of bad stock that fellow. A blasted FitzRichard all over again. If he takes over the place, he'll turn it into a Richard of Eastwell centre. Can't have that.'

'And that would have led him to *murder* Brenda?' Peter queried, wearing his 'please bear with me' expression.

Gerald didn't bear with him. 'It did, didn't it? Brenda would have stopped him from buying that wreck of a pub.'

'How?' Peter asked politely.

Gerald hesitated for a moment. 'She'd manage. She was strong-willed was Brenda.' He brooded for a moment. 'You've met my Sophy. She imagines she's something out of *Romeo and Juliet* herself. Wants to marry her Romeo. Rival houses. Same today. We're Randalls and that young idiot she fancies is a Plantagenet.'

'John Wilbourne cut his ties with the Randalls,' Peter pointed out.

Gerald fixed him with a look. 'And look what happened to him? Got himself murdered.'

'And you're sure that Colduggan was John's murderer?' Peter asked cautiously. 'Have you any evidence apart from motive?'

Gerald rose to his feet with great dignity in order to reply: 'Never let it be said that I jump to hasty conclusions. I have a plan. Always fancied one of those Poirot set-ups I see on TV. Get Colduggan here, invite all the other suspects to come along and I'll announce who the murderer really is.'

'That, in real life, could be dangerous,' Peter said.

Gerald chuckled. 'You two can come along if you like. Police hiding in the kitchen so they can overhear the confession. That's the thing. I'll let you know when I'm ready.'

'Do you think,' Georgia remarked carefully as they reached the rear of the Maid of Kent, where a few tables had been set in a forlorn hope of diners arriving, 'that there might be a touch of inbreeding in Cobshaw? *Two* manic characters, Percival and Gerald, both in a position where they might wreck Cobshaw's future?'

'That, dear daughter, could well be so,' Peter replied, stopping by one of the tables. 'And incidentally does it not strike you as incongruous that in two months' time we'll be holding a concert here for two world-famous musicians and an audience, all of whom will be expecting sanity?'

The sight of Percival waving at them vigorously prevented Georgia from answering, and for once she was glad. Fears about the concert were already bubbling up inside her. 'No outside service today,' Percival yelled at them.

'There is and we're staying put,' Peter shouted back. 'Come and join us.'

Percival wavered but decided to do so, albeit somewhat guardedly.

'Congratulations on the good news. You must be hard at work checking Howard Green's claim to be your sister's grandson,' Georgia said.

Percival glared at her, something to which she was becoming accustomed. 'Bernie's doing all that. He says he is, but how would I know? All I asked him,' he added plaintively, 'was when Serena's coming back home. She'd be old now of course. She's not coming, he told me. Long gone. I never heard anything from her. I didn't believe it. Not Serena. She'd have come back home if she could. He even showed me a certificate, he did. Serena Rose. Spinster it said.'

'A death or marriage certificate?'

Percival stared at them. 'Marriage. Chap called Marshall. This Howard Green fellow says he never knew his grandmother. Just found out about Serena when he was clearing out his parents' house. There was a photo of this place, he said, and a photograph of her best friend, Daisy something. And he showed me a photograph of *her*. But it wasn't *my* Serena. My Serena was happy as the day is long. Dancing in the sunshine. Not this one.'

He glanced around. 'You'd best come inside,' he said crossly, 'if you want a drink or anything.' But he didn't move.

Georgia judged that having begun to talk about Serena he was reluctant to stop. 'Why did she leave home though? Was it a love affair gone wrong?'

Percival ruminated. 'Don't think so. There was trouble though. Always is, with the Buckleys and Cooks. All's fair in love and war, that's what my dad used to say.'

* * *

'Any luck? Have you identified Burglar Bill yet?' Georgia called out, seeing Peter hard at work over Suspects Anonymous on his computer as she arrived at his office the next morning.

'Burglar Bill,' he informed her crossly, 'has failed to help our investigation, though to please Gerald Randall all the suspects have been lined up waiting for him to make his choice. In search of the missing link I've fed Buckleys and Cooks in too, plus Serena and Howard Green just in case. I feel I want to zoom in and question them all, but Suspects isn't programmed for that.'

'Suspects for which murder?' Georgia enquired. 'John Wilmot's or Brenda's?'

'Both, on the grounds that they might be linked. Suspects Anonymous didn't show much interest when I fed Serena's and Howard's names in, but it got quite excited over the Buckleys and Cooks. It's possible the fête intensified the division between the Planters and Tudors, and John Wilbourne was a Tudor, estranged or not. And naturally enough it pointed out the most likely suspects for his murder amongst those present at the play that evening were Rowena and, I'm afraid, Brenda.'

'Not credible,' Georgia said firmly. 'Brenda couldn't have killed him. Even by accident.'

'It's unlike you to be so biased. This was sixty years back when she was a young and passionate girl.'

'Still unlikely. Girls with crushes don't go around murdering the beloved; they sob their sorrows away. Anyway,' she said, determined to bring this to an end, 'even if I'm wrong about that, what about the murder of dear Cecilia, maid of Kent?'

'Can't we cross her off the list?' Peter asked plaintively. 'It was in 1553.'

Georgia considered this. 'I'd like to,' she said finally, 'but the fact remains that her true story is yet to be discovered.'

'Probably permanently buried along with her. As perhaps the true story of what happened on 22nd August 1959 lies buried with John Wilbourne. Let's hope not.' Peter stared at his screen. 'Gerald wasn't exactly forthcoming about the Randall family, save that John Wilbourne marched out of the family in a possible scandal. What about sticking to the highly theoretical line that the real Serena FitzRichard vanished into thin air and that Howard Green's grandmama was someone completely different? Just for the record,' he hastily concluded, no doubt seeing Georgia's despairing look.

She watched patiently as the figures paraded across the screen. The result was only a Sherlock Holmes-type figure who rushed after them across the screen waving a red herring.

'What did you click on to produce that?' she said gloomily. 'Howard Green?'

'Sometimes,' Peter remarked savagely, 'I find this app annoying. Brenda has been flagged up twice, and even Cecilia once.'

'Methinks, dear father,' Georgia said crossly, 'that the fault lies not in our stars but in ourselves. Somewhere we're not making the right links.'

'Time to do some hard work,' Peter agreed. 'Cobshaw parish registers.'

'Transcripts?'

'No, let's brave the real thing. The advantage is that we can see the whole picture then, rather than just checking one name. I've discovered that Cobshaw's lucky enough to be one of those few villages that still has both its own church and its own registers. We can study them right there, no need to go to the County Archives. Cobshaw can't hide its secrets forever.'

'It's having a damned good try,' Georgia muttered.

As she spoke his mobile rang and Peter's face changed. 'Elena,' he mouthed at Georgia as she listened with rising panic.

'What's wrong?' she asked, as soon as he put the phone down.

'Depends how you judge wrong. DI Jack Cotton's with her.'

'What on earth for?' At least it wasn't something worse.

'He rang the wrong doorbell apparently and she and Jack are having a nice chat.'

A nice chat? She exchanged uneasy glances with Peter.

Almost immediately, Jack Cotton strolled through the adjoining door and into the office. 'Hi,' he greeted them, 'Just dropped by to say thanks from the Gov for the bulletins. Keep on sending them if you like but probably no need now.'

'You've got your man?' Peter asked gravely.

It took more than that to throw Jack off piste again. 'Closing in.' He peered at the screen. What about this app I heard about from the Gov?' He peered at it. 'Bringing Sherlock Holmes in on the case, I see. Tell him we've moved on a bit since then.'

'Humour him,' Peter advised as Jack took his leave. 'He'll learn.'

'Quickly, I hope,' Georgia said, staring at the screen. At least he'd come. They'd almost given up waiting for him to contact them, but perhaps there hadn't been much to contact them about. 'Look at this, Peter. There's still a red herring flagged up. What does Sherlock know that we don't?'

'It's a computer,' Peter said patiently. 'It only uses stuff we feed in.'

Georgia sighed. There was no answer to that.

Chapter Eleven

'Do you find this somewhat daunting?' Georgia said after a minute or two. Peter had been silent for a remarkably long time after the church warden of St Nicholas's had conducted them to St Edith's Chapel on Wednesday morning. The warden had clearly been highly suspicious as to what their intentions might be towards the pile of registers they'd chosen from the iron chest in the vestry where they were safeguarded. Georgia therefore deduced that the warden was a Tudor sympathiser who had feared that two Planters might be planning a raid. The lady had now returned to the vestry, after sizing them up as unlikely candidates for running off with church property. She had even offered them a transcript of the registers which Peter had declined to Georgia's annoyance. The original, he had told her grandly, carried the atmosphere and the context, thus inspiring their detection skills.

St Nicholas's Church was modest in size compared with many Norman churches and was peacefully tucked away amidst its protective shield of yew trees. Nevertheless, its memorials and murals indicated its importance in the village. Cobshaw, they seemed to declare, had centuries of status. St Edith's Chapel seemed to be the domain of the Randall family, judging by the memorial plaques and one ornate tomb. Georgia saw at least two brasses on the floor, obviously dating back centuries, and no doubt concealed or buried under the pews there would be more. The two large stained-glass windows were spectacular, one very old, the other a nineteenth-century addition just as colourful.

'I do indeed find it daunting,' Peter said in answer to Georgia's question. 'And challenging.'

The silence in the church was oppressive as they opened the first of the six registers they had chosen. Even Peter looked overwhelmed. 'Just as well we only want to check the last hundred and fifty years or so. Impressive though that pile of registers looked, it would take us years to study them properly.'

The smell of the registers they had seen in the chest as they decided upon their chosen six was so redolent of past ages that Georgia rather regretted not having all the time in the world to study Cobshaw history from the year dot onwards. Brenda must have studied every page of these unique records. Even so, this was a huge task ahead. At a quick glance the handwriting was far from copperplate.

Georgia braced herself. 'OK, boss. Let's go. Which first and just what are we looking for?'

'I can't define that.'

'Not helpful.'

His turn to capitulate. 'Agreed, so let's put it this way. To understand John Wilbourne's death, it would help to see him in the context of Cobshaw as it was when he was living here. So let's start with the man himself. I'll check the baptism records for Randalls, as he must have been born with that name, and to be on the safe side under Wilbourne as well. He probably changed it when he left home,' Peter added. 'And keep an eye open for the other ladies and gents of interest to us. You check marriages either for him or for other Randalls last century and while you're about it the burials. Let's get the broad picture and look out for Cooks, Buckleys etcetera.'

'Including, I presume, the FitzRichards.' This was going to be quite a task.

'Agreed,' Peter said.

After two hours, Georgia began to despair. She had come up with very little of interest and her eyes were getting tired. Peter was scowling which suggested he was in the same position.

She could bear it no longer. 'Any luck?' she asked.

'Yes, but I'm not sure it helps much. John was baptised as John Randall in 1915 and I doubt if you'll find any sign of a marriage taking place here. I looked up his *Who Was Who* entry yesterday. He married Elizabeth Courtney in 1944 and they divorced in 1949. No children. Dead end. I also found our Mick's grandfather, Samuel Buckley, baptised in 1917 and the two Cook brothers Dave mentioned, Brian and George. Brian's the one who failed to rejoin his ship during the war. John would have been at school with both of them even if not in the same year.'

'He might have been sent away first to a prep school then a private one and anyway what does that tell us?'

'Give me time,' Peter said with dignity. 'What have you found for the FitzRichards? I've got Montague baptised in 1886, Percival in 1934.'

'Married to Serena's mum—his first wife Elspeth—January 1919. Married Percival's mum Agnes in 1932.'

'Anything in burials? Or anything about this Serena or other children around?' Peter enquired. 'I've found a baptism date for her in September 1919 so she did exist at least.'

'That's a relief,' Georgia commented ironically. 'Nothing under burials for her of course, or marriages, which ties in with her popping off to join the war effort. She would have been twenty when the Second World War broke out, and Percival would have been about five so those dates work. Then she met her husband to be, who was nothing to do with Cobshaw, and she presumably stayed away from it thereafter.'

'Why leave though?' Peter asked.

'If you came from a family like the FitzRichards you'd have done the same.'

'Very funny. Nevertheless, we're pinpointing a death in 1959.' He frowned. 'We shouldn't lose sight of the fact that in our enthusiasm for Cobshaw's history we're ignoring the fact that John can't have been universally popular as a Randall.

'Good morning.' The deep voice came from behind them. To Georgia's amazement, framed in the entrance to the chapel and leaning on his walking stick was Sir Edward Colduggan. 'Ah, Mrs Frost, or are you Georgia today?'

Introduction were hastily made. From the gleam in Peter's eye Georgia was conscious of the fact that he might be mentally engaged in summing Sir Edward up as Suspect Number One.

'My host,' Sir Edward informed them, 'is eager to entertain us all at Cobshaw Hall but I preferred to track you down here. Elena kindly informed me of your whereabouts. With Host Gerald's eagle eye on me, I fear I might be arrested for murder at any moment—quite without foundation—but here I am safe from persecution. I take it I might join you briefly?'

Despite this bland assurance that he had no desire to be cast in the role of murderer, Peter's eagerness to welcome Sir Edward made it all too clear to Georgia that Peter was mentally contemplating that very thing. As he was sitting down in one of the pews, Sir Edward's eyes fell on the volumes they were studying. 'Investigating poor John's murky past?'

'Background research is always useful,' Peter murmured.

'Indeed. However, when one hobbles across a stage in doublet, hose and pinched-toed footwear the knowledge that the research is authentic fails to charm.'

'But the end result would be inferior without it,' Peter parried.

Sir Edward smiled. 'A hit, a hit, a very palpable hit, So, now we have crossed swords, how is the hunt for John's killer going?'

Georgia managed a laugh. 'The hounds are spread out at the moment. Baffled at the lack of scent.'

'I am hardly in a position to provide that, although my alibi must seem very weak. Memory is a treacherous creature; it comes and goes of its own free will. Sometimes one reaches for it but finds it has eluded one's grasp and feared gone forever, only for it to reappear at the strangest moments.'

'Has yours reappeared more fully with regard to 1959?' Peter enquired politely.

'After nearly sixty years, that might be considered suspicious. When does a memory become a fantasy dreamed up in one's imagination? Most inconvenient for detectives. I pointed that out to Gerald, as he seems set on questioning me about it. At least in discussing it with you, I am fortunate in that you write books about your cases which gives more permanence. The publicity Gerald might bring upon me would only arise through my being found guilty of the charge of murder. I jest of course,' Sir Edward added gently. 'As I told Gerald, the solution to John's murder is glaringly obvious: look to the lady.'

Georgia seized on this. 'The Lady Rowena?'

'Perhaps, Georgia, but I had in mind dear Brenda. John was always a ladies' man, seemingly always in search of the perfect woman—no, that is wrongly expressed. In search of true love perhaps. But that can be elusive, so he searched widely but in vain. Note that his first marriage was relatively short. Five years, I believe, though I never met his former wife. His search for perfection in female form might be the reason for his choosing *Romeo and Juliet*. This is after all the village where he was born and where Brenda lived.'

'He was in love with Brenda?'

'That I cannot say. Brenda, however, was in love with him. I gather from Gerald that John paid at least one private visit to Cobshaw that summer, whether Rowena approved or not, and it could be that Brenda was the reason for it.'

'Just a minute, are you implying Rowena was not only in love with him but he was her lover?' Peter broke in.

'One cannot be certain, of course, but that appeared to be the case. However, that would not have hindered his pursuit of Brenda. Dear Rowena was also perpetually in love with someone—someone, dare I suggest, who could be of advantage in her career. Although most talented, Rowena was never set to be another Judi Dench herself, but was drawn to men with such gifts, in particular John. Even my humble self did not elude her favour.'

Which could account for Rowena's present lack of enthusiasm towards him. 'We heard that she and Brenda had a set-to after the performance that night,' Georgia said.

'And a bitter one, so I was later told,' Sir Edward replied. 'Alas, Rowena took exception to Brenda's rather obvious boasting about—as she saw it—her relationship with John.'

'What exact form did the set-to take?' Peter asked with interest. This would probably have been inside the pub, and so it would be interesting, Georgia thought, to hear what he had made of it, after Geoff's and Gerald's vivid descriptions of the battle outside. 'Another duel?'

'Far more primitive. I was inebriated but not so far gone at that point not to enjoy the spectacle of their physical wrestling. From my vantage point not under a table but nearly, I could see it at close quarters. Rowena was winning the fight before the publican thrust them outside. She would of course be the victor. Rowena does not take rejection lightly and I was annoyed with poor John for having neglected her that evening for Brenda, despite Rowena's magnificent performance on stage.'

'Was that a sign that he was moving on from Rowena?' Georgia asked.

'I doubt if he saw it in that light. His wife had long since departed from his life and he was a free man in that respect, whether divorced or not. Did you know that the great actor Edmund Kean had this overpowering sexual appetite that had to be satisfied even during time off-stage during performances? It is not an unknown situation in the stage world. John was not so extreme, but nevertheless the sexual as well as the romantic aspects of love dominated his life—second only to the stage of course.'

'But Brenda has now been murdered and we're told that Rowena had recently telephoned her. Could that have any relevance to John Wilbourne's murder?' she asked. A long shot but in deference to Suspects Anonymous she might as well ask.

'I'm interested to hear that, but it's hard to see that it would be relevant, unless one considers a scenario in which firstly Brenda killed John, secondly, Rowena made it clear she was aware of this and lastly that Brenda killed herself either in remorse or in fear of revelation. However, I feel that the answer does lie closer to home. I am informed by Rowena that the Maid of Kent is to be sold, and I gathered that the vital element is that it has to go to a buyer with Plantagenet ancestry, which has narrowed the candidates down to either the current landlord's daughter or a hotel mogul named Howard Green.'

Georgia was taken aback. 'But how could *Rowena* know all this?' It certainly hadn't been mentioned on their visit to her.

'From, I believe, Howard Green.'

Her head was spinning now. 'But do they know each other?'

'Apparently so.'

Sir Edward clearly decided to make his exit on this punch line, but then he paused. 'I do have an excellent alibi for the time of Brenda's death, although that will disappoint poor Gerald. He so longs to prove I am a mass murderer, not only of poor John but Brenda too. Alas, I cannot oblige. I was on the stage of the West London Theatre in the role of King Lear. My absence, I am sure, would have been noticed. And now I must make my exit, I fear. I have a rendezvous with the delightful Mrs Jill Frost.

'Incidentally,' he said as he rose to his feet, 'I take it you have heard the news? Gerald has. Percival FitzRichard is to announce the destiny of the Maid of Kent public house at two o'clock this afternoon. A strange family. I remember Montague, Percival's father of course, a splendid character straight out of Shakespeare. And Percival is pure Malvolio.'

'I take it you'll want to attend?' Georgia asked, after Sir Edward's departure—to an invisible flourish of trumpets judging by his body language.

'Of course,' Peter replied. 'No point going home first. We'll eat at the Maid. Nothing I like better than their splendid sausage and chips.'

The news must have travelled fast for when they arrived the Maid of Kent car park was full, apart from a disabled space that Georgia gratefully took.

Still musing on the coincidence—or otherwise—of Howard Green knowing Rowena, Georgia joined Peter on the terrace where there were still several tables available. A quick check through the door had revealed a crowded bar. On a sunny day the terrace would surely have been packed so it was clear that everyone was gathering inside for the 'entertainment'. There had been no sign of Bernie or Tony inside, but Percival himself came out to greet them. She suspected he'd been looking for an excuse to leave the bar—and she was right.

'Had to get outside,' he growled. 'That fellow Randall's there. Heard about what's to happen? Good. Thought I'd put an end to the speculation.'

'Can you give us a hint?' Peter joked.

Percival took this seriously. 'Not made my mind up yet.'

'Leaving it late, aren't you?'

'I always do things this way,' he replied complacently. 'Gets the best results.'

Georgia couldn't see the logic here, but that was immaterial where Percival was concerned. Logic was not his forte.

'You must have been hard at work checking whether Howard Green really does have Plantagenet blood,' she said.

Percival looked blank. 'Bernie's been doing all that. Anyway, he said he has.'

'We've been looking at the parish records for John Wilbourne and noticed that there was no record of your sister being married here,' Peter commented blandly. 'Of course, you did tell us that she left to join the war effort, but was there another reason? A sweetheart perhaps? This Mr Marshall who appears on the marriage certificate?'

Georgia held her breath. Peter was pushing it which with Percival was risky. Percival's face went blank. 'She never came home. I asked my father,' he added plaintively, repeating his usual story. 'When's Serena coming home?' I asked. "She's not," he said. That's all. Nothing more.'

'That's very sad.' Georgia shivered. Words were an inadequate response for such heartbreak and Peter clearly felt the same.

Percival nodded. 'Cut herself off from everyone, so he said. Even from you, little Percival. But I didn't believe it. Serena wouldn't do that. She loved me. She'd have come home.'

'What about her mother, Elspeth?' Georgia asked, thinking of the agony she must have gone through. 'Or was she no longer alive?'

'Long gone off to live with a rotter, Dad said. And then my own mum died not long after the war.'

Percival had said enough for Georgia to understand his idiosyncrasies. It can't have been an easy life for him.

'And your wife?' Peter asked quietly.

For a moment she thought he'd gone too far, but Percival didn't seem to mind. 'Went over to New Zealand with some chap and left Bernie with me. That's why Bernie's kids are out there. They went out there and never came back. Like my Serena. They none of them came back to me.'

Only his father and Bernie had remained here. That was sad. Time to change the subject, Georgia sensed. 'Did your father talk to you much about the night John Wilbourne disappeared?'

Percival scowled. 'No reason he should. Far as he knew the fellow left the village either that night or next morning early.' He had clearly tired of co-operation for he turned his back on them and stalked back into the pub.

Cod and chips had replaced sausages as the hot dish of the day so their lunch proved better than expected and by the time she and Peter had made their way back inside the pub it was nearly two o'clock and time for the fun to begin—fun for Peter and herself anyway, Georgia thought. Peering through the crush inside, she could see Bernie sitting on a bar stool with no sign of Tony although Jimmy was behind the bar. Howard Green was standing on its far side by the exit door she and Peter used, but Percival, although standing quite close to them, was almost hidden by the crowd. He looked like a small, pathetic figure facing a pack of hounds that might soon be released on him.

She was wrong. Nothing pathetic about Percival. He merely banged on the bar—with as far as Georgia could see, an old gong mallet—and as comparative silence fell, yelled:

'I'm selling the old Maid to Howard Green and that's that.'

He didn't waste time. After he'd thrown this cat amongst the pigeons, Georgia first lost sight of him, and then glimpsed him pushing his way through to the door by which Howard Green had been standing. When she next had a clear view she could see no sign of either of them.

After a stunned silence, the bar crowd broke into an uproar. Dave Cook was pushing his way towards Bernie, Mick Buckley was cheering, Gerald Randall was spluttering with laughter, and Louis, Sophy and Geoff Sanders were looking despairingly at the anger and gloating erupting around them.

'Let's get out of here,' Peter muttered. It wasn't easy or pleasant with angry faces turning furiously towards them as they manoeuvred the scooter past the bar to the door, almost as though they had played some part in this drama.

Still no sign of Howard Green, Georgia noticed, as she and Peter reached the corridor after battling their way through the crowd. He must have had the same fears as they did for neither he nor Percival were anywhere to be seen. Georgia cast a rueful eye on the Plantagenets looking down on them in the corridor, perhaps foreseeing their own end now that the Tudors were victorious. For all his claims to be a Plantagenet, Georgia couldn't see Howard Green going out of his way to stress their glories compared with the publicity value of the Tudors. Richard of Eastwell would get a poor showing in the new hotel.

Peter stopped the scooter at the first exit door they came to. 'Let's get out of here,' he said abruptly. 'This one will take us to the car park more quickly.'

The door led into the former stable yard, now used for workshops and garages, where Georgia spotted a parked Bentley. Howard Green's?

she wondered. The door of the largest garage was open and she could see inside Tony's beloved Porsche 356SC. What, she wondered, was going to happen to Tony and Bernie now the Green deal appeared to be going through? They weren't at retiring age yet so perhaps they had something else lined up. One thing was for sure: if there was a hitch and the deal collapsed, she couldn't see Tony selling his beloved Porsche to help restore the Maid.

As if on cue, Tony himself came out of the garage. He was obviously a refugee from the fray inside. 'How will Bernie take the news about the hotel?' Peter asked him curiously.

He shrugged. 'Philosophically, I expect, though Howard won't be top of her Christmas card list. I'll go back inside and offer free pints all round. That might help a bit. Bernie guessed that's what Percival would decide to do. All because of his fixation with that sister Serena of his. It's the Planters I'm worried about, though. Dave Cook's mob have been done out of their community centre.' He looked beyond them and Georgia turned to see Howard coming out of the pub. He looked surprised and not entirely happy to see them.

'Time to leave, I'm afraid.' He glanced at Tony. 'We'll talk later on.'

'Congratulations are in order,' Peter said heartily. 'But you've quite a task ahead.'

A diplomatic smile from Howard Green. 'An enjoyable one.'

'We've been talking to your friend Rowena Watts about John Wilbourne,' Peter said casually.

A slight pause. 'I know her slightly. You'll recall that it was she who told me about the Maid of Kent and that my Plantagenet grandmother was born here.'

'She probably knew that from her visit here in 1959?' Peter pressed on, despite the diplomatic smile on Howard Green's face rapidly disappearing.

'Perhaps. I really don't know. However, Daisy Watts, her mother, was a minor star of the musical stage early last century. And before you ask,' he added smoothly, 'Daisy Watts was best friends with Serena Marshall, maiden name FitzRichard. Does that complete your enquiries?' He pointedly studied his watch.

'For the moment, thank you.' Peter was adept at polite but meaningful messaging. But where, Georgia wondered, would this interesting revelation take them? It was too much of a coincidence not to have played its part in the story somehow. But what was it?

Chapter Twelve

'Daisy Watts, Rowena Watts, Howard Green, Brenda Randall—they're certainly sitting awkwardly together. How to put this daisy chain case together? Brenda must be part of it, though,' Peter reflected. 'Remember how you loved making daisy chains on our lawn?'

'When I was seven years old, yes.' Georgia was jerked back in time. It brought back memories, some good, some bad. Time doesn't always eliminate the ones you want to lose. Rick would have been four years old then, not into making daisy chains for himself but inquisitive about what she was doing. Always curious. Always there. Always happy, so it seemed now.

'The method's the same for us sleuths,' Peter continued. 'A slit in the stem of one of them, you pop the stem of the next one in and eventually you can join the two ends. Voilà! A daisy chain. Let's consider our new daisy.'

'Rowena?'

'Yes. Her latest appearance on the scene could be quite innocent. She knows Howard Green and told him about the pub quite casually either because she remembered it from her visit in 1959, or because she knew Howard's family through her mother's friendship with Serena.

Still, it's a coincidence, and possibly suggests a link between 1959 and today's events.'

They were back at the Maid of Kent the next day where they seemed to be accepted as regulars now that their mission was no doubt known to the whole village. Luckily today's mission dealt with 1959 and so they must be counted by most villagers as eccentric historians rather than spies—or so she hoped.

She and Peter were attending two meetings today and, with half an hour still to go before the first one began, they had retreated to the gardens to avoid being drawn into the infighting earlier than necessary. As accepted 'eccentric historians' they had been asked to attend, perhaps as outside witnesses again. This meeting was being held in the pub and had been organised by Gerald Randall. Yesterday's announcement had added fuel to the already glowing fire of opposition, and another meeting was taking place in the village hall, its purpose to uphold the rights of Cobshaw to the ownership of Cecilia's well.

Here in the Maid of Kent, however, Gerald was proclaiming the Randall estate's claim, intent on signing an agreement with Howard Green's company, giving it a leasehold on the well. This was asking for trouble, Georgia thought. The charitable explanation was that holding the meeting here in the pub was a move not only on Gerald's part but on Howard's, to demonstrate that both the Plantagenet and Tudor versions of Cecilia's story were to be honoured. Surely Gerald Randall would not stand for that though? Nor would Dave Cook on behalf of the parish council (and the Planters) stand for it. And nor, she suspected, would Percival who seemed to regard the well as his personal property. And then there was Mick Buckley's casual comment that the Buckleys had some sort of stake in it.

Already she could see Gerald Randall striding in a meaningful way towards them. He looked gleeful to say the least, twirling an antique walking stick in his hand, his beard positively bouncing up and down as he advanced.

'The council of war's upstairs,' he called out. 'Everything will be agreed by two o'clock. None of this Richard of Eastwell nonsense. The Planter rats are scuttling down to the village hall. Jolly good. We can get our business done here and transform this place back to Cobshaw Court in a jiffy as soon as Howard gets going. Let those Planters plant themselves elsewhere!'

'But Howard's a Plantagenet himself.' Georgia was taken aback by this onslaught.

Gerald snorted. 'He sees my point. Time the Randalls made a stand over our well, or before you can say Richard III those Planters will seize it, and our Cecilia will be reclaimed as a Plantagenet icon. That's what we're fighting against. Besides, the well's on Tudor land and that's final.'

With a flourish of his stick, Gerald turned his back on them and marched back to the pub, where she could see Mick Buckley waiting for him. Divided loyalties, she thought. Plantagenet by heritage, but in Tudor employ, and apparently it had long been so with the Buckleys.

That brought Georgia back to Sam Buckley and the elusive story of Serena FitzRichard who would have been a contemporary of his. A lot of girls volunteered for war service before it was compulsory, but they didn't permanently leave their homes on that account. There had to be something else. And that brought Georgia back to the most likely explanation: she'd fallen out with her father and a very possible reason for that might have been her choice of boyfriends. And *that* brought her back to the apparently unpopular Sam Buckley again. Were they a couple? Had that all come to a head at the fête that the young Percival so vividly remembered? Had Montague FitzRichard disapproved of Sam Buckley's Tudor leanings? But hadn't there been some reference earlier to Sam Buckley being as thick as thieves with Montague?

Or was the whole story simpler? Georgia played around with the idea that the reason for Sam Buckley's unpopularity was that he jilted Serena and later married someone else, leaving a broken-hearted Serena to leave the village.

All possibilities—but they were leading nowhere at present. Any link between Serena and Sam Buckley in 1939 to Brenda's death was so tenuous it easily broke in the cold light of facts.

She pulled herself back to the present. Peter was still musing on the politics awaiting them in the meeting. 'Difficult situation for our Mr Green,' he observed, 'being a Plantagenet by birth. That must be why he held back that information as long as he could.'

'And now he's aiming to please both factions. Difficult isn't the word. *Impossible* is.'

Georgia watched refugees from inside the pub now spilling on to the terrace, probably on their way, as Gerald predicted, to the village hall, and—hardly surprisingly—Geoff Sanders and Dave Cook were amongst them.

Peter had seen them too. 'Trouble ahead,' he predicted.

'Who for though? *Everyone* is up in arms one way or another, with the possible exception of Percival and Howard.'

Dave must have overheard her comment because he and Geoff halted and came over to them. 'Right,' he said. 'We're up in arms and with good reason. If the Randalls do what they threaten, Howard Green will forget he's a Plantagenet and become a dyed in the wool Tudor. That's their plan. They're taking *our* pond away. My dad told me there was something special about that pond—he'd been told that by my granddad—and now it was my job to make sure it stayed under the village's control. You can feel it's special when you're there, can't you?'

Geoff nodded slowly. 'We're its guardians, Dave, that's what my dad told me. I asked him guardians of what? "The past", he said.'

'And today it's still ours,' Dave said fiercely. 'If the Randalls or Howard Green try to take it from us….' he paused, 'we'll take it back. You'll see.'

'What if we can't?' Geoff grunted. 'Once that contract's signed it could be a goner.'

Dave grinned. 'We can take back our own property back. The parish council contracted to surround the well with a pond and it was our parents and grandparents built that wall. We'll take it back brick by brick.'

That, Georgia thought uneasily, sounded like the kind of fun that could turn into disaster. Dave seemed a reasonable man and was probably only using that threat as a bargaining tool, but he couldn't rely on his supporters being satisfied with that. Demolishing the pond's wall—especially if 'accidentally' the old wall round the well fell too—could affect not only the well and the land around but the water table below them.

A sudden roar from the bar of 'Up the Tudors!' prompted an equally loud response from the Planters. Those of them still inside the pub began to surge outside to join their fellows and together began the march to the village hall. Geoff Sanders regarded them in silence as they flocked past to accomplish their mission. From their angry faces and shouts, no holds would be barred.

'It's back,' he muttered.

'What's that, Geoff?' Dave asked quietly.

'The darkness. My dad said it would return, and now it's coming.'

In contrast to the village hall, the Maid of Kent meeting was to be held in the same upstairs room as the earlier one, but today it was looking almost festive with flowers, provisions for tea and coffee and even two bowls of strawberries. Civilised, Georgia thought—although how did one define that word at present? Civility in words and deeds could mask hidden passions but not always eradicate them.

Did Bernie have anything to do with this splendid array? Unlikely, Georgia felt. Perhaps this was courtesy of Gerald Randall and Bernie had gone on strike. She would, in her position, Georgia decided. There were a dozen or so people here, including Sophy. Percival, looking in one of his gloomy moods, was sitting on one side of Howard with Gerald on the other. Surprisingly, Sir Edward Colduggan was also present. What, Georgia wondered, was his interest in Cecilia's well, or was it merely curiosity that brought him here?

'Our Poirot Gerald refuses to let me leave the Hall,' he joked, when she asked him, 'and I admit I have no objection to staying on. The role of playing the unjustly accused victim is new to me, but I would assume it would be a passive one. My challenge therefore is to turn it into an active role.'

'Might one enquire how?' Peter asked gravely.

'One may not. The curtain has not yet risen.'

Then it was Sophy's turn to come over to them. 'Sorry about this,' she said ruefully, taking the seat next to Georgia. 'I'm accompanying Grandpa Randall today. Louis's gone to the village hall to be with his grandfather, so I thought I'd wave the flag for the Tudors here, while he waves for the Planters.'

'How's Gerald getting on with his investigations into Brenda's death?' Peter asked her.

She laughed. 'Poirot is playing Lord of the Manor today, so there's no news.'

'Sophy—' Georgia took the opportunity to ask—'did Brenda ever talk to you about Rowena Watts, who played Juliet the night of John Wilbourne's death?'

Sophy looked interested. 'No. There was some woman who rang

her recently. My aunt just described her as "that woman who thought she was God's gift to the stage". Could that have been her?' Seeing their reaction, she clasped her hand to her head and grimaced. 'Sorry. Didn't I tell you? I told the police. Don't know what it was about, but she seemed a bit upset about it.'

Georgia remembered Gerald Randall mentioning this phone call too, but 'God's gift to the stage' was new. 'You've no idea at all who it was?'

'She ordered me out of the room and said no more about it afterwards.'

'Did the police trace the call?'

'I don't know. I told that DI Cotton about it and he said he was following it up. Nothing heard since.'

It could well have been Rowena, Georgia thought, especially in view of what they now knew about the fight between the two women after the 1959 performance. Gerald was standing up now, so it was clearly time for the show to begin.

'*Mes amis,*' Gerald began solemnly, and Georgia groaned inwardly. Not here, *please*. Poirot was out of place. Was that why they had been asked to attend? She relaxed, however, as he continued gravely, 'I am to inform you that the remains of our dear departed John Randall, otherwise known as John Wilbourne, are to be interred in Cobshaw churchyard in four days' time, Tuesday, 11th June, where a service will take place. Afterwards, I propose we all return to the Hall as my guests,' he added in a tone heavy with mystery.

'Myself included, I trust, Gerald?' Edward Colduggan enquired.

'Yes, yes.' Gerald waved him aside, intent on his speech. 'There will be *other* guests too.'

Then that could well be Poirot time, Georgia thought resignedly. Perhaps it offered him the best chance of having all his suspects together, although in the circumstances to choose such a day seemed off beam. Sure enough, Gerald continued, 'You will join us, Peter and Georgia?'

'Thank you. We accept,' Peter said promptly. That surprised her but on reflection, he was right. From their point of view, although it might prove only a lot of nonsense, it was conceivable that useful information might emerge.

Gerald paused impressively. 'And that is when I shall unmask the person guilty of murdering dear John.'

Dear *John*? What was this? Georgia had been under the impression that the proposed gathering would centre on Brenda's death. Now what? She'd expected at the very least that Jack Cotton would be hiding in the next room, ready to jump out with handcuffs.

'And now, ladies and gentlemen,' Gerald continued blithely, 'I have to inform you that the time has come to act. For years we have generously allowed the entire village to trespass on Randall property. No longer shall that happen. Even as I speak our men are installing improved fencing for Cecilia's well and the land around it. I have come to an understanding with the new owner-elect of the Maid of Kent, formerly Cobshaw Court, whereby only hotel guests will be permitted to enter—and Randalls, of course.'

It was just as well that the Planters were busy protesting in the village hall and not present at this public declaration of war, Georgia thought. It was putting the seal on it, judging by the applause.

Sophy pulled a long face. 'Looks as if Louis and I are going to have to choose which family we belong to,' she whispered, 'or leave grandfather Sanders behind and make a run for it.'

'Delicate,' Peter said as they left. 'Our liaison officer hasn't been liaising as often as he should. That phone call could have been relevant to our case.'

Georgia tried to be fair. 'Anything to do with Brenda's death is police business only and our hunches aren't evidence.'

'I wish they were,' Peter said mournfully. 'I rang Jack Cotton while I was waiting for the lift down. They were already on to it, and he confirmed nothing was said on that phone call that referred to 1959 except that Rowena had explained that she had met Brenda then and wanted to say how terrible it was that John's remains had been found.'

'And that's all she would say to us if we asked her. It might even be true,' Georgia said reluctantly. 'Anyway, with luck she'll be coming to Cobshaw Hall after the interment on Tuesday—much better to tackle her then.' She paused. 'I know we're planning on popping in to the Maid of Kent theatre to size it up, but I'd like to whizz over and see what they're doing to the well. You never know, Cecilia might appear and give me a few clues about where she's buried and whether she's a Plantagenet or a Tudor.'

'If she does, you can have a girly chat with her. OK, I'll see you at the theatre when you've finished.'

Peter promptly set off to the garden exit door, while Georgia returned to the bar in the hope of seeing Bernie before she set off. It was noticeable that Bernie had not been present at the meeting. There she was, sitting in solitary state by a window and reading a newspaper. She looked up and reluctantly put the paper down. This must be an awful time for her, Georgia realised. With her father bent on selling to Howard Green and her own perfectly valid offer presumably spurned, she must feel rejected at the very least.

'Can I help you?' Bernie asked formally, without any indication that she wanted to do so.

'I wanted to say how sorry I am that the decision's gone against you. Any hope of this deal being scuppered?'

Bernie shrugged. 'I doubt it. Howard doesn't seem to care whether this place is falling down or not so it should go through quite quickly.'

'At least the village battle isn't taking place here.'

'That's a mercy. Running a Wild West saloon isn't my idea of fun.'

'There's going to be a fight over that well,' Georgia said ruefully.

'Yes, bloody Cecilia is the ruddy limit.' Bernie managed a grim smile. 'Without Dad's hand in things, I could have made something of this place with the cash Dave was going to raise.'

'How will you manage now?' Georgia dared to ask.

'Tony says he gets on all right with Howard so maybe we can both get jobs here, polishing boots most likely. I might cope for a while. There'll be a big make-over though, and once that's done we could both be on the scrapheap.'

'Because Howard Green will aim to turn it into a mini-Hilton?'

'That depends on whether Howard goes with the Plantagenets or sneakily plays up to the Tudors. He's got to decide one way or the other. Especially with that blasted well at stake.'

'What will your father do?' Georgia couldn't imagine Percival playing a role in a mini Hilton.

Bernie smiled. 'He's under the impression he'll be living in the hotel giving talks about the Plantagenets, poor old soul. I doubt if that's in Howard's plans.'

Georgia could see her point. The vision of a five-star hotel keeping Percival as a permanent resident didn't quite work.

She drove round to the well still meditating on Percival's possible future, but as soon as she drew near the site all thoughts of Percival vanished. Gone was the relatively low white fencing she and Peter had seen when they came here with Brenda. Instead, a formidable ten-foot-high barrier seemed to be surrounding the site. Having parked the car, she could see it was nearing completion. True, it was possible to see through the sturdy fencing, but the gate was already provided with a padlock. On the outside of the fencing there was a new tarmacked narrow footpath, either as a courtesy to those who wished to view it or to the prevailing legal footpath situation.

She wasn't the only person peering through the fence. Geoff Sanders was there, and as far as she could judge he was alone.

'A sad sight,' she called out to him.

He turned and walked slowly towards her, not, it seemed for once, out of belligerence. 'Always has been in my time. Not many folks come here, and those that do have reason, no doubt.'

'Because of this well?' she asked. It was becoming frighteningly clear that there was indeed a darkness surrounding this well that stemmed from the past and had long been buried. That was obvious because it was the older people in the village who were most affected. Certainly today Geoff Sanders seemed to be lost in a world of his own, a world in which she did not figure.

'Maybe. How would I know? Always been a dark place, here.'

'For the Randalls or the Planters, or both?'

'Both, my dad said. But who knows now, missus? What happened is long gone. I were only a nipper, so I never knew. Never.'

Georgia held her peace. She sensed that his being 'only a nipper' line was a definite self-defence mechanism—but against what?

By the time she got back to the Maid of Kent, nearly an hour had passed and she thought Peter might have driven home as they'd come in separate cars. But his car was still in the car park, so she walked through the gardens to the theatre. There she saw him hunched up over the scooter near the remaining beech tree staring down at the stage, as though Juliet were gazing lovingly down from her balcony at her Romeo beneath.

'Penny for them,' she said fatuously, when he didn't reply to her shout of arrival.

'Worth more than that, my love,' Peter retorted. 'I'm reliving the night of 22nd August 1959.'

'With what in mind specifically?'

'What jealousies, what petty rivalries, what unavenged wrongs might have existed amongst the cast as they put them aside and united in a superb performance about two lovers in a play by William Shakespeare?'

Peter sounded unusually serious, so Georgia replied in the same vein. 'More than we'll ever know? That isn't much, I grant you.' She looked at the stage below, envisaging how it was in 1959. 'Edward Colduggan longs to play Romeo, not Mercutio, but is held back by John Wilbourne,' she said slowly. 'And Rowena Watts is John's lover, making her fiercely jealous of any rivals. More might have been going on, but if so we haven't heard about it. In the audience however there are plenty of hidden emotions. We know the Randalls have them galore, and the Cooks, Buckleys and Sanders all nurse their own. All centred on John Wilbourne, magnificent actor and perhaps sex-driven middle-aged man.'

Peter pounced on that. 'We know he was super attractive to women, but are we sure he was emotionally as well as sexually involved? Evidence, please.'

'Well, there's Rowena—'

'We don't know he returned her passion. Or Brenda's. Case dismissed.'

'Worried about your concert?' Tony Beane had come up behind them, making Georgia jump.

'It does cross our minds with this sale going through,' Peter said cheerfully.

'Thought it was Georgia on your mind,' Tony grinned as he cracked the familiar joke. 'Don't worry. I doubt even my father-in-law could get the sale through in two months. The surveyors will be crawling through every cavity and testing every beam for death watch beetles.'

'How did they get that name?' Georgia remarked idly. 'I've always wondered. Because they bring death to the beams or walk at dead of night?'

'The beams have got plenty of life in them even if some of it's woodworm. But they're good for another few hundred years,' Tony said. 'Mind you, not all the beams are exposed and I find new ones from time to time. Medieval mysteries, they are. I'm still hoping to find Cecilia tucked away some time or other.' He pulled a face. 'Better get my skates on or I'll lose the chance.'

'Bernie said you both might get jobs in the new hotel, for a while at least.'

'Did she?' he shrugged. 'Why not? Got to keep the old Porsche in the style to which it's become accustomed. Trouble is, Bernie doesn't want to upset the Planters but you can't please everyone. Anyway, no need to worry about that concert. It will be good publicity for the new hotel.'

Georgia hadn't thought of that. Two celebrated musicians, a distinguished audience. But she felt inexplicable anger at Rick's concert being publicity. Would *he* have wanted that? Then she came to her senses. He wouldn't have cared a jot. Nevertheless, a shadow remained. Perhaps Cobshaw's darker side was beginning to get to her.

Chapter Thirteen

A private reburial service at the graveside. That's what she and Peter had expected. But never underestimate Gerald Randall. Looking round St Nicholas's Church, Georgia estimated there were at least 150 people here, including Cobshaw villagers and a great many whom she did not recognise—probably the theatre dignitaries who had gathered in force for this Service of Reinterment. Peter's was not the only mobility scooter here and across the aisle there was at least one wheelchair.

Dave Cook and his family were sitting in front of Peter and herself at the rear of the church. 'Planters at the back, Tudors at the front,' he had joked as they had arrived.

As the coffin containing the remains of Sir John Wilbourne was borne in, Edward Colduggan and Gerald were walking directly behind it, and they were followed by six more mourners, amongst whom was Rowena Watts.

No doubt about it, this was a fully-fledged performance that Gerald had mounted. The press were here as well, with TV cameras operating from the small gallery where perhaps a rood screen had once stood. The service included eulogies to John Wilbourne's achievements and also short extracts from the Shakespearian roles for which he was known.

The service should have been moving, given that there were people here today who had actually known John Wilbourne, but somehow it wasn't. To Georgia, it had the air of being a staged performance, in which each member of the audience was playing a part. Moreover, this service was only one scene in this story. She felt guilty about thinking this, but a glance at Peter told her that he felt the same. His eyes had their professional alertness, and their own thoughts on those mourning John Wilbourne would be shared privately later.

The reinterment itself was to be private, but as guests invited to Cobshaw Hall they could go there to await their host. And then, Georgia thought with foreboding, the final act of this performance would begin.

A butler greeted them when she and Peter arrived at the Hall, which added to the staged atmosphere. Was that purely her imagination, Georgia wondered, or was it an entrée to the main performance? Surely not all of the fifty or so mourners present could be Poirot-style suspects either for Brenda's or John Wilbourne's murders? She tried to dismiss this out of place levity, but the sense of this being a theatrical performance still remained. The large framed photographs of John Wilbourne in his most famous roles contributed to that, but didn't entirely account for it.

The reinterment must have been a brief service, for only fifteen minutes later the Randall clan arrived. Eight in all, of whom she recognised only Gerald and Sophy. Now it was time for Peter and herself to play their parts. The first surprise was that Percival FitzRichard was here—the last person Georgia would have expected to see at a Randall gathering and the only Planter as far as she could see.

'A Tudor beanfeast, that's all this is,' Percival muttered to her.

Unfortunately for him, Gerald overheard this. 'Typical Plantagenet,' he snorted. 'What do you want? Bosworth field all over again? Too bad, we Tudors won.'

Percival looked as though he were about to explode, but to give him credit, he rallied. 'Not today, Randall,' he replied with dignity, sweeping off his ancient Homberg hat (from which he had obviously refused to be parted at the door). Georgia watched him as he stalked off towards the long table in the entrance hall, which was well stocked with drinks and sandwiches.

A change of subject was obviously called for. 'Who else is here who would have remembered John Wilbourne?' she asked Gerald.

Gerald looked pleased. 'You'll find out. Have to keep some surprises up my sleeve. This is the last chapter, eh?'

Georgia was already dizzy—and it wasn't the alcohol. She was steering clear of that. Abstinence hadn't helped though. In the half hour since they'd been here, she had met nobody who could be deemed a 'surprise' and she was beginning to think that they'd been wrong to hope for a conclusion to this case today. Perhaps Gerald had no such Poirot plan in mind for today. No unfortunate soul would be exposed as the murderer. No police would rush in for a triumphant denouement. Perhaps all these people were here only to remember John Wilbourne, whether they knew him in the flesh or only on stage or film.

This huge room, dating back to the eighteenth century, must once have been a grand drawing-room and in a way it still was. Its Persian rugs, Chinese fire screens and Indian jardinières contrasted with the serviceable Chesterfield sofas and very English Queen Anne tables, and yet somehow the combination worked. Georgia could see Sir Edward sitting in an easy chair, and Percival scowling by a window. Rowena Watts was busy sweeping from group to group and Peter was impatiently waiting for the opportunity to talk to her.

A rap on the table signalled that Gerald was about to speak. The noise of chatter gradually quietened. Was this one of the surprises he'd planned? Georgia held her breath as he began to thank everyone for attending, including—judging by his pause this was his pièce de résistance—'Mrs Elizabeth Atkins, John Wilbourne's former wife.' He waved his hand towards the wheelchair's occupant.

A surprise indeed, and a huge step forward for Marsh & Daughter. Georgia could sense Peter's excitement was as great as her own. Edward Colduggan, she deduced, could well have played an active role in this development. She could see Elizabeth Atkins clearly now, frail and hunched but very much part of the proceedings. She must be well over ninety, if she married John in 1944. This, Georgia thought, was where the performance ended and real life might take over. She debated whether she and Peter should barge over to talk to her or wait for a better moment. Their host settled it for them.

His speech concluded, Gerald made straight for them. 'I've good news, Elizabeth would like to speak with you.' He beamed as though he were solely responsible for bestowing this honour upon them.

Peter gravely thanked him before he and Georgia made their way through the throng of guests to join Elizabeth. Despite her age, her neat grey hair, keen eyes, and smile left Georgia in no doubt that this was no ordinary courtesy on Elizabeth's part.

Somehow, seeing her made it easier for Georgia to imagine John Wilbourne as a young man. The dozen or so photographs that Sophy had lent to Peter and herself now came alive even though they had mainly been of his schooldays or family groups. There were only two of his acting career—one of his first Hamlet, taking a bow with Ophelia at the end of the performance and one of a very early Romeo with his then Juliet. In one of the family group photographs, however, John was pictured with a young woman who might be Elizabeth, Georgia thought, and here she was with them now.

'You're Marsh & Daughter,' she greeted them with obvious pleasure. 'I've read some of your books. You establish the truth behind mysteries of the past, don't you? And Gerald told me you are doing your best to unravel what happened to my John.' There was an urgency in her voice, Georgia noticed, even though she spoke in little more than a whisper.

'We are indeed Marsh & Daughter,' Peter replied, and Georgia could see that the two had already bonded. That didn't always happen with Peter. 'I believe his death was a deliberate murder, not just an accident hastily covered up. Were you present the evening of the play?'

'No. We'd married in 1944, a wartime marriage when haste was advisable and as a result of that haste came divorce in 1949.'

'You fell out of love?'

Elizabeth laughed at that. 'Not me. Nor John. He only had one true love though, and that was the stage. I couldn't live with it. There were three in our marriage, as Princess Diana so memorably said. He had a great passion for women—always blondes like myself, which I took as a compliment—but he moved from woman to woman. Always fair-haired. Like that woman over there.'

Georgia followed the direction of her eyes. It led to Rowena Watts, who had given one of the tributes at the service. She was a blonde, though surely by now coloured by art and not nature. Perhaps Brenda too had once been blonde, although when she and Peter met her she had been steely grey. No colourings for Brenda, who believed in plain truth, Georgia reflected.

'Do you know of anyone who could have hated him so much as to kill him?' Peter asked gently.

She considered this, relaxed now. 'No, but he had a strange side did my John. He truly loved the stage, but on occasion he would wander off as though in search of some role, whether in film, on stage or TV, that he longed to conquer. When he apparently disappeared in 1959, I assumed that's what had happened for a while.'

'Not another woman?'

'Possibly, but that would have bored him in the end. He was fully aware that he was God's gift to women and that he could move on when he chose and so he took advantage of it. At first, it counted in my favour that I wasn't part of his theatrical world. I was the exception—but it didn't work out. Over there—' she indicated Rowena again—'she was one of his ladies. He'd have tired of her though. I didn't remarry until after John's disappearance, and I had heard about Rowena's role in his life. But she was very young then, of course. Naughty of John.' She paused and the urgency returned as she added, 'Find out what happened, Mr Marsh, Miss Marsh. Did *she* take revenge on him?'

'That we don't yet know. But we will,' Peter assured her.

Elizabeth's attention flickered towards Gerald who was bearing down on them again, and Peter adroitly manoeuvred them in the direction of Rowena Watts before Poirot could take centre stage. Rowena, to Georgia's surprise, looked pleased to see them. That might have been because she had been talking to Edward Colduggan, and perhaps that had not worked out too well. Perhaps today both were being forced to remember earlier and not necessarily pleasant times. On one's own it is easier to ignore the past, as Georgia knew all too well from the disaster of her own first short marriage. But being faced with a very living memory of that day in 1959 might be a different matter for both Rowena and Sir Edward, thrusting them back to who they were when they first knew each other. Georgia remembered once meeting two war veterans, one a sergeant, the other his commander, a major. Despite the decades that had passed since they served together, each of them slipped uncomfortably back into their former roles.

Could that be the case with these two? Edward Colduggan was an established young actor in those days, and Rowena a relative newcomer aged nineteen or twenty, perhaps in her first starring role.

'A lovely service,' the mature Rowena observed warmly to them.

'Your tribute in particular,' Peter said. 'Both gracious and informative.'

Rowena inclined her head. 'An honour.' A pause. 'Are you any further ahead in your investigation?'

'It's a slow process,' Peter fenced, speedily switching the focus. 'Partly owing to the death of Brenda Randall of course, or Brenda Parsons as she was in 1959. We're told you telephoned her shortly before her death.'

She smiled—prepared of course for this. It was not a surprise to her. 'Merely to commiserate with her on the discovery of John's remains. We shared an admiration for him.'

Plus a big fight over him, Georgia thought. 'I do hope we'll be seeing more of you now that Howard Green is buying the old pub,' she said earnestly. 'He tells us you know each other.'

'You may indeed see me again,' Rowena said, a trifle coolly. 'Howard is proposing to offer me slots for recitations, or perhaps perform in plays here on the history of Cobshaw and the Maid of Kent. I'm hoping my schedule will permit me to take him up on his offer.'

A sure sign that such offers weren't too common now, Georgia thought, and then upbraided herself for being catty.

'About the Plantagenets?' Peter asked.

'Of course,' Rowena almost snapped, before retrieving the situation, clearly on guard now. 'My mother was a close friend of Serena FitzRichard, who was, as you must know by now, born in the Maid of Kent pub.'

'Did your mother know Serena FitzRichard before she married? She left here at some point after the war started in 1939, but we're interested in finding out why she left. Just wanting to help the war effort,' Georgia asked, 'or because of a broken relationship with a villager, perhaps someone called Sam Buckley?'

Rowena's willingness to co-operate was waning rapidly. 'I don't recall why she left, but then I never met her. She died in the 1950s, I believe. Why are you are so interested in all these details, when you claim to be investigating John's death?'

Peter speedily dealt with that. 'There's an old nursery rhyme which tells us that for want of a nail in the end the kingdom was lost. We like collecting nails just in case.'

'This one is more likely a nail in the coffin for your case,' Rowena retorted. 'What *is* your case exactly? Does Brenda Randall's murder come into it?'

'We're leaving that to the police and our host,' Peter said lightly. 'He seems intent on solving both.'

'A dangerous path,' she commented, but they had lost her attention. Rowena was peering at something happening at the doorway into the entrance hall.

The noise level in the room was rising, Georgia realised, and there was movement. Peter immediately began pushing forwards towards the source of the hubbub as guests crowded round the doorway.

'Time for Poirot's big reveal?' Peter hissed back at her as she managed to reach him.

Perhaps, but there was no sign of Gerald, and the racket coming from the entrance hall intensified. Surely that was Gerald himself shouting—and banging too? The crowd parted just enough for Georgia to see him framed in the doorway, yelling in anger. This was surely nothing to do with Poirot.

'Here, you, Marsh! Where the devil are you?'

'Over here,' Peter shouted sharply, as his scooter was held back by the crowd. 'What's wrong?'

Georgia tried to push a way through for Peter to follow her, her alarm rising. This wasn't like Gerald and now that she and Peter were closer she could see that Sophy, who was supporting Gerald, was looking very white.

'The fools,' Gerald snarled to them and the now silent guests. 'The police. They've arrested Mick Buckley for Brenda's murder. They've got the wrong man and I haven't even made my speech.'

Chapter Fourteen

'So where,' Peter asked blankly, as they left the Hall, 'does that leave us? Better or worse off? And why on earth arrest Mick Buckley?'

Georgia groaned. 'For worse, if the police really have enough evidence to charge him. *If* he's guilty it could leave us out on a limb. They'll say it's mere coincidence that Brenda was killed so soon after John Wilbourne's remains were found.'

'We'd have to prove them wrong. But what possible motive could Mick have for Brenda's murder? Just so that he and his family could move into Cobshaw Cottage?'

'Murder has been committed for less,' Georgia replied. 'I agree though. He's too fond of his own skin to risk it.'

'A spur of the moment attack on his part?'

'Anything's possible but strangling someone with a scarf isn't that spur of the moment. And incidentally,' Georgia added, slowing down to permit a hedgehog to conclude his stately crossing of the road, 'where is our liaison officer? It's Jack Cotton's case and we're not officially involved.' The call to Gerald had been Mick's permitted call from the police station to appeal for his help. As they left the Hall, Gerald had been calling his Canterbury solicitors, while Sophy had rushed round to support Mick's wife.

'I agree Jack's within his rights,' Peter conceded. 'Mick's arrest and Brenda's death are outside our permitted line of enquiry. And we haven't yet found any link between her murder and Wilbourne's. There may not be one.'

'Even so,' Georgia said in frustration, 'a hint from him would have been helpful. Instead, they've slammed the door on us and Jack Cotton is helping to keep it shut.'

'He's young,' Peter said indulgently. 'For Jack, history is over and done with. Only the present counts—and his own future. Nevertheless, Mick Buckley's arrest is a major development so I can't see why—'

She guessed what was coming. 'Because we don't know what evidence Jack is basing it on. I know but—'

'A call to Will?'

'Diplomatically risky.'

'True. Jack it is then. I'll ring from the office then you can hear what's going on—unless you need to get home.'

A vision of Luke who would undoubtedly be patiently awaiting her arrival was guiltily pushed aside. The chances were small, but if there was any way at all of getting more news or even background on Mick Buckley she wanted to know right away.

Unfortunately, there proved to be another hitch. As she and Peter arrived at Haden Shaw, they found Elena awaiting their arrival. She flew into the office as soon as she heard their return.

'Darlings,' she said soberly. 'Such terrible news.'

'Mick Buckley,' Georgia said. 'Yes, we're trying to—'

'Who? No. *Jill.*'

'What about her?' Georgia asked, alarmed. She had a horrible feeling that she wasn't going to like this.

'She's been offered her old position back at that university in the States. It's the last straw. Mark is so upset. He can't and doesn't want to go. She wants to leave in time for the autumn semester.' Elena burst into tears.

That meant Jill would be leaving this summer to get settled in with the children. How *could* she? 'Does Luke know about this yet?' Georgia asked anxiously as she tried to comfort her mother.

'I don't know. It was Mark who rang me.'

'I have to go,' Georgia said abruptly, as the ramifications of this news threatened to overwhelm her. She needed to be at Luke's side as soon as she could.

'You go, I'll ring Jack Cotton,' Peter said, as she hugged Elena in a vain attempt at convincing her all would be well.

Her journey back to Medlars seemed endless, and Luke must have heard the car for he was waiting at their front door. 'Yes, I've heard,' he said without preamble. One look at her face must have told him why she was here.

'Can you do anything?' she asked hopelessly. Fond though she was of Jill, the lady was not for turning, as Margaret Thatcher famously said.

'I can try.' The tone of his voice confirmed that he thought the situation was as bad as she did.

'And the children?'

'She'll sort that out. When she's set on something she gets it done.'

'The lady with a tiger's heart at times,' Georgia said bitterly. 'Shakespeare always has a word for it.'

'I seem to remember Coriolanus addressed his wife as "My Gracious Silence",' Luke said gloomily. 'No such luck where Jill's concerned.'

'There's still time.' But they both knew that time wasn't what was needed. The silence was broken by the phone ringing.

'I rang Jack Cotton,' Peter said without preamble when she answered it. 'Depressing. Superficially friendly, but the door's locked. Then Will rang me back. Less depressing. He was in co-operative mode, but for our ears only. Mick Buckley had a meeting with Brenda that evening. He was seen going to the well with Brenda around nine o'clock, and several witnesses heard him declare his intention of doing so.'

'What on earth were they doing there at that time?'

'Mick Buckley isn't the brightest of people, but he surely could have thought up a better story than the one he's produced,' Peter said. 'You'll love it. It was to discuss a mutual way forward for the future of the well.'

'But they're both Tudor sympathisers, so they wouldn't have fallen out about it.'

'Ah, but the ownership is now in open dispute. The Buckleys do still have a claim on it.'

Georgia remembered Mick's passing remark about that. 'Surely he wouldn't pursue that? He works for the Randalls and wants Gerald's help over his arrest.'

'It's a good bargaining chip if one wanted a pay rise—or a new home,' Peter pointed out. 'Will and Jack think he was using the claim on the well angle to "persuade" Brenda to move out of Cobshaw Cottage so he could move in. And then there's the question of Cecilia's remains, which weren't—in Mick's view—buried there, but Brenda believed they might have been. That was on the grounds that Cecilia was murdered by Plantagenet sympathisers who might have wanted to add to their hatred of the Tudors by burying her either in or close by the well of which she was so fond. That's why she wouldn't ever be moving from Cobshaw Cottage, she told Mick. It was her duty to protect the well.'

'I suppose that's a convincing story,' Georgia said doubtfully. 'But why did he have to meet her at that time of night?'

'Brenda was, according to Mick's story, in a strange mood, describing the well as Cecilia's sacred place. Mick disagreed, saying his father brought him up to avoid the place as it was sinister, not sacred. She insisted they went to the well together and she would explain to him exactly where she believed Cecilia's remains could be. Something to do with the alignment of the stars. Unlike Mick, his father had also been convinced the remains were at the well.'

'What happened when Mick got to the well though?' Georgia asked. 'What's the police's story? Did he lose his temper with Brenda and strangle her?'

'According to him, he did lose his temper but stomped off and left her there alive.'

'Do we go with that?' Georgia asked, thinking about it from their own point of view. If Mick had indeed strangled Brenda then there was no link with John Wilbourne. If he didn't... that vital link still had to be found.

A pause. 'Let's sleep on it,' Peter said at last. 'And as regards Jill,' he added reluctantly, 'we can't do much about it, my love, except mop up the pieces afterwards.'

Georgia tossed and turned. 'A plague o' both your houses.' She must have cried out in her sleep, because Luke leaned across with a comforting arm, which half woke her up.

'Forget Shakespeare,' he murmured. 'Worry about him tomorrow.'

And now tomorrow had come, she thought ruefully on Wednesday morning. She'd go straight over to join Peter. Luke was burying himself in work, with another local history on links with Jane Austen and Charles Dickens to get ready for press. It was familiar territory: problems with length, photographs, copyrights, quotations etc. How at the moment she envied him.

'The link,' Peter declared as soon as she arrived at Haden Shaw.

'You've found it?' she asked incredulously.

'No,' he admitted. 'Not *the* link. But if it's actually in the deeds that only a Plantagenet can inherit, then Howard Green's claim could be invalidated. Just suppose Brenda had discovered that possibility. Then there would be a motive for silencing her. Agreed?'

Georgia frowned. 'No. How could it be invalidated? Even if it could, as a Tudor herself Brenda would have been pleased he wasn't a Plantagenet.'

'She wouldn't have been pleased if it scuppered the whole deal or if he insisted on going ahead regardless. And Brenda wasn't the kind of person to turn a blind eye, whatever was at stake. She'd have spilled the beans.'

'She didn't spill any to us,' Georgia pointed out crossly. Where was this red herring leading?

'But she was very, very worried about something when we met her. And I think it was this.' Peter waved his notebook in triumph. 'We only found records of Serena's baptism, but I've managed to look at her birth certificate—she was born in the village of Harting, not a million miles from Cobshaw.'

'I don't see the connection,' she said obstinately. 'That doesn't mean she was illegitimate. We know that it was Montague and his wife Elspeth who were his parents in the baptism register, but whose name was on the birth certificate?'

'Montague FitzRichard. Mother Elspeth FitzRichard.'

'I'm lost. What's the problem?'

'There may be none,' Peter said smugly. 'But consider two factors: Serena was born in July 1919. Her baptism was September 1919. The marriage between Montague and Elspeth had taken place in January 1919.'

'Five or six months. Premature birth?'

Peter remained undaunted. 'Possibly. Second factor: Serena has an interesting second forename, Serena Fairlee FitzRichard. And, in another triumph of investigation, I discovered there was a gentleman by the name of Fairlee in the 1911 census, living in Harting.'

Georgia considered this. 'That still doesn't prove anything. And anyway, how would this have any connection to a murder in 1959?'

'Don't get impatient. I don't know of any connection. But it's another link in the chain, even if that chain is loose.'

She struggled to see where he might be heading: 'You mean a chain linking John Wilbourne and Rowena Watts to Brenda Randall and Howard Green. If so, the link between them has to be the Maid of Kent—and I mean the pub, not Cecilia.'

Peter sighed. 'Dear partner in crime, you're right. Though we can include Cecilia if you wish.'

On Wednesday morning, Peter broke the news to Georgia that Jill was willing to meet them for a coffee at her Canterbury home to discuss her plans, and after lunch they would be meeting Rowena Watts at her Canterbury hotel at her request. Reason unknown. This was irritating, although Georgia conceded that the less time she had to get worked up before they met Jill the better.

'I'll drive,' Peter told her appeasingly. 'You can buy lunch.'

The morning's discussions with Jill left both Peter and Georgia depressed—and not because of any heated clashes. There were none. All arguments against her plans were given due consideration by Jill, but politely rejected as invalid, until Georgia was at screaming point. Family visits were usually fun, but today the children were at school and she was painfully aware that time could be running out for their usual chats, romps and games.

The meeting with Rowena Watts at her five-star hotel was equally frustrating. It wasn't clear why she had asked to see them, which made

Georgia suspicious. Rowena hadn't shown much enthusiasm for chatting to them at Cobshaw Hall, and so Georgia suspected that she saw this as a legitimate opportunity for her to delve back into past recollections, one or more of which had made her uneasy. Talking about them might smooth the rough edges of her memory, and there was always the hope that lurking amongst those memories might be a few gems of vital information about John Wilbourne. Polite conversation over tea and coffee in the hotel lounge, however, produced nothing for a while. And then it spilled out from Rowena in a rush.

'I saw you talking to Elizabeth at Gerald's reception,' she said abruptly. 'She had no idea what John was truly like. They were married for a very short time and she had nothing to do with the stage, its loves, its passions, its problems, its rewards. But I shared so much with John, we were both lovers and partners.' There was a defiant note in her voice.

'There was a big age difference between you,' Peter stated more bluntly than Georgia would have dared.

'Age is immaterial to those who love the stage,' Rowena retorted immediately.

'We've been told that Brenda Randall—Parsons as she was then—was also in love with John and that's why you and she had a fight on the night that John disappeared,' Peter persevered.

This was also dismissed. 'Unfortunately, yes. John had no regard for her, however. On the contrary. She was harassing him unbearably with her attentions and then had the nerve to attack me.' She hesitated. 'I wanted to ask you—is it correct that the Maid of Kent can only be bought by someone with Plantagenet blood in their veins?'

'Apparently so,' Peter told her, 'so it's lucky that your mother was friendly with Serena FitzRichard otherwise Howard might never have discovered the connection with the Maid of Kent.'

Rowena stared at them as though this had occurred to her for the very first time, but her reply was a lacklustre, 'I suppose so.'

When they finally left Canterbury, it was late afternoon. 'What on earth was all that about?' Georgia said, as Peter started up the engine. 'It gets us no further, save that perhaps she too has doubts about this Plantagenet blood, but that means she can't have any firm evidence. We're on our own over that.'

'I agree. This strikes me as a pretty useless day all round so far,' he replied. 'We got nowhere with Jill and nothing positive from Rowena. She strikes me as a lady who's settling old scores and living in her own fantasy that John Wilbourne was in love with her—nothing can come between that and her illusions.'

'Illusions about what happened in 1959?'

'Who knows?' A pause. 'Fancy a drink? We'll be passing the old Maid shortly.'

'Why not?' Georgia replied obligingly. Perhaps Peter had something in mind, she realised, although personally she could do without another trip to the Maid of Kent.

When they arrived, Percival and Howard Green were sitting outside in the early evening sunshine. Georgia groaned. She could do without this too, but it was too late to turn round.

Percival waved a lordly hand. 'Over here. Come and join us. We've something to celebrate, haven't we, Howard?'

'We have indeed.' Howard stood up to greet them. 'The contract for the Maid of Kent is signed and sealed.'

That was quick work. Georgia was amazed. That meant they probably already had it drawn up and ready to sign last week.

'Plantagenets win,' Percival crowed. 'There'll be a separate deal for the well with the hotel owning it, and the blasted Randalls will be allowed to trample all over it whenever they like. I suppose that's fair enough.'

Was it? Georgia's alarm bells were ringing. 'But what about the village's claim to own it?' she asked, trying not to display her reservations too obviously 'And what about the Buckleys' claim?'

Percival speedily dismissed this. 'Nothing to that. Can't trust the Buckleys. One of them did a bit of work for my dad once.'

So much for the Buckleys being as thick as thieves with Percival's father, Georgia thought. They'd obviously fallen out—could that have been over Serena? she speculated. Another leap, of course, but worth bearing in mind.

Howard remained diplomatic. 'The Buckley claim to the well is disputed. As for the village, there is a public footpath alongside the area we will own, which allows views of the well. So, it's all settled, isn't it, Percival?'

'Done and dusted,' he replied complacently, rising to his feet. 'I'll be off to spread the news.' He paid his farewells and set off happily towards the bar.

Georgia watched him go, realising to her surprise that she was developing rather an affection for Percival FitzRichard and she hoped he wasn't going to fall headlong into a heffalump pit of Howard Green's design.

Peter didn't waste time. 'Do you have any doubts over your Plantagenet heritage?' he asked Howard bluntly. 'It seems very likely there are some.'

Howard's smile wavered. 'Ah. I see the detectives have been at work. Now that Mr FitzRichard has left us, allow me to explain the position, Mr Marsh. Should there be any suggestion that Serena was not Montague FitzRichard's daughter, I would point out that there is no legal proof of that.'

'A DNA test, perhaps?' Peter murmured.

'Even if it revealed that I lacked any FitzRichard genes, that would not affect a legal birth certificate.'

'But what about Bernie's offer—?' Georgia began. 'It would affect that.'

'That's all settled. She and Tony will continue to work for the new hotel.'

Very well, she'd probably lost that point, Georgia conceded, but there were others. At least Bernie and Tony would have a future—and Tony could continue to show off his Porsche. And, she thought, it was now clear that there was indeed every chance that Serena was not Montague's child.

'And Brenda?' Georgia asked. 'Could that be what was troubling her in those last few days?'

Howard was still unfazed. 'I've no idea, alas. However, Mrs Randall's concern over the question of my Plantagenet blood is sadly irrelevant, especially as Mr Buckley has now been arrested for her murder.'

She'd lost ground again, Georgia thought ruefully. Why were slick businessmen always able to slip their poison into their prey like snakes? At least the Buckleys and the Cooks of this world fought in the open. She was becoming aware of a rumbling like thunder in the distance. What else was this dispiriting day going to produce?

'Incidentally,' Howard said, preparing to follow Percival inside, 'if it's of any interest to you both, let me add to your research. John Fairlee of Harting was a gardener and a married man.'

Peter was good at keeping his cool and was clearly managing to do so now, Georgia thought thankfully.

'The baby,' Howard continued smoothly, 'was born in the home of Elspeth's mother. Montague FitzRichard himself registered the birth.

And now, if you'll excuse me, I shall look around my company's latest real estate acquisition. Changes will have to be made.'

'The Plantagenet rooms renamed as Tudors?' Peter asked straight-faced.

Howard did not bother to reply. The rumbling noise was growing now and it wasn't thunder. It was human noise. Alarmed, Georgia stood up to look in the direction from which it seemed to be coming and in the distance she could see a large group of people advancing up the road. Fifty, perhaps more, with banners held high. Were they heading for the Maid of Kent, she wondered uneasily, or for the turn leading to Cobshaw Hall? Whichever it was, they were probably Planters and this was no place for the Marshes to be caught, here with the Tudor opposition. They risked finding themselves trapped in yet one more battle zone, and this time it threatened to be more serious. It was no place for Peter's scooter either. Time to go—quickly.

As they drove along the road to Haden Shaw, they passed the open gates to Cobshaw Hall, and in the distance Georgia could see the group must already have reached the junction with the track to Cobshaw Cottage. Her alarm grew. Even in the car, they could hear the noise. It was increasing all the time with voices cheering and chanting, the sound of a mob bent on its mission.

Chapter Fifteen

'Trouble ahead!' Georgia jumped out of the car as soon as Peter pulled up. With Peter in full accord, she'd turned round and driven into the Hall's grounds to see what was happening and they had pulled up at the junction. It clearly wasn't the Hall that the mob was making for. Dusk was beginning to fall now and as she peered into the fading light there was no doubt what its target was. The well. The noise coming from that direction was already loud and increasing all the time with shouting, chanting and what sounded like the banging of pans. In front of her she could see stragglers hurrying towards the mob along the track in front.

'They're carrying hammers,' Peter yelled. 'I'll call the police.'

Go or stay? Georgia did her best to push fear aside. *Think!* Something was coming to a head tonight, something that might help find Brenda's killer, or perhaps explain the darkness that had hung over Cobshaw so long, or even find the truth about John Wilbourne's murder. She had to stay, even though every gremlin in town was dancing up and down inside her. Peter must go, but she'd surely be safe if she could get into the woodland and out of the way of the mob. And the police would be here soon. In a split second she had made her decision.

She leapt out of the car and leant through the open window. 'You drive back to the Maid of Kent, Peter. I'll see what's happening and come over to join you. It's only a five-minute walk. We can have supper there, if you're hungry.' She saw the lingering doubt on his face. 'Don't worry—I'm not their target.'

Peter still looked doubtful, but she was adamant. If this mob turned nasty, she could gauge the danger and make a quick getaway, but Peter might get caught on his scooter or in the car.

'I don't want to leave you,' he said anxiously. 'But there's no need for you to stay. I'm firming up on who killed Brenda, and as far as we know this place doesn't have anything to do with John Wilbourne.'

'We can't rule it out,' she said, finally convincing him. Right, she told herself. Time to dismiss gremlins and *go*. She set off in the wake of the crowd, acting on instinct. As she ran towards the crowd ahead of her, she was fighting second thoughts on the wisdom of what she was doing. It was worth the risk. It had to be as Brenda's murder was surely linked to the well and therefore perhaps John Wilbourne's too.

How had it happened that way? It wasn't as if this well was a sacred shrine, save for both Planters and Tudors connecting it with their own history. The Planters, however, seemed to think of it as a place haunted with its own secrets, a place to be avoided rather than respected. The obstinacy of the Tudors in clinging to their claim of ownership was even more puzzling. True, there was a commercial aspect for them if they turned it into a tourist attraction, but that didn't exactly satisfy her as an explanation.

No more time for that now. The noise ahead had turned into a steady chant and was growing louder still. As she reached Cobshaw Cottage Georgia could see the track to the well was blocked solid with protesters waving their banners. Peter was right. It looked as if they were armed with hammers What in heaven's name were they planning? She was beginning to pick up the words of the chant. Innocent enough words, but with a chilling edge of menace:

'Ding dong bell

'*Planters'* well.'

There was even more noise now and frequent crashes, with shouts taking the place of the chanting. What to do? There were more protesters than she'd thought. If she pushed ahead, she'd be swamped by this crowd, swept along with it, learn nothing and put herself in danger. She was scared enough already without taking greater risks.

Then she noticed that much of the fencing lining the road ahead had been torn down. Could she make it? Yes. A quick sprint and she could get to the shelter of the trees. The mob wasn't after her; it was intent on its own mission, she told herself. She'd risk it. *Now*! Deafened by the chanting, she edged to the side of the crowd now surging around her and then on to the grassy bank near the first pile of fencing. Grabbing a torn-down tree branch to steady herself, she managed to heave herself over it and then ran for the nearest bushes. Safety! Now to find out what was going on. She stumbled through the undergrowth to a point where she could glimpse the pond and the well in its middle.

She could see the mob too. It was spreading out around the pond's fencing and already showing signs of attacking it. And all the while that chanting continued. What was going on? There must be at least a hundred people here, maybe more, and she was increasingly aware that her high heels and a skirt weren't suitable attire for a free-for-all such as this threatened to be. The chanting was turning back into a general din, the shouting and yelling intensifying. She pushed her way through a few more bushes and now she could see all too clearly what was happening.

'There she goes,' came a distinct cry amid the general racket. Was that Louis Sanders' voice? She could just about make him out in the dusk, punctuated with flickering lamp lights and torches. Cheers were mixed with the shouts and there were other sounds she couldn't immediately identify. Then she saw all too clearly that men with sledgehammers were hard at work knocking down the wall around the pond, and she could hear the sound of water beginning to gush out. Where she stood the ground was slightly raised, but near the pond some of the crowd were edging back away from the water's onslaught. Others were pushing their way forward over the rubble and towards the well at the centre.

Both men and women were wading through the remaining water, more and more of them as the pond walls continued tumbling. Cheers deafened her ears together with shouts of 'Ours'—'We paid for it, we keep it'. She couldn't see him, but she recognised Dave Cook's voice appealing for calm, but it had no effect. Fear flooded back as a surge of protesters swept up from behind her, forcing her forwards with them until she was close to a point where another section of wall had just been demolished. The remaining water was gushing out as the hammers struck the clay-lining. As the protesters in front of her pushed back to avoid it, Georgia felt herself being knocked off balance on to the broken bricks and rubble, grazing her knees as she fell forward on to the stones and mud.

And then she saw it. The water had either dislodged or revealed what had been lying beneath it.

Bones. A human hand outstretched.

The police were here now, thank heavens. Georgia was still weeping with relief at their arrival. Her yells to stop the sledgehammers' work had at last succeeded and Dave had regained command, establishing some sense of calm and guarding the area around the bones. The water from the pond had mostly drained out now, leaving a muddy plateau in the increasing darkness, although police lights were puncturing the gloom. Some of the protesters had drifted away after the initial chaos, leaving only a hard core of observers. To most of the crowd what she had seen were merely old bones, she realised. But the hand was probably part of a human skeleton, yet to be unearthed. Already slightly more of the hand had been exposed by the water, indicating that the arm bones lay beyond.

At first a murmur had run round the crowd: 'Cecilia!'

Could this possibly be the remains of a sixteenth-century woman? Had Cecilia really been found at last? Georgia was no expert, but that hand and what she had seen of the arm didn't look over four centuries old. Nevertheless, it was odd that its discovery had brought such an almost ominous silence from the crowd.

Why? she wondered. A human hand would surely normally have brought forth lots of speculation on whose it was and what it was doing here. But there was nothing normal about Cecilia's well and this pond. Most of the crowd had drifted away after the initial uproar and those who remained here were probably all Planters, though a low murmuring was replacing the silence. No Randalls would be present. They were probably still in Cobshaw Hall oblivious to what was going on.

Jack Cotton had appeared rapidly after the arrival of the first policeman—perhaps, Georgia guessed, because of the coincidence of this discovery so soon after Brenda's death. When he noticed her, she expected his usual offhand reaction, but this time she was mistaken. He looked genuinely concerned when he saw her. 'You don't look too good,' he said. 'Want us to run you home when we're done? That won't be long.'

'Thanks, but no. Peter—' She realised to her horror that she had forgotten him, and he was no doubt tranquilly still awaiting his supper. 'He's at the Maid of Kent. I'll call him. What's happening?'

'We've dug further,' he told her. 'There's talk of its being the hand of this Cecilia woman who keeps popping up in this place and we've had a hard job dissuading the locals to keep away.'

Cecilia? That didn't make sense. 'She'd have been lying here since Tudor times if it's hers, and she'd have been found when they built the pond.'

'The archaeologist is here now,' he replied. 'He'll give us a clue about the date. They don't look like ancient bones to me, though.'

Georgia thought once more of the strange atmosphere during her wait for the police to arrive. It had been a desolate sight. Mud, pools of water, broken bricks—and the onlookers. They weren't talking. Just waiting, it seemed to her. What for? Mere curiosity? Were they expecting something—or had it just been uncovered?

The waiting dragged on. 'You all right, Geoff?' Dave asked at one point. Georgia hadn't noticed him earlier, but of course all the Planters would be present.

Geoff Sanders didn't answer. He was staring at the remains of the pond and Georgia remembered his stories about it and the fête before the war. 'I was here as a nipper. I remember that all right,' he said at last.

Here we go again! But this time, Georgia thought, it might be different. Perhaps the reason for the villagers' avoidance of the well might at last come to light.

'Wouldn't let me stay here,' Geoff reminisced. 'Dad yelled at me. Bad times, eh, Dave?'

Dave managed a grin. 'I wasn't around when you were a nipper, Geoff. But my mum and dad wouldn't let me come here either. I thought they were scared I'd drown in the pond, but it wasn't that. It was village feud stuff, even then.'

Georgia looked at the scene around them: police moving around, more cars drawing up, newcomers arriving and the Planters just standing waiting. For what though?

'The parish council built the pond around that well,' Dave continued. 'But why? I've looked at their minute books but there's no clue to that.'

Geoff took his time to reply. 'Like I said,' he mumbled at last, almost as if talking to himself alone. 'Yes, they were bad times before that. Night of the fête, it was. It all went wrong.' He was beginning to get fired up. 'You remember?'

'I know something happened that night,' Dave said wearily. 'But I wasn't there. I wasn't even born then. My dad told me that well was special and it had to be protected always. He was on the council and after the war ended got that wall built round the pond to protect it. Old Jacob Randall was still alive then and agreed to it. All for it, he was, my dad said. It was for the villagers, both Planters and Tudors. But now the Tudors are selling it—and the Planters have been making their protest here tonight. Why? We've kept the well safe, just as my dad wanted. But knocking the wall down this way shows the truce they had when they built it is over. What was it all about, this truce? Do you know, Geoff?'

'We was all there, Dave. We still are because of our dads and granddads,' Geoff muttered as much to himself as Dave. 'Sam Buckley and all. He was there. She wasn't coming. Gave him the wrong message, so my dad said. Locked up she was. Said his lass weren't coming, weren't marrying him. So off he went. Never got over it. And then the war came.'

So that was it. Georgia felt like weeping on Serena's behalf. At last, the story was trickling out or at least part of it. If the 'she' was Serena then she'd been locked up, presumably in her room; Sam had been given a message that she had changed her mind so he had given up hope. Either then, or if he was called up for the war not long afterwards, he had married someone else. And Serena had left Cobshaw. That was all there was to Serena's story. A story that took Marsh & Daughter no further. No wonder Suspects Anonymous had been turning up so many red herrings in this case. They had just helped them add another to their list.

Georgia felt deflated. She just couldn't get enthused about the end of the story. It had come to a dead end, and yet she couldn't forget the Serena of Percival's memories, dancing, full of love and happiness, but instead she was doomed to the opposite at least until she left Cobshaw. But was that a romantic image of her own making? she wondered. Real life wasn't like that. No, sometimes real life *was* like that, she reminded herself. And for Marsh & Daughter on this occasion it was just another red herring.

The Maid of Kent was a short trek across the fields, but finally Georgia had accepted Jack Cotton's offer of a lift there and was glad she had done so. Peter's car was still in the car park thankfully, and the lights were on in the bar. There was no sign of him when she went in however, or of anybody else. No customers, no one at the bar. Probably because of the mob of course. There had been no reply to her phone which was odd. Nothing too unusual, she told herself. Peter often left his phone in his car, as taken in the context of the rest of the evening everything seemed odd.

Maybe Peter was with Bernie or Percival, or out with Tony in the garage. Late for that though. When she opened the door to the corridor it was in darkness, with no indication that anyone was around. She tried shouting but that brought forth nothing, so Peter must have gone to talk to Percival in his office, unless they'd gone to the private apartments upstairs. No, as he was expecting her Peter wouldn't have gone up there. With the help of her torch she managed to find the corridor light switch. The door leading to the garage was locked, which ruled out the possibility of Peter being with Tony out there, so she made her way to Percival's office. No reply to her knock on the door there and no light showing.

Had someone given Peter a lift home? If so, why? Could he have been taken ill? She felt panic rising. She'd had no text from him, so she rang Luke—who had heard nothing from him either. This was not good, or was she just tired from the whole evening's events and seeing bogeys where none existed?

Georgia felt her stomach tightening. Then she realised Percival and Peter must be together in Richard's Room. Of course. They could well have retreated there for a talk—that must be the answer. She wasn't sure she could remember the way as another fork presented itself and she was grateful for her torch so that she didn't have to search for more switches. Past Henry V, past the Princes in the Tower, and round the corner. It was looking so familiar now—and to her relief the door was open and the lights were on inside.

That was the end to normality. The room had changed. The pathway she remembered through the room was blocked with scattered boxes, ornaments, books and papers together with an overturned table. The huge armed statue of the man she had mistaken for Richard of Eastwell on her first visit was still there but was lunging towards a gaping hole next to the fireplace where the mural had been but was now swung back. It had not been part of the wall, but some kind of concealed entrance.

And there was something else amiss. Something that filled her with terror. She could see Peter's scooter lying upended in front of her and from inside that hole she could hear faraway voices. Where though? And what was that hole for? He couldn't have moved into that hole himself—he'd been dragged. *Dragged?* What did that imply? Was he dead?

Numb with fear, she rushed forward, realising the hole was the beginning of a short tunnel. She could hear Peter yelling out, now, surely in pain and fear, but *alive*. She needed help. Was it Percival in there? Tony? Bernie? A villager? Some of them must be within hearing distance—the private rooms weren't far away. But she had to get to Peter *now*. Phone? Take too long. Scream, shout, and *go*. A rush back to the entrance. Crying out for help, rushing to reach Peter, through the stifling hot stone-walled tunnel, still screaming as she made her way half crouching towards whatever awaited her.

The tunnel ended in a dark stone-walled room and there in the dim light coming from a lantern she could see Peter. And the worst nightmare of all hit her. He was lying flat on his back desperately trying to ward off his attacker, who was bent on strangling him. She had to get there! Quickly! Georgia's head swam. This is for real. He's kneeling on Peter's chest, he'll suffocate, he's seized his throat… Her feet were struggling to scramble over the uneven stones at the doorway into the room. Now she was there, in the room, only to be thrust aside by Bernie who miraculously appeared behind her and threw all her weight at Peter's would-be killer.

'Get out!' Bernie shouted at her. 'I'll deal with this. Call the police.'

What to do? She had to trust her? Whose side was Bernie on? She'd no choice. Georgia stumbled back along the tunnel. The police must still be nearby. Her adrenaline was working overtime. Ring Jack Cotton, dial 999, rush back to help Bernie.

Never had she needed Luke so much. Georgia could see Bernie shivering, white as chalk with Percival's arm round her. Georgia was numb, unable to think, unable to move from the armchair in the snug where the police had shepherded them, after a quick check by the paramedics.

'*Tony*,' Bernie was saying over and over again. 'Why?'

Georgia had no reply, herself in shock. Tony, Bernie's apparently placid, obliging, understanding, supportive husband, devoted to her and beyond that devoted to his Porsche. There was, she began to realise, only one reason for his attacking Peter—that Peter's solution to Brenda's murder on which he was 'firming up' had turned out to be correct.

'He must have been a Tudor, Bernie love,' Percival kept murmuring to his daughter.

Georgia looked at them dully. Tudors and Planters and their obsessions could wait. Peter was alive, that was all that mattered. Her call to Jack Cotton had brought him over in minutes. Peter was in hospital. Elena had been notified.

'He went crazy, pulled me off the scooter—that wall painting just slid open and he hauled me along. Dumped me down and was starting to strangle me,' Peter had managed to croak before the ambulance left. 'Look after Bernie, not me. I thought he was a sane murderer in his own way, but he's a madman. If it hadn't been for her and Jack Cotton that would have been the end of me.'

Jack Cotton. The young DI whom she'd once thought so offhanded, who had today been first on the scene, whom Georgia had met at the doorway, and with whom she'd raced through the pub and followed into that tunnel to find Bernie lying dazed on the floor while Tony was again intent on strangling Peter. Not once Jack Cotton arrived and went into action.

'Martial arts. Trained in Japan,' he told her briefly, as she had incoherently tried to thank him, while the back-up police dragged Tony away and the paramedics were dealing with Peter.

Peter had managed to gasp out a few words to her, describing

Tony as a *sane* murderer. Georgia had been struggling only with the nightmare of what she had just seen, her father about to be strangled. Now she had to go further into the nightmare—Tony had strangled Brenda, murdered her and tossed her into the pond. Was that *sane*?

Georgia had seen Tony's bewildered face while she was in that terrible room with Bernie as they tried to subdue him while waiting for the police. Bernie had been in her office behind the bar when Georgia had been calling out for help, and now looked on the point of complete collapse. And no wonder. Her husband Tony, whom she must have thought supported her in every way, was a murderer.

Tony had looked so genuinely puzzled as the police hauled him out and were about to escort him away. 'Can't you see, Bernie?' he said. 'We had everything tied up, you and me managing this hotel. I could have kept the Porsche, you'd have been proud of me. I'd have been someone in this village, not just running around at your dad's beck and call. But that woman Brenda was going to ruin the whole thing. She kept saying Howard had got it wrong and he hadn't any Plantagenet blood in him as Serena was not Montague's daughter. I couldn't let her do that, could I?' And now Bernie had to face the future, Georgia thought. Percival's arm was still tightly around her.

'My Brenda had principles,' he said to his daughter sadly. 'She would have told me about him not being one of us, a Plantagenet, even if that meant the end of all she wanted for the poor old Maid. If only she'd married me like I wanted and not that Tudor bloke. Tony wasn't like my Brenda, though. He wouldn't let his great chance of mixing with the posh nobs slip through his fingers just for the sake of a bit of history. Eh, Bernie?' Sadness changed to his familiar glare. 'He's a good-for-nothing Tudor at heart, he is.'

Just as Georgia thought she couldn't stand any more of this, blessedly she could see Luke coming through the door. *Luke.* Home. Tomorrow she could start again. But not tonight.

'Percival wants to pay us a visit,' Peter had told Georgia on the phone from hospital two days later. He had called to say that thankfully he'd had the all-clear and to ask for a lift home. 'I told him he could come at eleven o'clock Saturday.'

She and Luke had duly brought Peter home yesterday and were now in his office awaiting the arrival of Percival FitzRichard. Their temporary reprieve from Planters and Tudors was clearly over, Georgia thought wryly. She was still suffering from her bruises, although they were nothing compared with Peter's. He had won the battle with both his carer Margaret and with Elena (the issue being as to whose 'care' he was under) by disobeying orders from both not to think of work. And here he was. Georgia had had a similar battle with Luke who had insisted on driving her over to Haden Shaw.

'I know you've had two clear days to recover, but the after-effects of shock last a long time,' he said firmly. 'And,' he'd added to lighten her mulish mood, 'you and Peter have signed a contract with me for *The Case of the Missing Knight.* I have to look after my authors.'

He was right in one respect, Georgia thought. The after-effects of Wednesday night were not going to vanish yet.

'I'd worked it out,' Peter had told her in a still croaking voice. Luke had driven him home yesterday with her anxiously at Peter's side. 'The police had arrested Mick Buckley because of his meeting with Brenda that evening. He'd boasted freely about it in the pub. Tony must have decided his chance had come to rid himself of her meddling—whatever form that took—because he wasn't on duty that evening. When I told him I knew he'd killed Brenda, he was quite open with me about it—chiefly I suppose because he then planned to do the same to me,' he added wryly. 'I realised that there were only a certain number of people whom Brenda would trust enough to talk to by that well in the evening even if they turned up out of the blue, as Tony did after Mick's departure. Apart from Howard himself, Tony was the obvious candidate for having something material to lose if Howard's Plantagenet ancestry was a fake.'

'I see that,' Georgia had agreed. 'But it brings us back to the old question: why push her into the pond if he'd already killed her?' She'd been going to use the word strangled, but Peter's ordeal was still too raw to revive images of what he and Brenda had endured.

'I managed to get some kind of answer to that. He just shrugged, Georgia. I gathered it had been an act of contempt because she put principle before her own wishes.'

Now, they were safely here in Haden Shaw, back in the world of the Plantagenets and Tudors, Georgia thought with relief. Their only immediate problem was why Percival wanted to see them so urgently. They didn't have long to wait. At eleven o'clock promptly, Percival duly arrived, driving himself over in his ancient Morris Minor.

'I've come,' he informed them majestically, having divested himself of his raincoat and even the old Homburg hat, 'to make an apology for mistreatment on my premises by one of my staff.'

'Accepted,' Peter said graciously, while Georgia tried to keep a straight face. 'How's Bernie?'

'She'll recover,' Percival replied airily. 'I told her Tony was a Tudor all along, so that makes it easier for her. Says she might move away though. That's the reason I've come—as well as the apology,' he added quickly. 'I want you to dissuade her.'

'That's too difficult for comparative strangers like us to do,' Peter replied promptly, much to Georgia's relief.

'No, no. She respects you. Anyway, I have a plan,' Percival added smugly. 'I've heard from the police. They're charging Tony with Brenda's murder, so Bernie needs something to take her mind off all this upset. And I've a good plan for that.'

'Going to New Zealand to see her family?' Georgia asked.

'Bollocks. That's running away. No, much better to take her mind off things.'

'Additional staff to train?'

Percival brushed this aside. 'Yes, yes, but I mean something worthwhile. The bones! The hunt. What do you think of that, eh?' He sat back in triumph.

Bones? What on earth did he mean? Georgia was flummoxed. The hunt for what? 'But the bones found in the pond haven't been identified yet,' she began, 'and that's the—'

'*Cecilia's* bones,' Percival broke in eagerly. 'You could pretend to find them, Peter.'

Peter for once was thrown. '*Me*? But the police are handling that.'

'Not the bones in the pond. I mean hunt for Cecilia's in the room where Tony was having a go at you—my dad kept quiet about it. Never allowed me in there. You can tell Bernie you noticed something odd there while you were in it and go inside with her to track them down. They have to be somewhere like that. Call the press in to watch you. TV too. You can find something or other to satisfy them. And after all, Cecilia's around here somewhere. What do you say to that for a plan?'

'The answer's no,' Peter said forthrightly.

Chapter Sixteen

'First it's Percival and now we've had another summons from Gerald Randall,' Peter groaned. Percival had now left, and they still had a case to solve: John Wilbourne's. Georgia was all too well aware of that. 'It seems that despite all this kerfuffle Gerald is *still* intent on playing Poirot,' Peter continued. 'Can you believe it? He wants us to meet him on Tuesday afternoon, and I presume that's when he is going to announce he's solved the case of John Wilbourne, now that poor Brenda's seems wound up. Good luck to him, say I. Maybe he can work out what happened to his brother-in-law better than we can. You'll have to drive because of my aches and pains, but let's accept the invitation and we can pick up the pieces afterwards.'

'Who else is invited?' she asked with some trepidation.

'Sir Edward is still staying with him and we know that Rowena is still finding Canterbury a city of fascination. Which of course it is, but I somehow doubt she is merely sight-seeing for the fun of it. What can we deduce from that?'

A no-brainer. 'That both are interested in what we—or Gerald— might or might not have discovered?' Georgia pondered this for a moment and remembered her earlier brief plan. 'How about seeming to pander to Gerald by suggesting we hold a full reconstruction of the night of John Wilbourne's disappearance? Gerald could hold it at the Hall. Or,' it occurred to her, as the idea grew in her mind, 'we could rope Percival in—a good idea anyway—and use the open air theatre.'

Peter gazed at her as though she had solved the whole mystery in one go. 'Now that is what I call a brilliant idea—although it has the potential of going pear-shaped.'

'If that happens, we won't have lost anything. More to the point, though, would we gain anything from putting on this show?'

'We might. That's if we ensure the right people are there in the best Poirot tradition.' Peter paused for a moment. 'Let's go with it. I'll ring Gerald and Percival. By the way,' he added, 'Will Whittan dropped by last night. There was an almost complete skeleton recovered from the pond and it's been confirmed they aren't bones of antiquity, so there'll be an inquest. In all probability, they're twentieth century.'

'Not Cecilia's then,' Georgia said.

'Not unless she's changed century and sex too. They're male remains. Nothing to link them to our case though, as we would have heard if anyone disappeared from the village in 1959. Which we haven't. All we have is the implication that these bones found at the well might have something to do with that fête. That was twenty years earlier, of course, but we do have both a drama over the possible love affair of Serena and Sam Buckley, plus an unsolved mystery that happened about that time. A missing person: Dave Cook's uncle Brian. But that was during the war. I don't see how that could be tied up with our other glimpses into the fête. Sam Buckley, Serena FitzRichard and messages going astray?'

'It's worth thinking about though. We don't know exactly when he went missing so the bones at the well could be his in the absence of any other candidates,' Georgia said.

'Or Brian Cook might simply have been a war deserter who just couldn't face joining his ship. Possible. Either way, it's odd that no one noticed that he'd vanished from village life.' Peter had his 'cap that if you can' voice.

She did cap it. 'Not if he lived alone.'

'Hypothesis is the soul of sloppiness.'

'Or a flame of hope,' she maintained obstinately. 'I admit that doesn't help us over John Wilbourne.'

Peter was showing more interest. 'I grant you that anything we learn about that fête could be relevant. Percival and Geoff both seem to muddle up 1939 and 1959 in their minds. That could just be because Percival's so set on the loss of his sister, but 1939 was obviously a dark time in the village, if only because of that fête plus the shadow of war. However,' he said, 'back to 1959. What about this reconstruction? Sure we want to risk it?'

'If the Cobshaw war breaks out in earnest we can always creep away.'

'Coward,' her father retorted amiably.

'We're closed.' That was the answer to Peter and Georgia's first knock on the Maid of Kent's door on Sunday morning. Their second knock was answered by a reluctant Bernie whose face changed when she saw them. 'The bar's *closed*. Can't face it yet.'

'This is a private visit,' Peter explained. 'No need for the bar. I emailed your father about an event in the theatre on Tuesday afternoon to do with our John Wilbourne case.'

'That's something I can do without,' Bernie replied grimly.

'It wouldn't involve either you or Tony,' Georgia said gently.

'Everything involves him.'

'Not the case of John Wilbourne,' Peter said.

Bernie wavered, then: 'Come on in,' she said. 'I'll cope. Dad's too occupied with that ghastly room. Still banging on about Cecilia. She probably jumped on a boat and emigrated.'

As soon as they were seated in the empty bar, she burst out with, 'You know what upsets me most about Tony? He never told me he'd found that tunnel or the room at the end of it. Ridiculous, isn't it? I didn't know it was there and Dad's told me he was allowed in and when he did venture in it just looked full of useless junk. Tony must have cleared it out when he was crawling all over the place in one of his "I'm a master carpenter" periods.' She stopped abruptly. 'I don't want to talk about him.'

'I'd rather not talk about him either,' Peter said mildly.

Bernie was silent for a moment, then burst out with, 'It was that Porsche. Even if that wretched car had been worth enough to have bought this place, that wouldn't have suited Tony. He'd have been the owner of a failing pub, no cash left to restore it further and no car left to boast about. He must have reckoned that Howard Green's deal was his last chance for stardom.' She hesitated. 'This concert of yours in August—'

'You want us to cancel it?' Georgia had been dreading this.

'No. That concert's going ahead no matter what. The sale completion date isn't till September so I'm not letting those Tudors have it all their own way. The concert will take my mind off things.' She grimaced. 'Apart from Tony, I've got other problems. Such as whether Dad and I decide to challenge the sale legally if it turns out Howard Green's lied about having Plantagenet blood as he hinted to me smugly was the case—something about Dad's half-sister not being Montague's child. I'm sick of it all, but I've got to keep that Plantagenet flag flying for Dad's sake.'

'Does your father feel the same about the concert?'

'You bet he does. He sees it as his last hurrah before the takeover.'

Georgia relaxed. That at least was good news. 'How about the reconstruction of the events of 1959 we're planning for Tuesday?' she asked. 'Is your father okay with that? We haven't heard from him.'

'The blighter didn't even mention it to me,' Bernie said resignedly. 'I'll see that he's on board if you tell me what you want. Jimmy and I can manage any chairs or whatever. Who's coming?'

'We're passing the word round,' Peter told her. 'We'd like to see who from the village is interested first. Can we hold a preliminary meeting here for that on Monday?'

'It's going to be quite a show,' Bernie replied wryly. 'Have the meeting here if you want to. Who's playing Brenda on Tuesday?'

'Not sure yet.'

'Then I'll bloody well play her,' Bernie said defiantly. 'Wonder what Tony would make of that.'

For all Bernie's courage, Georgia could see tears in her eyes.

Chapter Seventeen

It seemed as though the whole of Cobshaw wanted to please Peter, as if to atone for such an attack happening on a visitor to their territory. The numbers that were drifting through the bar door on Monday were thankfully manageable however, to Georgia's relief. There was even hope that the Planters versus Tudor hatchet had been buried, at least temporarily, with Sophy and even Mick here to represent the Tudors, now charges against him had been dropped. He still looked very shaken, and his wife was with him looking belligerently protective. Louis, Geoff and Dave Cook were here for the Planters. Jack Cotton (who was now their new best friend) was also here, though keeping a low profile.

By the time Georgia arrived, Peter had already begun. With his usual sang-froid he had driven himself into the centre of operations, with chairs drawn up in a semi-circle around him. She took a seat on one side, preferring an onlooker's position which might be more useful than claiming centre stage.

There was only one snag. Contrary to her expectations Peter wasn't focussing on the reconstruction of 1959. Instead, to Georgia's concern, he currently appeared to be delving into last Wednesday's dramas. Typical of Peter. Presumably this must be part of his plan, but she was uneasy about it. 'Those bones found in the pond,' he was saying. 'One of you at least must suspect whose they are. Your families must have talked about it. If you're ever to have a united village, tell us. Have it out *now*.'

'Some tramp,' Mick muttered.

'Yeah. It were an accident,' Geoff Sanders roared out at last, as no one else stepped forward. 'My dad said that. I'd been to the fête in the grounds of the Hall. Some lady gave me a lollipop, and then there was that play.'

'Play? If you mean *Romeo and Juliet* that was years later,' Peter said patiently. 'We're all talking about the 1939 fête.'

'I were a nipper. There was a fight, Dad said.'

'Who was fighting?'

'Somewhere near that well it was,' Geoff growled. 'Weren't no pond then. Planters and Tudors. Them Randalls. Up near the well. The day of the fête.' This came out in short jerks, as though he were remembering it little by little. '"All's fair in love and war." That's what my dad said.'

Georgia pictured a small boy, clutching the hand of his father, scared and puzzled. Geoff seemed to be remembering things that had stuck in his mind, which perhaps he had not understood fully at the time. Perhaps he was still puzzled. Did 'love and war' carry any relevant meaning for that evening so long ago? Was it a reference to a fight going on for the love of Serena? Was there more to that love story than its being a fairy tale with a dark ending?

'I followed them all,' Geoff continued, still lost in the past. 'It were all dark, it was. Then my dad saw me and took me away. Told me it was all about Mrs Wilson. She was ill, so she was lying down by the well.'

'Who's she?' Dave asked blankly.

'She worked up at the Hall. Cooked for them. She made me buns. I liked her.'

'Those bones can't be hers, Geoff,' Dave pointed out patiently. 'We know they're a man's.'

Georgia was jolted alert. Could she have been right in her earlier guess? 'Do you remember exactly what your dad said, Geoff?'

A scowl. 'I told you, missus. He said it was the cook lying down by the well.'

Dave looked white with shock. 'Or did he say *Cook* was lying down?'

Geoff stared at him belligerently. 'I was only a kid, Dave. A nipper.'

Guess confirmed. Georgia's head was spinning and Peter looked thrown. Hypothesis sometimes work out but this one had seemed to have had only a remote chance of being fact. But now…

Dave put that guess into his own words. 'Brian Cook,' he said slowly. 'My great-uncle. I reckon that's who it was. Went missing. Lived out on Hunters Farm. Never turned up at his ship. What happened, Geoff? Killed in a punch-up, was he? *Who did it*? And what's all this about all's fair in love and war?'

'Best you don't ask, Dave.' Geoff replied. 'It were an accident, like my dad said.'

Mick Buckley pushed his way through to them. 'My granddad Sam was in the fight there that night. That's what you're all thinking, aren't you? First it's me supposed to be a murderer, now it's old Sam.' Mick was speaking very quietly, Georgia realised, not with his usual bluster. 'Perhaps it was. How would I know, Dave? My dad told me my granddad was mixed up in some rumpus that evening, and old Montague FitzRichard who he did some work for tried to sort it out.'

He looked round at his audience, then back to Dave. 'So what do we do now, Dave? It may be your great-uncle dead, my granddad who might have killed him. Or maybe someone else did. No one knows now. The inquest's going to be an open verdict. There's this DNA stuff to find out who it was died, but even that's likely to be a wash-out.'

Dave took his time. 'I reckon we'll just leave it then. We'll never know who did it, anyway. I doubt if you can tell us any more, can you, Geoff?'

Geoff stared at him. 'Some dead roots aren't worth the price of digging up, Dave. That's what my dad said. If he knew about all this it's gone with him.'

'And yourself, Geoff?'

'I were only a nipper.'

Dave nodded his head. 'Fair enough. Fancy a pint, Mick? Reckon you can do with one after all you've been through.'

The relief that ran round the pub was almost tangible, and Georgia felt her own tension falling away. But the puzzle still remained. Sam Buckley (probably) and Brian Cook had a fight and Brian died but, terrible though that was, why did it result in Serena deciding to leave the village, leave Sam and join the war effort?

'Why,' Peter whispered quietly to her, as the crowd relaxed, 'was the death concealed? It must have been known to far more people than the two families involved and therefore there must have been an unspoken agreement to keep silent on the issue. That suggests to me that even if it was Sam who struck the fatal blow it had been a general free-for-all. And what were they clashing over? Serena?'

'Brian would be the one picking the fight,' Georgia whispered back. 'It was Sam whom Serena loved. So if it was Brian who died, why did Serena and Sam break up?' She stopped as a new interpretation hit her. Or had they got the story wrong? Could it be Brian, not Sam, whom Serena loved? With whom she was perhaps planning to leave the village. Without whom she could not bear to stay here. Had they been planning to marry, after which Brian would join his ship and

Serena join the war effort? With Serena locked in her room, had the 'wrong message' in this story been to ensure that *Brian* and Serena's plans were foiled so tragically?

'It *was* the other way around,' she began excitedly to explain to Peter. But she was interrupted.

Percival suddenly came to life again. 'That Sam Buckley,' he shouted, 'did odd jobs at the Maid. My dad was good at sorting things out. Things happened round that well, he said. That well was dangerous. That's why the pond was built around it.'

There was a dead silence. The temporary armistice was shattered. There were too many unanswered questions.

'Or was that to hide where my great-uncle's body lay?' Dave said evenly. 'He must have been buried in haste—I went up to take a look when they said nearly the whole skeleton was there. No coffin. Just wrapped up in some kind of carpeting, so the forensic chap said.'

'It must have been an accident, Dave,' Mick repeated shakily.

'I'd like to know why, Mick. Over a woman, was it? Anyone know anything about this?' Dave asked calmly.

Georgia held her breath in the heavy silence that followed. Someone here might *know* what happened. Serena? Once again it was Percival who broke the silence, as he said anxiously, almost crying:

'My Serena. Dancing at the fête, she was. With Brian Cook, with everyone. Mr Cook, I called him. Happy as the day is long, she was. *Serena's staying in her room, Percival.* That's what he said, my dad. *No more dancing.*'

Peter glanced at her and Georgia nodded. Time to speak out. 'Why was that, Percival?' she asked. 'Because your father didn't like Brian Cook and Serena loved him? Was that why she was locked up?'

But Percival had had enough, shaking his head. 'It was an accident, everyone said. I was a kid.'

Dave sighed. 'So that's it. An accident.' He pulled himself together and looked round. 'What do you think? The well has given up its secrets. That must have been why I was told it had to be protected. I thought he meant just the well but he meant the wall round the pond too. That's why it was built and we've just knocked it down. We didn't know, that's why. None of us did. We just thought the place was spooky and that well was special because of Cecilia.' He paused, then continued firmly, 'I reckon that with no one perhaps knowing for sure who struck the blow that killed Brian as the whole lot of them were involved in the fight, the Planters and Tudors together thought this was the best answer. With war breaking out even the vicar wouldn't have known why my great-uncle wasn't around anymore.'

He looked round at his silent audience. 'I reckon it's time to bury our dead. I'll be talking to Howard and Gerald—we want no more Planters and Tudors. Not after this. Centuries it's been going on, and it stops now.'

At least the sun was out, Georgia thought gratefully, otherwise she would be dreading this reconstruction even more than she already was. It had seemed such a good idea, but now that the day was here and the hour would be upon them this afternoon, Georgia wasn't so sure.

Tony had now been charged with Brenda's murder, and the provisional ending of the well story and possible reconciliation between Planters and Tudors (at least to the extent of a workable relationship) had shone a light on the sad story of Serena and Brian Cook. Nothing was proven, but it fitted—almost. That final question mark must wait. Today required all their attention.

What was glaringly obvious was that John Wilbourne's death remained an unsolved puzzle. Theories swirled endlessly round. The case was like a pyramid. Its base had been firmly established; the sides were being constructed but the peak remained tantalisingly out of reach.

Here she was sitting with Peter in a row of chairs forming a semi-circle set back from the stage, having arrived early for the reconstruction. The participants in it, Georgia hoped, knew what they would be doing, even though there was no script to this. Memory was all and the stakes were high. A parade of people following the same movements as on a night sixty years ago suddenly seemed an impossible challenge, especially as it included two elderly eccentrics, one determined to play Poirot and the other obsessed by the Plantagenets.

She was beginning to have stage fright. Why did she and Peter ever start this? Would there be some kind of magic wand that Peter could wave in his planned summing-up?

Bernie had told them that persuading Percival and Gerald to hold the reconstruction here rather than at the Hall had been difficult, but an even more difficult question, so Georgia and Peter had found, was whether Gerald should hold the balance of power or Percival? Gerald had maintained that as host to Sir Edward and his role (self-appointed) as Poirot gave him managerial rights, but Percival claimed owner's prerogative. It had taken delicate negotiations to reach a scenario in which neither of them would have the upper hand. Peter would be in the chair, with the role of stage director.

This waiting was the worst part of today's 'performance'. It was hard to believe that in two months' time they would be sitting here enjoying Rick's concert.

'This reconstruction won't be like the original evening in so many ways,' she said to Peter as they waited. 'For a start, there's the light. In 1959 it was dark and we're here in the sunshine.'

Peter had been deep in his own thoughts, but he came to with a start. 'Dark,' he said. 'He said it was nearly *dark*.'

'What was?' Even as she spoke, she realised what he must be thinking. 'Of course!' she grappled feverishly with what this might imply, struggling to assemble the facts behind Peter's reasoning. 'The fête and the gathering at the well. There's a gap of several hours.'

'In which a play took place,' Peter said simply. 'Percival referred to one and I assumed he was mixing up 1959 with 1939. But suppose there really was a performance of some kind?'

'How much would that affect what we've been piecing together?' she asked, still struggling to take this on board.

'Perhaps quite a lot. It's important anyway. Why otherwise would Percival mention it? It could be relevant.'

Err on the side of caution, Georgia decided. 'Surely he would have told us before now if it was?'

'Perhaps he did and we didn't pick up on it. Remember when he first told us about Serena? He said "before the show". We thought he was getting mixed up with 1959, but he wasn't. He was back twenty years earlier with his Serena. And, Georgia—' Peter's eyes gleamed with excitement—'talking of performances—'

'Those photos,' they said in unison.

'Steady the Buffs, as you used to say,' Georgia added shakily. 'There were only a couple that were of John Wilbourne's acting career, but one—'

'Was of *Romeo and Juliet*,' he finished for her. 'And the Juliet was not Rowena Watts. Which means the photo was not of the 1959 performance.'

'Undated,' Georgia continued, scrabbling in her memory. 'In theory it could have taken place anywhere and anytime, but the word Cobshaw was scribbled on the back, which defines it as 1939.'

They looked at each other. 'Could it be,' Georgia said slowly, 'that our missing link is hidden somewhere inside this tangle?'

Chapter Eighteen

Sometimes the vital piece of a jigsaw falls neatly into place. It isn't necessarily the last piece, but it pulls the picture together. Then you fit the remaining pieces around it, but that tends to be easier because the end is in sight. Was that so now? Georgia's pessimism had vanished. At least there was a possible link to cling to.

The reconstruction had begun and with that link in mind her hopes were rising that it was going to produce positive results. She couldn't see how—but nevertheless she was going to pay *very* close attention to it:

For never was a story of more woe
Than this of Juliet and her Romeo.

Sir Edward was currently on stage declaiming the prince's closing speech in *Romeo and Juliet,* as a prelude to the reconstruction of what had taken place in 1959. Elated by their new theory, Georgia watched what then happened. The chosen characters in this prelude—Rowena as Juliet, Sir Edward as Mercutio, Louis playing John Wilbourne's Romeo, Percival and Montague FitzRichard (the latter played by Jimmy the barman), Gerald Randall, Dave Cook, Mick and

Geoff—now appeared for their final curtain. After that they would make their way to an area in the gardens that had been roped off to represent the bar of the Maid of Kent in the re-enactment. Onlookers were sitting in the theatre auditorium and the 'jury'—herself and Peter—were now stationed higher up at a point where it was possible to see both the stage and 'the bar'.

Gerald had been sitting with them, until he departed for his grand entry on to the stage. It had been agreed that if 'Poirot' was to make his speech then it should come first and not last—in case, Peter had explained diplomatically—the reconstruction ended in disarray and his speech was either curtailed or ignored.

Gerald was now striding on to the stage smartly dressed in modern clothes—he had fought valiantly to appear in 1920s costume and moustache, but Director Peter had pointed out that Poirot would strongly have disapproved of such an impersonation.

'*A plague o' both your houses,*' Gerald began in thrilling tones.

Georgia could almost hear the gnashing of Peter's teeth. 'I wasn't allowed to see his speech,' he muttered. 'I fear the worst. We've already got enough Shakespeare.'

Fortunately, the Shakespeare was temporary. 'This is Cobshaw's plague too but, *mes amis,* I am here as a physician to cure it.' Gerald's moment had come. He was Poirot. He carefully removed his glasses, looked at his audience and smiled. Georgia tried not to cringe.

'We're in for a bumpy ride,' Peter whispered to her gloomily.

'The death of my dear half-brother, John Wilbourne,' Gerald continued, 'who disgraced the family name and died so tragically is my concern today. I owe it to his family to reveal the truth of that terrible evening to you.'

'Bumpiness approaching fast,' Georgia whispered.

'John suffered a severe penalty for his double crime,' Gerald continued with a flourish. 'The double crime was his disgracing the family firstly by desiring to be an actor and secondly by choosing to marry beneath him, a woman who was not a Tudor.'

'Here we go!' Peter was suddenly alert. 'He can't mean Elizabeth or Rowena. Brenda?'

'She would have been a very young bride. The other Juliet, the one in the photo perhaps?'

Georgia could say no more. Gerald was in full flow: 'John was cast out of the house by my father, bent on his disastrous career choice. And then he returned here, with but one thought in mind. Revenge! He would marry and bring shame on the family.'

She couldn't hold back. 'Who's he chosen to pick on now?' she said. This wasn't 1959, it had to be pre-1944 when he married Elizabeth. 'His Juliet,' she asked, 'the one we saw in the photograph?' Then the impact of Gerald's words hit her. *Returned here* and *revenge*. What for? Just to break the news to his family of his marriage, or had he been in love with someone else before that? A villager. Suppose—'

'Have we been barking up completely the wrong tree?' Peter cut in sharply.

Her head really was spinning now, and her heart was pounding. She braced herself. Surely this was too much of a leap. But she made it, just as Peter voiced it for her: '*Serena.*'

The truth can be obvious when it chooses to appear, Georgia thought, lamenting her stupidity for not having made the possible connection earlier. It had been lying there for a long time, just one mental leap away. Percival talking about his sister Serena's joy at the fête, John's return here in 1959 with that play so relevant to his own life, the message gone astray, the fight between the Planters and Tudors, and Shakespeare's Capulets and Montagues.

When it came to choosing a wife, she realised, John had chosen a

Planter and 'disgraced' the family. And that also explained a lingering question about their previous thesis: why would Serena's father have objected so much to Brian Cook when they were both Planters? Now it was clear. Whatever reason for the fight between Sam Buckley and Brian Cook it had not been for love of Serena. Had it been simply part of a general scrap between Tudors and Planters or had it been specifically because of John Wilbourne and Serena's love for each other? That could indeed be the reason as something had obviously gone wrong with their affair. What, for instance, did Geoff's mention of 'the wrong message' mean?

Georgia sat bemused and then came to with a start when Gerald raised his voice, seemingly winding up to his triumphant conclusion:

'But, *mes amis,* this is not so, because of their *alibi.* Can these be wrong? No, they are not wrong. The truth is, *mes amis,* this was an Impossible Murder. That is what I can prove. And why is it impossible? Because John Wilbourne killed *himself.* He is the murderer. Why did he do this terrible deed? Because in 1939 he had come to the village to kill Sam Buckley. But he made a mistake and in error killed poor Brian Cook instead. He was haunted by this terrible error and in 1959 returned here to kill himself.'

'How on earth did he dream up this fairy tale?' Peter whispered to Georgia as she sat there aghast.

'Ah, *mes amis,*' Gerald swept on, 'you will ask how then did he come to be buried? The answer is simple. In the howling wind and pouring rain he plunged a dagger into himself in a remote spot where he was gradually buried by the growth of the trees that sheltered his lonely soul. He lay where he had chosen to die—'

'*No!*'

Rowena Watts walked onto the stage. For a moment Georgia thought this was all a part of Gerald's plan, but soon changed her mind.

'Mr Randall,' Rowena began, 'you are vastly mistaken and I really cannot allow anyone to believe what you have so falsely claimed. So it's time for *my* big speech. And here's where it starts—totally unrehearsed. John would never have committed suicide, and John would never have killed anyone. I knew him, I loved him, and he was incapable of violence of any kind. Is that clear?'

She looked round her audience defiantly. 'I loved him, but unfortunately he didn't love me, or indeed any woman save one. I never met her but, my goodness, I heard about her from my mother and I've read many of her letters, so I know the story backwards, forwards and indisputably. This girl was the one love of John's life, the first and I believe only one. He was fond of Elizabeth, he was fond of me, but he had no real love to give.' Rowena paused, looking as if she were surprised to find herself where she was.

'One day John told me the whole sad story,' she continued, 'which he had kept to himself for years. His heart belonged to Serena FitzRichard. Her family was against her marrying John because of a village feud, and so they planned to meet after a performance of *Romeo and Juliet* in the grounds of Cobshaw Hall. John left his motor car at Cobshaw Halt Station and the plan was that she would steal away from the crowd after the performance, join him, and they would elope. But she never arrived. Someone called Sam Buckley delivered what he said was a message from her to tell John that she had changed her mind and wasn't coming.

'In fact,' Rowena continued steadily, 'I discovered through my mother that Serena had been locked in her room by her father, and it was Montague FitzRichard who ordered Buckley to take the message, though I gathered Buckley was only too willing to do so. John told me he wrote to her afterwards, but not surprisingly the letters never reached Serena, probably intercepted by her father. As the war had come by then John was moving from town to town and country to country and wouldn't have received the letters she wrote to him. Their lives had changed, but, as I know to my cost, not their feelings for each other. Serena FitzRichard left no room in John's heart for anyone else. It wasn't until a few months before his death that he discovered the truth. That, I fear, was from me. Serena had died some years before and when he mentioned the name of his beloved Serena it drove me too far and I told him the whole story. The performance of *Romeo and Juliet* on this stage was his revenge.'

Gerald Randall had already left the stage and Georgia thought that Rowena was about to follow suit. She hadn't finished, however, although there was a break in her voice.

'And if you want to know why I haven't revealed this before, the answer is simple. I was too jealous. Jealous then, and jealous now. I had known my mother had a friend called Serena but when I discovered that she was the Serena, possessor of John's heart, it was even worse. It seemed to me that her image pursued me everywhere. It still does. Even now.'

She fell silent, until Sir Edward Colduggan walked on to the stage and gently led her away.

Peter's office had seldom hosted such a venerable guest. Georgia was well aware that Elena was hovering with anticipation on her side of the communicating door—which, Georgia noticed, was slightly open, probably with Elena glued to it in the hope of being invited in. Maybe afterwards. Not now. Definitely not now.

Sir Edward had requested this appointment, and it was to be in Peter's office, he stipulated, the official address for Marsh & Daughter. Neither Peter nor Georgia could be certain, but it was obvious this was going to conclude the story of John Wilbourne.

Dave Cook had come to visit them, his mission to convey what the village had agreed must have taken place at the well that night after the 1939 fête. It had been thrashed over, he assured them, with both Planters and Tudors *together*. The probability was, it had been agreed, that Sam Buckley's duplicity must have led to a general brawl resulting in Brian Cook's death, but there was no one alive today to testify as to who had been directly responsible. With war about to break out and some of the contenders probably awaiting the inevitable call-up papers, there must have been a consensus, spoken or unspoken, for silence. Hence the sense of mystery and darkness about the well that they had handed on to their descendants.

Serena had been popular in the village, Dave had explained, and Brian Cook might well have squared up to Sam Buckley in a rage, when he found out about the deliberate foiling of Serena's plans. Brian was once a barman at the Maid of Kent where he could have been a friend or early sweetheart of Serena's and furious on her behalf. But so could a number of other people have been similarly enraged. The reason that Sam was so cock-a-hoop over having messed up John Wilbourne and Serena's plans wasn't known, but payment by Montague FitzRichard was top of the list of possibilities. Another was that Sam was hoping to grab Serena for himself, especially with the hope of inheriting the Maid of Kent. A public interment service, Dave had assured them awkwardly, would be held for his great-uncle's remains and both Randalls and Cooks would be present.

Sir Edward arrived by taxi precisely on time and looked round Peter's office with great interest, after being seated in the armchair, which was guaranteed to put its users at ease. That and a tray of coffee and Elena's best Kentish cookies.

'Is this your stage, Mr Marsh?' He was studying the lines of books behind Peter's desk. A good way of describing this office, Georgia thought. The stage where Peter performed.

'This and the room next door with the files,' Peter replied genially. 'One can't keep everything digitally. Once technology outstrips what we work with today, we'd land up in another Dark Ages.'

'Nor can one keep everything in one's head,' Sir Edward commented. 'Which is why I requested this meeting.'

'For which Georgia and I are most grateful,' Peter replied formally, but sincerely.

'And I trust of course that you have no recording devices here?'

'No phone recorders, no other recorders, no flapping ears.'

Apart, Georgia thought, from Elena, but she was no threat.

'Then the truth, if you please,' Sir Edward requested. 'Do either of you still harbour a suspicion that I killed John—presumably out of jealousy or perhaps because I had a yen for Rowena?'

'I do not,' Peter replied.

'Nor I,' Georgia said, 'but you may have been holding back to make your entrance.'

Sir Edward smiled. 'Elegantly put. If so, that is only because suspicion is not certainty. I do moreover have a story to tell. Do you know Gilbert and Sullivan's operetta *The Yeoman of the Guard*?'

'I certainly do,' Peter replied promptly. 'I sang in it once. Chorus only.'

'Then you will recall poor Jack Point's song of the merryman moping mum,' Sir Edward continued:

Whose soul was sad and whose glance was glum
Who sipped no sup and who craved no crumb
As he sighed for the love of a lady.

'That, Peter and Georgia, was Sir John Wilbourne, whose tale of love you have heard from Rowena, now seconded by me. However, there was something she could not even bear to tell you herself. Betrayed on a day in August 1939, John's letters were unanswered and Serena, as you know, left home a month or two later. She stayed with Rowena's mother for a while.'

'Until she was married?' Peter asked.

'Not quite. She stayed until her baby was born.'

Baby? 'But when…' Georgia began.

'She left home when she realised she was pregnant,' Sir Edward told them. 'She was carrying John's son. Their romance did not spring out of nowhere on the day of the fete; John had left Cobshaw, so he told Rowena, because of a family row over his courting Serena. The relationship did not die when he left home though, and somehow they managed to keep seeing each other. The performance of *Romeo and Juliet*, which he managed to arrange with the company he was then with, would have provided a dramatic exit from Cobshaw life for both Serena and himself as they had planned to elope. And that is why he chose that play again when he returned in 1959 to take his revenge. I see now why Romeo was at his theatrical best that evening.'

'Which leads us to how this began,' Peter said. 'Who killed John Wilbourne?'

Sir Edward smiled. 'The truth then, as far as this can be established. I do indeed remember nothing about that evening after that stupid duel I fought with John. I was maddened by his upstaging me that evening, although I realise now that he must have been obsessed with his return to Cobshaw for personal reasons. I might also have imagined the cause of my fury. How irrelevant a matter of upstaging is in hindsight, and how emotional a matter it can be at the time it occurs. However, one thing has always puzzled me.'

'The swords?' Peter said.

Sir Edward nodded. 'Indeed. The swords. I remember the duel, and I remember Montague coming to break it up, and I remember I walked off the stage with my sword still clutched in my hand. Stage sword of course. John just threw his down on the stage. I remember the look of fury on his face. I took that at the time as a sign of his dislike of me, and of his being robbed of a chance to shine in our petty make-believe duel. I'm quite sure that I did take my sword back to the pub as I still had it with me the next morning. I remember nursing it all the way back to London as the company kept a strict financial eye on stage properties. So mine could not have been the sword found near John's remains. That must have been the one he had flung on the stage. I surmise he returned there, seized the sword and fled, pursued by his killer armed with a more lethal weapon.' He looked at Peter and Georgia expectantly.

Georgia scrambled through her memory. Of course. But a *sword*.

'A sword,' Peter said, obviously coming to the same conclusion as her. 'Not a stage sword, but a real blade that could kill. Like the Plantagenet knight's arming sword in Richard of Eastwell's room at the Maid of Kent. Grabbed on the spur of the moment to kill John Wilbourne who had come to track down the man who had ruined his life. *Montague FitzRichard.*'

'Indeed,' Sir Edward said gravely.

Peter had been mulling it over, Georgia realised. Not merely an ordinary kitchen knife for Montague, but a Plantagenet weapon of war against the Tudor John Wilbourne.

'He would have been hell bent on revenge for his daughter being led astray, as he saw it, by daring to love a Tudor,' she said, working it out step by step. 'John must have tackled him after the show, Montague saw his chance, perhaps insisting on a duel, grabbed his arming sword. Perhaps he told John that it was your stage sword that you'd brought back to the pub, so John went to pick up his from the stage not realising that Montague's sword was all too real. Whether he had any different plans in mind for revenge we'll never know.'

'John was indeed hell bent on revenge in 1959,' Sir Edward said. 'Now, too late, I realise that. *I am fortune's fool*, John cried out as Romeo that night. And indeed he was.'

'The irony is,' Peter pointed out gleefully, 'that it's 99% sure that thanks to her mother Elspeth, Serena FitzRichard had no Plantagenet blood in her. Elspeth had had that pre-marital affair with John Fairlee of Harting and hastily married Montague FitzRichard. Years later John Wilbourne was wrongly accused by the Randalls of wanting to marry a Plantagenet which Serena was not, and much later still poor old Howard Green can't claim Plantagenet blood through his grannie Serena.'

'And,' Georgia added, 'it's possible that Brenda already knew about Serena's parentage before that phone call from Rowena Watts just before her death, because the evidence wouldn't have been hard to track down with her research abilities. What Rowena telephoned Brenda about would really have shaken her though. Rowena was the daughter of Daisy Watts, Serena's great friend, who knew Serena's story and the fact that she had a baby by John Wilbourne. In due course that baby married Paul Green, the hotel magnate, and they had a child, Howard. Knowingly or unknowingly, therefore, Howard is a Tudor, and not a Plantagenet, since Serena had no Plantagenet blood. His Tudor heritage would have worried Brenda immensely because of the contract he was signing. Because of her principles she would have told Howard the truth, even though it would probably scupper the whole deal with Percival. Tony wouldn't have risked that.'

'Howard is indeed a Tudor.' Sir Edward rose to take his leave, then paused. 'Incidentally, when I disturbed you in the Randall chapel some days ago, one of its stained glass windows caught my attention—forgive me, but they are a hobby of mine. The chapel walls are built with Kentish ragstone and no doubt date from a very early period. As you may know, much of our heritage of stained glass church windows was destroyed in the late 1530s during the period of the dissolution of the monasteries, but a gradual restoration was begun by Queen Mary during the 1550s. That could account for this particular window, in which the patron saint of music, Saint Cecilia, appears in one corner. Quite a coincidence in a chapel devoted to the Randalls, don't you think?'

Peter's eyes gleamed. 'You think it's a deliberate pointer?'

Sir Edward nodded. 'In my opinion the FitzRichards' belief that she is buried in the Maid of Kent, particularly in that room where you suffered, Peter, is misplaced. Why not try under the floor of the Randalls' chapel?'

'Phew!' Georgia sank back in her chair after Sir Edward had left. 'It seems to me this case has lunged forward rather like that knight in Richard's Room.'

'I prefer not to remember that gentleman,' Peter said wryly.

'Apologies. But we do seem to have lunged forward only to find the answer under our noses, including now perhaps Cecilia's resting place.'

'Plus the answers to all our questions,' Peter added soberly. 'We're planning to call our book *The Case of the Missing Knight,* Georgia. A paradox in a way. John Wilbourne is no longer missing. His story can now be told.'

Epilogue

The glorious voice of Josephine Mantreau singing the haunting 'Scarborough Fair' died away in the still evening air. It had been Rick's favourite song, her final offering in this wonderful concert, preceded with Lucien Marques playing his cello in Saint-Saëns' 'Swan'. There remained only Sir Edward Colduggan to draw an end to a magical evening with—of course—Shakespeare.

> *Our revels now are ended…*
> *We are such stuff as dreams are made on*
> *And our little life*
> *Is rounded with a sleep. And then came Sir Edward's own*
> *words: Sleep well, Rick Marsh.*

Georgia was spellbound. The stage, with the huge beech tree guarding it, and the sound of that music had made the evening not only a tribute to Rick but to John Wilbourne as well. For Peter, Elena and herself it had been an unforgettable and moving experience shared not only with Luke and his family but with—as it had turned out—a great many of Cobshaw's villagers as well. Tudors *and* Planters. Dave had been as good as his word. A public interment service had taken place for Brian

Cook. Dave had also sorted out something with the Randalls together with the Buckleys and Howard Green. Once rebuilt, Cecilia's well and the pond around it would be open to all. Not only that, but Bernie had agreed to stay on and manage the new hotel—which Howard planned to make welcoming for the community. And there was more.

'Couldn't believe it at first,' Dave had said to them, when he called to impart his progress over the future of Cobshaw. 'Howard just threw this out as calmly as though he'd been planning it all along. "Dave," he said, "how about getting together over a big extension of the Maid for a new community meeting place for clubs and dances and so on?"'

One way or another, the future of Cobshaw looked promising.

As for Peter and herself, Georgia wasn't too sure. With the concert over, the spotlight would return to family issues, which were far from promising. Here in the twilight, preparing to go to the late supper arranged (in consultation with Howard and Gerald) at the speedily transformed Maid of Kent bar, they were all too conscious that this could be the last such event for the Frost and Marsh families as a unit. Jill would soon be leaving for the States, and indeed her happiness was noticeable.

But on the way to supper, Jill said casually, 'By the way, folks, I won't be leaving for the States for a while. I'm keeping everything on hold. I have a new project.'

Georgia was dizzy with relief. There might be time to talk some sense into her. 'What is this new project, Jill?'

'I'm writing Edward Colduggan's biography.'

'What would Rick have made of that?' Peter asked when they'd recovered from the shock.

Georgia knew the answer. 'He would have laughed.' *Sleep well, dear Rick.*

Historical Note

The story of Richard of Eastwell (alternatively Richard Plantagenet) is a fascinating one, not least because apart from the generally accepted information that Richard was buried in Eastwell churchyard in Kent on 22nd December 1550, the rest of his life is known to posterity only through tradition and hearsay. There are gaps in his story as the written reports of his life over the centuries rely on that. They therefore vary greatly in detail and have been pieced together by many scholars with intriguing results and theses. *The Lost Prince* by David Baldwin (The History Press, 2007) is full of information on Richard of Eastwell, including his thesis that Richard might have been the younger son of King Edward IV, who has hitherto been thought to be one of the Princes in the Tower murdered, arguably, by Richard III. There are many other modern excellent histories of the Plantagenets.

In the 1730s Francis Peck included Richard's story in his collection *Desiderata Curiosa* and in 1744 *The Parallel* was anonymously published, a collection of stories of concealed births and disputed successions; the story was also handed down by the family who owned Eastwell Park. The latter was recorded in a letter written in 1733 by clergyman Dr Thomas Brett, who recalled the family tradition being related to him in 1720. Sir Thomas Moyle, according to tradition, employed Richard at some time in the 1540s (one source suggests 1542-3) and one day discovered him reading Horace's poems in Latin, strange for a stonemason in those days. Sir Thomas was living then in a manor house by the lake in Eastwell Park and was building his new mansion in the grounds. Eastwell Park is now a luxury hotel, and Eastwell church's ruins are not far away. Although a tomb in the churchyard claims to be Richard's, the site of Richard's grave is not certain.

With such a rich field of doubt as to the exact story of Richard of Eastwell, I'm far from being alone in featuring Richard in fiction. When I first came across the story years ago in *Kent Lore* by Alan Bignell (Robert Hale, 1983) it fascinated me so much that I wrote a short story in which Richard of Eastwell turned out to be the elder of the two princes in the tower, Edward V of England. That story is entirely fictional, however, with no supporting evidence. In this current novel I have followed in traditional footsteps over Richard's story as far as his meeting with his father Richard III at Bosworth, picking up the traditional route again at the point where Sir Thomas Moyle employs him to work on his estate (either as a stonemason or overseer according to varying theses). Richard's life at Cobshaw, including the existence of a granddaughter, is fictional, as is the whole story of Cecilia.

There is some evidence that there was indeed a private marriage in 1472 between Richard III (as he later became) and Anne Neville whom he publicly married two years later. *The Parallel* refers to marriage in 1474 to 'a lady of quality' (*The Lost Prince, op, cit*).

I have used the name Plantagenet in its wider sense to cover the eras up to the reign of Richard III and have not delved deeply into the fascinating but tangled ancestry web of the Tudors and Plantagenets, Beauforts and Nevilles.

Finally, another long-standing tradition is that Richard of Eastwell wrote his own autobiography, but hard evidence is there none. Possibly, therefore, he wrote about his days in Cobshaw…

CPSIA information can be obtained
at www.ICGtesting.com
Printed in the USA
BVHW081103250422
635249BV00008B/189

9 781839 014734